AROUND THE WORLD IN SEVENTY-TWO DAYS AND TEN DAYS IN A MAD-HOUSE
BY

Nellie Bly

Around the World in Seventy-Two Days

Chapter 1: A Proposal to Girdle the Earth.

WHAT gave me the idea?

It is sometimes difficult to tell exactly what gives birth to an idea. Ideas are the chief stock in trade of newspaper writers and generally they are the scarcest stock in market, but they do come occasionally,

This idea came to me one Sunday. I had spent a greater part of the day and half the night vainly trying to fasten on some idea for a newspaper article. It was my custom to think up ideas on Sunday and lay them before my editor for his approval or disapproval on Monday. But ideas did not come that day and three o'clock in the morning found me weary and with an aching head tossing about in my bed. At last tired and provoked at my slowness in finding a subject, something for the week's work, I thought fretfully:

"I wish I was at the other end of the earth!"

"And why not?" the thought came: "I need a vacation; why not take a trip around the world?"

It is easy to see how one thought followed another. The idea of a trip around the world pleased me and I added: "If I could do it as quickly as Phileas Fogg did, I should go."

Then I wondered if it were possible to do the trip eighty days and afterwards I went easily off to sleep with the determination to know before I saw my bed again if Phileas Fogg's record could be broken.

I went to a steamship company's office that day and made a selection of time tables. Anxiously I sat down and went over them and if I had found the elixir of life I should not have felt better than I did when I conceived a hope that a tour of the world might be made in even less than eighty days.

I approached my editor rather timidly on the subject. I was afraid that he would think the idea too wild and visionary.

"Have you any ideas?" he asked, as I sat down by his desk.

"One," I answered quietly.

He sat toying with his pens, waiting for me to continue, so I blurted out:

"I want to go around the world!"

"Well?" he said, inquiringly looking up with a faint smile in his kind eyes.

"I want to go around in eighty days or less. I think I can beat Phileas Fogg's record. May I try it?"

To my dismay he told me that in the office they had thought of this same idea before and the intention was to send a man. However he offered me the consolation that he would favor my going, and then we went to talk with the business manager about it.

"It is impossible for you to do it," was the terrible verdict. "In the first place you are a woman and would need a protector, and even if it were possible for you to travel alone you would need to carry so much baggage that it would detain you in making rapid changes. Besides you speak nothing but English, so there is no use talking about it; no one but a man can do this."

"Very well," I said angrily, "Start the man, and I'll start the same day for some other newspaper and beat him."

"I believe you would," he said slowly. I would not say that this had any influence on their decision, but I do know that before we parted I was made happy by the promise that if any one was commissioned to make the trip, I should be that one.

After I had made my arrangements to go, other important projects for gathering news came up, and this rather visionary idea was put aside for a while.

One cold, wet evening, a year after this discussion, I received a little note asking me to come to the office at once. A summons, late in the afternoon, was such an unusual thing to me that I was to be excused if I spent all my time on the way to the office wondering what I was to be scolded for.

I went in and sat down beside the editor waiting for him to speak. He looked up from the paper on which he was writing and asked quietly: "Can you start around the world day after tomorrow?"

"I can start this minute," I answered, quickly trying to stop the rapid beating of my heart.

"We did think of starting you on the City of Paris tomorrow morning, so as to give you ample time to catch the mail train out of London. There is a chance if the Augusta Victoria, which sails the morning afterwards, has rough weather of your failing to connect with the mail train."

"I will take my chances on the Augusta Victoria, and save one extra day," I said.

The next morning I went to Ghormley, the fashionable dressmaker, to order a dress. It was after eleven o'clock when I got there and it took but very few moments to tell him what I wanted.

I always have a comfortable feeling that nothing is impossible if one applies a certain amount of energy in the right direction. When I want things done, which is always at the last moment, and I am met with such an answer: "It's too late. I hardly think it can be done;" I simply say:

"Nonsense! If you want to do it, you can do it. The question is, do you want to do it?"

I have never met the man or woman yet who was not aroused by that answer into doing their very best.

If we want good work from others or wish to accomplish anything ourselves, it will never do to harbor a doubt as to the result of an enterprise.

So, when I went to Ghormley's, I said to him: "I want a dress by this evening."

"Very well," he answered as unconcernedly as if it were an everyday thing for a young woman to order a gown on a few hours' notice.

"I want a dress that will stand constant wear for three months," I added, and then let the responsibility rest on him.

Bringing out several different materials he threw them in artistic folds over a small table, studying the effect in a pier glass before which he stood.

He did not become nervous or hurried. All the time that he was trying the different effects of the materials, he kept up a lively and half humorous conversation. In a few moments he had selected a plain blue broadcloth and a quiet plaid camel's -hair as the most durable and suitable combination for a traveling gown.

Before I left, probably one o'clock, I had my first fitting. When I returned at five o'clock for a second fitting, the dress was finished. I considered this promptness and speed a good omen and quite in keeping with the project.

After leaving Ghormley's I went to a shop and ordered an ulster. Then going to another dressmaker's, I ordered a lighter dress to carry with me to be worn in the land where I would find summer.

I bought one hand-bag with the determination to confine my baggage to its limit.

That night there was nothing to do but write to my few friends a line of farewell and to pack the hand-bag.

Packing that bag was the most difficult undertaking of my life; there was so much to go into such little space.

I got everything in at last except the extra dress. Then the question resolved itself into this: I must either add a parcel to my baggage or go around the world in and with one dress. I always hated parcels so I sacrificed the dress, but I brought out a last summer's silk bodice and after considerable squeezing managed to crush it into the hand-bag.

I think that I went away one of the most superstitious of girls. My editor had told me the day before the trip had been decided upon of an inauspicious dream he had had. It seemed that I came to him and told him I was going to run a race. Doubting my ability as a runner, he thought he turned his back so that he should not witness the race. He heard the band play, as it does on such occasions, and heard the applause that greeted the finish. Then I came to him with my eyes filled with tears and said: "I have lost the race."

"I can translate that dream," I said, when he finished; "I will start to secure some news and some one else will beat me."

When I was told the next day that I was to go around the world I felt a prophetic awe steal over me. I feared that Time would win the race and that I should not make the tour in eighty days or less.

Nor was my health good when I was told to go around the world in the shortest time possible at that season of the year. For almost a year I had been a daily sufferer from headache, and only the week previous I had consulted a number of eminent physicians fearing that my health was becoming impaired by too constant application to work. I had been doing newspaper work for almost three years, during which time I had not enjoyed one day's vacation. It is not surprising then that I looked on this trip as a most delightful and much needed rest.

The evening before I started I went to the office and was given £200 in English gold and Bank of England notes. The gold I carried in my pocket. The Bank of England notes were placed in a chamois-skin bag which I tied around my neck. Besides this I took some American gold and paper money to use at different ports as a test to see if American money was known outside of America.

Down in the bottom of my hand-bag was a special passport, number 247, signed by James G. Blaine, Secretary of State. Someone suggested that a revolver would be a good companion piece for the passport, but I had such a strong belief in the world's greeting me as I greeted it, that I refused to arm myself. I knew if my conduct was proper I should always find men ready to protect me, let them be Americans, English, French, German or anything else.

It is quite possible to buy tickets in New York for the entire trip, but I thought that I might be compelled to change my route at almost any point, so the only transportation I had provided on leaving New York was my ticket to London.

When I went to the office to say good-bye, I found that no itinerary had been made of my contemplated trip and there was some doubt as to whether the mail train which I expected to take to Brindisi, left London every Friday night. Nor did we know whether the week of my expected arrival in London was the one in which it connected with the ship for India or the ship for China. In fact when I arrived at Brindisi and found the ship was bound for Australia, I was the most surprised girl in the world.

I followed a man who had been sent to a steamship company's office to try to make out a schedule and help them arrange one as best they could on this side of the water. How near it came to being correct can be seen later on.

I have been asked very often since my return how many changes of clothing I took in my solitary hand-bag. Some have thought I took but one; others think I carried silk which occupies but little space, and others have asked if I did not buy what I needed at the different ports.

One never knows the capacity of an ordinary hand-satchel until dire necessity compels the exercise of all one's ingenuity to reduce every thing to the smallest possible compass. In mine I was able to pack two traveling caps, three veils, a pair of slippers, a complete outfit of toilet articles, ink-stand, pens, pencils, and copy-paper, pins, needles and thread, a dressing gown, a tennis blazer, a small flask and a drinking cup, several complete changes of underwear, a liberal supply of handkerchiefs and fresh ruchings and most bulky and uncompromising of all, a jar of cold cream to keep my face from chapping in the varied climates I should encounter.

That jar of cold cream was the bane of my existence. It seemed to take up more room than everything else in the bag and was always getting into just the place that would keep me from closing the satchel. Over my arm I carried a silk waterproof, the only provision I made against rainy weather. After-experience showed me that I had taken too much rather than too little baggage. At every port where I stopped at I could have bought anything from a ready-made dress down, except possibly at Aden, and as I did not visit the shops there I cannot speak from knowledge.

The possibilities of having any laundry work done during my rapid progress was one which had troubled me a good deal before starting. I had equipped myself on the theory that only once or twice in my journey would I be able to secure the services of a laundress. I knew that on the railways it would be impossible, but the longest railroad travel was the two days spent between London and Brindisi, and the four days between San Francisco and New York. On the Atlantic steamers they do no washing. On the Peninsular and Oriental steamers-which everyone calls the P. & O. boats-between Brindisi and China, the quartermaster turns out each day a wash that would astonish the largest laundry in America. Even if no laundry work was done on the ships, there are at all of the ports where they stop plenty of experts waiting to show what Orientals can do in the washing line. Six hours is ample time for them to perform their labors and when they make a promise to have work done in a certain time, they are prompt to the minute. Probably it is because they have no use for clothes themselves, but appreciate at its full value the money they are to receive for their labor. Their charges, compared with laundry prices in New York, are wonderfully low.

So much for my preparations. It will be seen that if one is traveling simply for the sake of traveling and not for the purpose of impressing one's fellow passengers, the problem of baggage becomes a very simple one. On one occasion-in Hong Kong, where I was asked to an official dinner-I regretted not having an evening dress with me, but the loss of that dinner was a very small matter when compared with the responsibilities and worries I escaped by not having a lot of trunks and boxes to look after.

Chapter 2: The Start.

ON Thursday, November 14, 1889, at 9.40.30 o'clock, I started on my tour around the world.

Those who think that night is the best part of the day and that morning was made for sleep, know how uncomfortable they feel when for some reason they have to get up with-well, with the milkman.

I turned over several times before I decided to quit my bed. I wondered sleepily why a bed feels so much more luxurious, and a stolen nap that threatens the loss of a train is so much more sweet, than those hours of sleep that are free from duty's call. I half promised myself that on my return I would pretend sometime that it was urgent that I should get up so I could taste the pleasure of a stolen nap without actually losing anything by it. I dozed off very sweetly over these thoughts to wake with a start, wondering anxiously if there was still time to catch the ship.

Of course I wanted to go, but I thought lazily that if some of these good people who spend so much time in trying to invent flying machines would only devote a little of the same energy towards promoting a system by which boats and trains would always make their start at noon or afterwards, they would be of greater assistance to suffering humanity.

I endeavored to take some breakfast, but the hour was too early to make food endurable. The last moment at home came. There was a hasty kiss for the dear ones, and a blind rush downstairs trying to overcome the hard lump in my throat that threatened to make me regret the journey that lay before me.

"Don't worry," I said encouragingly, as I was unable to speak that dreadful word, goodbye; "only think of me as having a vacation and the most enjoyable time in my life."

Then to encourage myself I thought, as I was on my way to the ship: "It's only a matter of 28,000 miles, and seventy-five days and four hours, until I shall be back again."

A few friends who told of my hurried departure, were there to say good-bye. The morning was bright and beautiful, and everything seemed very pleasant while the boat was still; but when they were warned to go ashore, I began to realize what it meant for me.

"Keep up your courage," they said to me while they gave my hand the farewell clasp. I saw the moisture in their eyes and I tried to smile so that their last recollection of me would be one that would cheer them.

But when the whistle blew and they were on the pier, and I was on the Augusta Victoria, which was slowly but surely moving away from all I knew, taking me to strange lands and strange people, I felt lost. My head felt dizzy and my heart felt as if it would burst. Only seventy-five days! Yes, but it seemed an age and the world lost its roundness and seemed a long distance with no end, and-well, I never turn back.

I looked as long as I could at the people on the pier. I did not feel as happy as I have at other times in life. I had a sentimental longing to take farewell of everything.

"I am off," I thought sadly, "and shall I ever get back?"

Intense heat, bitter cold, terrible storms, shipwrecks, fevers, all such agreeable topics had been drummed into me until I felt much as I imagine one would feel if shut in a cave of midnight darkness and told that all sorts of horrors were waiting to gobble one up.

The morning was beautiful and the bay never looked lovelier. The ship glided out smoothly and quietly, and the people on deck looked for their chairs and rugs and got into comfortable positions, as if determined to enjoy themselves while they could, for they did not know what moment someone would be enjoying themselves at their expense.

When the pilot went off everybody rushed to the side of the ship to see him go down the little rope ladder. I watched him closely, but he climbed down and into the row boat, that was waiting to carry him to the pilot boat, without giving one glance back to us. It was an old story to him, but I could not help wondering if the ship should go down, whether there would not be some word or glance he would wish he had given.

"You have now started on your trip," someone said to me. "As soon as the pilot goes off and the captain assumes command, then, and only then our voyage begins, so now you are really started on your tour around the world."

Something in his words turned my thoughts to that demon of the sea-sea-sickness.

Never having taken a sea voyage before, I could expect nothing else than a lively tussle with the disease of the wave.

"Do you get sea-sick?" I was asked in an interested, friendly way. That was enough; I flew to the railing.

Sick? I looked blindly down, caring little what the wild waves were saying, and gave vent to my feelings.

People are always unfeeling about sea-sickness. When I wiped the tears from my eyes and turned around, I saw smiles on the face of every passenger. I have noticed that they are always on the same side of the ship when one is taken suddenly, overcome, as it were, with one's own emotions.

The smiles did not bother me, but one man said sneeringly:

"And she's going around the world!"

I too joined in the laugh that followed. Silently I marveled at my boldness to attempt such a feat wholly unused, as I was, to sea-voyages. Still I did not entertain one doubt as to the result.

Of course I went to luncheon. Everybody did, and almost everybody left very hurriedly. I joined them, or, I don't know, probably I made the start. Anyway I never saw as many in the dining room at any one time during the rest of the voyage.

When dinner was served I went in very bravely and took my place on the Captain's left. I had a very strong determination to resist my impulses, but yet, in the bottom of my heart was a little faint feeling that I had found something even stronger than my will power.

Dinner began very pleasantly. The waiters moved about noiselessly, the band played an overture, Captain Albers, handsome and genial, took his place at the head, and the passengers who were seated at his table began dinner with a relish equaled only by enthusiastic wheelmen when roads are fine. I was the only one at the Captain's table who might be called an amateur sailor. I was bitterly conscious of this fact. So were the others.

I might as well confess it, while soup was being served, I was lost in painful thoughts and filled with a sickening fear. I felt that everything was just as pleasant as an unexpected gift on Christmas, and I endeavored to listen to the enthusiastic remarks about the music made by my companions, but my thoughts were on a topic that would not bear discussion.

I felt cold, I felt warm; I felt that I should not get hungry if I did not see food for seven days; in fact, I had a great, longing desire not to see it, nor to smell it, nor to eat of it, until I could reach land or a better understanding with myself.

Fish was served, and Captain Albers was in the midst of a good story when I felt I had more than I could endure.

"Excuse me," I whispered faintly, and then rushed, madly, blindly out. I was assisted to a secluded spot where a little reflection and a little unbridling of pent up emotion restored me to such a courageous state that I determined to take the Captain's advice and return to my unfinished dinner.

"The only way to conquer sea-sickness is by forcing one's self to eat," the Captain said, and I thought the remedy harmless enough to test.

They congratulated me on my return. I had a shamed feeling that I was going to misbehave again, but I tried to hide the fact from them. It came soon, and I disappeared at the same rate of speed as before.

Once again I returned. This time my nerves felt a little unsteady and my belief in my determination was weakening, Hardly had I seated myself when I caught an amused gleam of a steward's eye, which made me bury my face in my handkerchief and choke before I reached the limits of the dining hall.

The bravos with which they kindly greeted my third return to the table almost threatened to make me lose my bearings again. I was glad to know that dinner was just finished and I had the boldness to say that it was very good!

I went to bed shortly afterwards. No one had made any friends yet, so I concluded sleep would be more enjoyable than sitting in the music hall looking at other passengers engaged in the same first-day-at-sea occupation.

I went to bed shortly after seven o'clock. I had a dim recollection afterwards of waking up enough to drink some tea, but beyond this and the remembrance of some dreadful dreams, I knew nothing until I heard an honest, jolly voice at the door calling to me.

Opening my eyes I found the stewardess and a lady passenger in my cabin and saw the Captain standing at the door.

"We were afraid that you were dead," the Captain said when he saw that I was awake.

"I always sleep late in the morning," I said apologetically.

"In the morning!" the Captain exclaimed, with a laugh, which was echoed by the others, "It is half-past four in the evening!"

"But never mind," he added consolingly, "as long as you slept well it will do you good. Now get up and see if you can't eat a big dinner."

I did. I went through every course at dinner without flinching, and stranger still, I slept that night as well as people are commonly supposed to sleep after long exercise in the open air.

The weather was very bad, and the sea was rough, but I enjoyed it. My sea-sickness had disappeared, but I had a morbid, haunting idea, that although it was gone, it would come again, still I managed to make myself comfortable.

Almost all of the passengers avoided the dining-room, took their meals on deck and maintained reclining positions with a persistency that grew monotonous. One bright, clever, American-born girl was traveling alone to Germany, to her parents. She entered heartily into anything that was conducive to pleasure. She was a girl who talked a great deal and she always said something. I have rarely, if ever, met her equal. In German as well as English, she could ably discuss anything from fashions to politics. Her father and her uncle are men well-known in public affairs, and by this girl's conversation it was easy to see that she was a father's favorite child; she was so broad and brilliant and womanly. There was not one man on board who knew more about politics, art, literature or music, than this girl with Marguerite hair, and yet there was not one of us more ready and willing to take a race on deck than was she.

I think it is only natural for travelers to take an innocent pleasure in studying the peculiarities of their fellow companions. We were not out many days until everybody that was able to be about had added a little to their knowledge of those that were not. I will not say that the knowledge acquired in that way is of any benefit, nor would I try to say that those passengers who mingled together did not find one another as interesting and as fit subjects for comment. Nevertheless it was harmless and it afforded us some amusement.

I remember when I was told that we had among the passengers one man who counted his pulse after every meal, and they were hearty meals, too, for he was free from the disease of the wave, that I waited quite eagerly to have him pointed out, so that I might watch him. If it had been my pulse, instead of his own, that he watched so carefully, I could not have been more interested thereafter. Every day I became more anxious and concerned until I could hardly refrain from asking him if his pulse decreased before meals and increased afterwards, or if it was the same in the evening as it was in the morning.

I almost forgot my interest in this one man, when my attention was called to another, who counted the number of steps he took every day. This one in turn became less interesting when I found that one of the women, who had been a great sufferer from sea-sickness, had not undressed since she left her home in New York.

"I am sure we are all going down," she said one day in a burst of confidence, "and I am determined to go down dressed!"

I was not surprised after this that she was so dreadfully sea-sick.

One family who were removing from New York to Paris, had with them a little silver skye terrier, which bore the rather odd name of "Home, Sweet Home." Fortunately for the dog, as well as for those who were compelled to speak to him, they had shortened the name into "Homie."

"Homie's " passage was paid, but according to the rules of the ship, "Homie" was confined to the care of the butcher, much to the disgust of his master and mistress. "Homie" had not been accustomed to such harsh measures before, and the only streaks of happiness that came into his life were when permission was obtained for him to come on deck. Permission was granted with a proviso that if "Homie" barked he was to be taken instantly below. I fear that many hours of "Homie's " imprisonment might be laid at our door, for he knew how to dig most frantically when anyone said, "Rats," and when he did dig, he usually punctuated his attempt with short, crisp barks. With dismay we daily noted "Homie's " decrease in flesh. We marveled at his losing weight while confined in the butcher's quarters, and at last put it down to sea-sickness, which he, like some of the passengers, confined to the secrecy of his cabin. Towards the end of the voyage, when we were all served with sausage and Hamburger steak, there would be many whispered inquiries as to whether "Homie" had been seen that day. So anxious became those whispers that sometimes I thought they were rather tinged with a personal concern that was not wholly friendship for the wee dog.

When everything else grew tiresome, Captain Albers would always invent something to amuse us. He made a practice every evening after dinner, of putting the same number of lines on a card as there were gentlemen at the table. One of these lines he would mark and then partly folding the card over so as to prevent the marked line from being seen. would pass it around for the men to take their choice.

After all had marked, the card was passed to the Captain, and we would wait breathlessly for the verdict. The gentleman whose name had been marked paid for the cigars or cordials for the others.

Many were the discussions about the erroneous impression entertained by most foreigners about Americans and America. Some one remarked that the majority of people in foreign lands were not able to tell where the United States is.

"There are plenty of people who think the United States is one little island, with a few houses on it," Captain Albers said. "Once there was delivered at my house, near the wharf, in Hoboken, a letter from Germany, addressed to,

'CAPTAIN   ALBERS,
FIRST HOUSE IN AMERICA.'"

"I got one from Germany once," said the most bashful man at the table, his face flushing at the sound of his own voice, "addressed to,

'HOBOKEN, OPPOSITE THE UNITED STATES.'"

While at luncheon on the 21st of November, some one called out that we were in sight of land. The way everyone left the table and rushed on deck was surely not surpassed by the companions of Columbus when they discovered America. I can not give any good reason for it, but I know that I looked at the first point of bleak land with more interest than I would have bestowed on the most beautiful bit of scenery in the world.

We had not been long in sight of land until the decks began to fill with dazed-looking, wan-faced people. It was just as if we had taken on new passengers. We could not realize that they were from New York and had been enjoying (?) a season of seclusion since leaving that port.

Dinner that evening was a very pleasant affair. Extra courses had been prepared in honor of those that were leaving at Southampton. I had not known one of the passengers when I left New York seven days before, but I realized, now that I was so soon to separate from them, that I regretted the parting very much.

Had I been traveling with a companion I should not have felt this so keenly, for naturally then I would have had less time to cultivate the acquaintance of my fellow passengers.

They were all so kind to me that I should have been the most ungrateful of women had I not felt that I was leaving friends behind. Captain Albers had served many years as commander of a ship in Eastern seas, and he cautioned me as to the manner in which I should take care of my health. As the time grew shorter for my stay on the Augusta Victoria, some teased me gently as to the outcome of my attempt to beat the record made by a hero of fiction, and I found myself forcing a false gaiety that helped to hide my real fears.

The passengers on the Augusta Victoria all stayed up to see us off. We sat on deck talking or nervously walking about until half-past two in the morning. Then some one said the tugboat had come alongside, and we all rushed over to see it. After it was made secure we went down to the lower deck to see who would come on and to get some news from land.

One man was very much concerned about my making the trip to London alone. He thought as it was so late, or rather so early, that the London correspondent, who was to have met me, would not put in an appearance.

"I shall most certainly leave the ship here and see you safely to London, if no one comes to meet you," he protested, despite my assurances that I felt perfectly able to get along safely without an escort.

More for his sake than my own, I watched the men come on board, and tried to pick out the one that had been sent to meet me. Several of them were passing us in a line just as a gentleman made some remark about my trip around the world. A tall young man overheard the remark, and turning at the foot of the stairs, looked down at me with a hesitating smile.

"Nellie Bly?" he asked inquiringly.

"Yes," I replied, holding out my hand, which he gave a cordial grasp, meanwhile asking if I had enjoyed my trip, and if my baggage was ready to be transferred.

The man who had been so fearful of my traveling to London alone, took occasion to draw the correspondent into conversation. Afterwards he came to me and said with the most satisfied look upon his face:

"He is all right. If he had not been so, I should have gone to London with you anyway. I can rest satisfied now for he will take care of you."

I went away with a warm feeling in my heart for that kindly man who would have sacrificed his own comfort to insure the safety of an unprotected girl.

A few warm hand clasps, and interchanging of good wishes, a little dry feeling in the throat, a little strained pulsation of the heart, a little hurried run down the perpendicular plank to the other passengers who were going to London, and then the tug cast off from the ship, and we drifted away in the dark.

Chapter 3: Southampton to Jules Verne's

"M R. & MRS. JULES VERNE have sent a special letter asking that if possible you will stop to see them," the London correspondent said to me, as we were on our way to the wharf.

"Oh, how I should like to see them!" I exclaimed, adding in the same breath, "Isn't it hard to be forced to decline such a treat?"

"If you are willing to go without sleep and rest for two nights, I think it can be done," he said quietly.

"Safely? Without making me miss any connections? If so, don't think about sleep or rest."

"It depends on our getting a train out of here to-night. All the regular trains until morning have left, and unless they decide to run a special mail train for the delayed mails, we will have to stay here all night and that will not give us time to see Verne. We shall see when we land what they will decide to do."

The boat that was landing us left much to be desired in the way of comfort. The only cabin seemed to be the hull, but it was filled with mail and baggage and lighted by a lamp with a smoked globe. I did not see any place to sit down, so we all stood on deck, shivering in the damp, chilly air, and looking in the gray fog like uneasy spirits.

The dreary, dilapidated wharf was a fit landing place for the antique boat. I silently followed the correspondent into a large empty shed, where a few men with sleep in their eyes and uniforms that bore ample testimony to the fact that they had slept in their clothes, were stationed behind some long, low tables.

"Where are your keys?" the correspondent asked me as he sat my solitary bag down before one of these weary looking inspectors.

"It is too full to lock," I answered simply.

"Will you swear that you have no tobacco or tea?" the inspector asked my escort lazily.

"Don't swear," I said to him; then turning to the inspector I added: "It's my bag."

He smiled and putting a chalk mark upon the bag freed us.

"Declare your tobacco and tea or tip the man," I said teazingly to a passenger who stood with poor, thin, shaking "Homie" under one arm, searching frantically through his pockets for his keys.

"I've fixed him!" he answered with an expressive wink.

Passing through the custom house we were made happy by the information that it had been decided to attach a passenger coach to the special mail train to oblige the passengers who wished to go to London without delay. The train was made up then, so we concluded to get into our car and try to warm up.

A porter took my bag and another man in uniform drew forth an enormous key with which he unlocked the door in the side of the car instead of the end, as in America. I managed to compass the uncomfortable long step to the door and striking my toe against some projection in the floor, went most ungracefully and unceremoniously on to the seat.

My escort after giving some order to the porter went out to see about my ticket, so I took a survey of an English railway compartment. The little square in which I sat looked like a hotel omnibus and was about as comfortable. The two red leather seats in it run across the car, one backing the engine, the other backing the rear of the train. There was a door on either side and one could hardly have told that there was a dingy lamp there to cast a light on the scene had not the odor from it been so loud. I carefully lifted the rug that covered the thing I had fallen over, curious to see what could be so necessary to an English railway carriage as to occupy such a prominent position. I found a harmless object that looked like a bar of iron and had just dropped the rug in place when the door opened and the porter, catching the iron at one end, pulled it out, replacing it with another like it in shape and size.

"Put your feet on the foot warmer and get warm, Miss," he said, and I mechanically did as he advised.

My escort returned soon after, followed by a porter who carried a large basket which he put in our carriage. The guard came afterwards and took our tickets. Pasting a slip of paper on the window, which backwards looked like "etavirP," he went out and locked the door.

"How should we get out if the train ran the track?" I asked, not half liking the idea of being locked in a box like an animal in a freight train.

"Trains never run off the track in England," was the quiet, satisfied answer.

"Too slow for that," I said teasingly, which only provoked a gentle inquiry as to whether I wanted anything to eat.

With a newspaper spread over our laps for a table-cloth, we brought out what the basket contained and put in our time eating and chatting about my journey until the train reached London.

As no train was expected at that hour, Waterloo Station was almost deserted. It was some little time after we stopped before the guard unlocked the door of our compartment and released us. Our few fellow-passengers were just about starting off in shabby cabs when we alighted. Once again we called goodbye and good wishes to each other, and then I found myself in a four-wheeled cab, facing a young Englishman who had come to meet us and who was glibly telling us the latest news.

I don't know at what hour we arrived, but my companions told me that it was daylight. I should not have known it. A gray, misty fog hung like a ghostly pall over the city. I always liked fog, it lends such a soft, beautifying light to things that otherwise in the broad glare of day would be rude and commonplace.

"How are these streets compared with those of New York?" was the first question that broke the silence after our leaving the station.

"They are not bad," I said with a patronizing air, thinking shamefacedly of the dreadful streets of New York, although determined to hear no word against them.

Westminster Abbey and the Houses of Parliament were pointed out to me, and the Thames, across which we drove. I felt that I was taking what might be called a bird's -eye view of London. A great many foreigners have taken views in the same rapid way of America, and afterwards gone home and written books about America, Americans, and Americanisms.

We drove first to the London office of the New York *World*. After receiving the cables that were waiting for my arrival, I started for the American Legation to get a passport as I had been instructed by cable.

Mr. McCormick, Secretary of the Legation, came into the room immediately after our arrival, and after welcoming and congratulating me on the successful termination of the first portion of my trip, sat down and wrote out a passport.

My escort was asked to go into another part of the room until the representative could ask me an important question. I had never required a passport before, and I felt a nervous curiosity to know what secrets were connected with such proceedings.

"There is one question all women dread to answer, and as very few will give a truthful reply, I will ask you to swear to the rest first and fill in the other question afterwards, unless you have no hesitancy in telling me your age."

"Oh, certainly," I laughed. "I will tell you my age, swear to it, too, and I am not afraid; my companion may come out of the corner."

"What is the color of your eyes?" he asked.

"Green," I said indifferently.

He was inclined to doubt it at first, but after a little inspection, both the gentlemen accepted my verdict as correct.

It was only a few seconds until we were whirling through the streets of London again. This time we went to the office of the Peninsular and Oriental Steamship Company, where I bought tickets that would cover at least half of my journey. A few moments again and we were driving rapidly to the Charing Cross station.

I was faint for food, and while my companion dismissed the cab and secured tickets, I ordered the only thing on the Charing Cross bill of fare that was prepared, so when he returned, his breakfast was ready for him. It was only ham and eggs, and coffee, but what we got of it was delicious. I know we did not get much, and when we were interrupted by the announcement that our train was starting, I stopped long enough to take another drink of coffee and then had to run down the platform to catch the train.

There is nothing like plenty of food to preserve health. I know that cup of coffee saved me from a headache that day. I had been shaking with the cold as we made our hurried drive through London, and my head was so dizzy at times that I hardly knew whether the earth had a chill or my brains were attending a ball. When I got comfortable seated in the train I began to feel warmer and more stable.

The train moved off at an easy-going speed, and the very jog of it lulled me into a state of languor.

"I want you to see the scenery along here; it is beautiful," my companion said, but I lazily thought, "What is scenery compared with sleep when one has not seen bed for over twenty-four hours?" so I said to him, very crossly:

"Don't you think you would better take a nap? You have not had any sleep for so long and you will be up so late to-night, that, really, I think for the sake of your health you would better sleep now."

"And you?" he asked with a teasing smile. I had been up even longer.

"Well, I confess, I was saying one word for you and two for myself," I replied, with a laugh that put us at ease on the subject.

"Honestly, now, I care very little for scenery when I am so sleepy," I said apologetically. "Those English farm houses are charming and the daisy-dotted meadows (I had not the faintest conception as to whether there were daisies in them or not), are only equaled by those I have seen in Kansas, but if you will excuse me?–" and I was in the land that joins the land of death.

I slept an easy, happy sleep, filled with dreams of home until I was waked by the train stopping.

"We change for the boat here," my companion said catching up our bags and rugs, which he hauled to a porter.

A little walk down to the pier brought us to the place where a boat was waiting. Some people were getting off the boat, but a larger number stood idly about waiting for it to move off.

The air was very cold and chilly, but still I preferred the deck to the close, musty-smelling cabin beneath. Two English women also remained on deck. I was much amused at the conversation they held with some friends who had accompanied them to the boat, and now stood on the wharf. One would have supposed, by hearing the conversation that they had only that instant met and having no time to spend together, were forced to make all further arrangements on the spot.

"You will come over to-morrow, now don't forget," the young woman on the boat called out.

"I won't forget. Are you certain that you have everything with you?" the one on the wharf called back.

"Look after Fido. Give him that compound in the morning if there is no appearance of improvement," the first one said.

"You will meet me to-morrow?" said number two on shore.

"Oh yes; don't forget to come," was the reply, and as the boat moved out they both talked at once until we were quite a distance off, then simultaneously the one turned to her chair and the other turned around and walked rapidly away from the wharf.

There has been so much written and told about the English Channel, that one is inclined to think of it as a stream of horrors. It is also affirmed that even hardy sailors bring up the past when crossing over it, so I naturally felt that my time would come.

All the passengers must have been familiar with the history of the channel, for I saw everyone trying all the known preventives of seasickness. The women assumed reclining positions and the men sought the bar.

I remained on deck and watched the sea-gulls, or what I thought were these useful birds-useful for millinery purposes-and froze my nose. It was bitterly cold, but I found the cold bracing until we anchored at Boulogne, France. Then I had a chill.

At the end of this desolate pier, where boats anchor and where trains start, is a small, dingy restaurant. While a little English sailor, who always dropped his h's and never forgot his "sir," took charge of our bags and went to secure accommodations for us in the outgoing train, we followed the other passengers into the restaurant to get something warm to eat.

I was in France now, and I began to wonder now what would have been my fate if I had been alone as I had expected. I knew my companion spoke French, the language that all the people about us were speaking, so I felt perfectly easy on that score as long as he was with me.

We took our places at the table and he began to order in French. The waiter looked blankly at him until, at last, more in a spirit of fun than anything else, I suggested that he give the order in English. The waiter glanced at me with a smile and answered in English.

We traveled from Boulogne to Amiens in a compartment with an English couple and a Frenchman. There was one foot-warmer and the day was cold. We all tried to put our feet on the one foot-warmer and the result was embarrassing. The Frenchman sat facing me and as I was conscious of having tramped on someone's toes, and as he looked at me angrily all the time above the edge of his newspaper, I had a guilty feeling of knowing whose toes had been tramped on.

During this trip I tried to solve the reason for the popularity of these ancient, incommodious railway carriages. I very shortly decided that while they may be suitable for countries where little traveling is done, they would be thoroughly useless in thinly populated countries where people think less of traveling 3,000 miles than they do about their dinner. I also decided that the reason why we think nothing of starting out on long trips, is because our comfort is so well looked after, that living on a first-class railway train is as comfortable as living at a first-class hotel. The English railway carriages are wretchedly heated. One's feet will be burning on the foot-warmer while one's back will be freezing in the cold air above. If one should be taken suddenly ill in an English railway compartment, it would be a very serious matter.

Still, I can picture conditions under which these ancient railway carriages might be agreeable, but they are not such as would induce a traveler to prefer them to those built on the American model.

Supposing one had the measles or a black eye, then a compartment in a railway carriage, made private by a tip to the porter, would be very consoling.

Supposing one was newly wed and was bubbling over in ecstacy of joy, then give one an English railway compartment, where two just made one can be secluded from the eyes of a cold, sneering public, who are just as great fools under the same conditions, although they would deny it if one told them so.

But talk about privacy! If it is privacy the English desire so much, they should adopt our American trains, for there is no privacy like that to be found in a large car filled with strangers. Everybody has, and keeps his own place. There is no sitting for hours, as is often the case in English trains, face to face and knees to knees with a stranger, offensive or otherwise, as he may chance to be.

Then too, did the English railway carriage make me understand why English girls need chaperones. It would make any American woman shudder with all her boasted self-reliance, to think of sending her daughter alone on a trip, even of a few hours' duration, where there was every possibility that during those hours she would be locked in a compartment with a stranger.

Small wonder the American girl is fearless. She has not been used to so called private compartments in English railway carriages, but to large crowds, and every individual that helps to swell that crowd is to her a protector. When mothers teach their daughters that there is safety in numbers, and that numbers are the body-guard that shield all woman-kind, then chaperones will be a thing of the past, and women will be nobler and better.

As I was pondering over this subject, the train pulled into a station and stopped. My escort looking out, informed me that we were at Amiens. We were securely locked in, however, and began to think that we would be carried past, when my companion managed to get his head out of the window and shouted for the guard to come to our release. Freed at last, we stepped out on the platform at Amiens.

Chapter 4: Jules Verne at Home

M. JULES VERNE and Mme. Verne, accompanied by Mr. R. H. Sherard, a Paris journalist, stood on the platform waiting our arrival.

When I saw them I felt as any other woman would have done under the same circumstances. I wondered if my face was travel-stained, and if my hair was tossed. I thought regretfully, had I been traveling on an American train, I should have been able to make my toilet *en route*, so that when I stepped off at Amiens and faced the famous novelist and his charming wife, I would have been as trim and tidy as I would had I been receiving them in my own home.

There was little time for regret. They were advancing towards us, and in another second I had forgotten my untidiness in the cordial welcome they gave me. Jules Verne's bright eyes beamed on me with interest and kindliness, and Mme. Verne greeted me with the cordiality of a cherished friend. There were no stiff formalities to freeze the kindness in all our hearts, but a cordiality expressed with such charming grace that before I had been many minutes in their company, they had won my everlasting respect and devotion.

M. Verne led the way to the carriages which waited our coming. Mme. Verne walked closely by my side, glancing occasionally at me with a smile, which said in the language of the eye, the common language of the whole animal world, alike plain to man and beast:

"I am glad to greet you, and I regret we cannot speak together." M. Verne gracefully helped Mme. Verne and myself into a coupé, while he entered a carriage with the two other gentlemen. I felt very awkward at being left alone with Mme. Verne, as I was altogether unable to speak to her.

Her knowledge of the English language consisted of "No" and my French vocabulary consisted of "Oui," so our conversation was limited to a few apologetic and friendly smiles interluded with an occasional pressure of the hand. Indeed, Mme. Verne is a most charming woman, and even in this awkward position she made everything go most gracefully.

It was early evening. As we drove through the streets of Amiens I got a flying glimpse of bright shops, a pretty park, and numerous nurse maids pushing baby carriages about.

When our carriage stopped I got out and gave my hand to Mme. Verne to help her alight. We stood on a wide, smooth pavement, before a high stone wall, over the top of which I could see the peaked outlines of the house.

M. Verne was not long behind us. He hurried up to where we were standing and opened a door in the wall. Stepping in I found myself in a small, smoothly paved court-yard, the wall making two sides and the house forming the square.

A large, black shaggy dog came bounding forward to greet me. He jumped up against me, his soft eyes overflowing with affection, and though I love dogs and especially appreciated this one's loving welcome, still I feared that his lavish display of it would undermine my dignity by bringing me to my knees at the very threshold of the home of the famous Frenchman.

M. Verne evidently understood my plight, for he spoke shortly to the dog, who, with a pathetic droop of his tail, went off to think it out alone.

We went up a flight of marble steps across the tiled floor of a beautiful little conservatory that was not packed with flowers but was filled with a display just generous enough to allow one to see and appreciate the beauty of the different plants. Mme. Verne led the way into a large sitting-room that was dusky with the early shade of a wintry evening. With her own hands she touched a match to the pile of dry wood that lay in the wide open fireplace.

Meanwhile M. Verne urged us to remove our outer wrappings. Before this was done a bright fire was crackling in the grate, throwing a soft, warm light over the dark room. Mme. Verne led me to a chair close by the mantel, and when I was seated she took the chair opposite. Cheered by the warmth I looked quietly on the scene before me.

The room was large and the hangings and paintings and soft velvet rug, which left visible but a border of polished hard wood, were richly dark. On the mantel, which towered above Mme. Verne's head, were some fine pieces of statuary in bronze and, as the fire gave frequent bright flashes as the flames greedily caught fresh wood, I could see another bronze piece on a pedestal in a corner. All the chairs artistically upholstered in brocaded silks, were luxuriously easy. Beginning at either side of the mantel they were placed in a semi-circle around the fire, which was only broken by a little table that held several tall silver candlesticks.

A fine white Angora cat came rubbing up against my knee, then seeing its charming mistress on the opposite side, went to her and boldly crawled up in her lap as if assured of a cordial welcome.

Next to me in this semi-circle sat Mr. Sherard. M. Jules Verne was next to Mr. Sherard. He sat forward on the edge of his chair, his snow-white hair rather long and heavy, was standing up in artistic disorder; his full beard, rivaling his hair in snowiness, hid the lower part of his face and the brilliancy of his bright eyes that were overshadowed with heavy white brows, and the rapidity of his speech and the quick movements of his firm white hands all bespoke energy-life-with enthusiasm.

The London correspondent sat next to Jules Verne. With a smile on her soft rosy lips, Mme. Verne sat nursing the cat which she stroked methodically with a dainty, white hand, while her luminous black eyes moved alternately between her husband and myself.

She was the most charming figure in that group around the wood fire. Imagine a youthful face with a spotless complexion, crowned with the whitest hair, dressed in smooth, soft folds on the top of a dainty head that is most beautifully poised on a pair of plump shoulders. Add to this face pretty red lips, that opened disclose a row of lovely teeth, and large, bewitching black eyes, and you have but a faint picture of the beauty of Mme. Verne.

This day when she met me she wore a sealskin jacket and carried a muff, and on her white head was a small black velvet bonnet. On taking her wraps off in the house I saw she wore a watered-silk skirt, laid in side plaits in the front with a full straight black drapery, that was very becoming to her short, plump figure. The bodice was of black silk velvet.

Mme. Verne is, I should judge, not more than five feet two in height; M. Verne about five feet five. M. Verne spoke in a short, rapid way, and Mr. Sherard in an attractive, lazy voice translated what was said for my benefit.

"Has M. Verne ever been to America?" I asked.

"Yes, once;" the answer came translated to me. "For a few days only, during which time I saw Niagara. I have always longed to return, but the state of my health prevents my taking any long journeys. I try to keep a knowledge of everything that is going on in America and greatly appreciate the hundreds of letters I receive yearly from Americans who read my books. There is one man in California who has been writing to me for years. He writes all the news about his family and home and country as if I were a friend and yet we have never met. He has urged me to come to America as his guest. I know of nothing that I long to do more than to see your land from New York to San Francisco."

"How did you get the idea for your novel, 'Around the World in Eighty Days?'" I asked.

"I got it from a newspaper," was his reply. "I took up a copy of Le Siécle one morning, and found in it a discussion and some calculations showing that the journey around the world might be done in eighty days. The idea pleased me, and while thinking it over it struck me that in their calculations they had not called into account the difference in the meridians and I thought what a denouement such a thing would make in a novel, so I went to work to write one. Had it not been for the denouement I don't think that I should ever have written the book."

"I used to keep a yacht, and then I traveled all over the world studying localities; then I wrote from actual observation. Now, since my health confines me to my home, I am forced to read up descriptions and geographies."

M. Verne asked me what my line of travel was to be, and I was very happy to speak one thing that he could understand, so I told him.

"My line of travel is from New York to London, then Calais, Brindisi, Port Said, Ismailia, Suez, Aden, Colombo, Penang, Singapore, Hong Kong, Yokohama, San Francisco, New York."

"Why do you not go to Bombay as my hero Phileas Fogg did?" M. Verne asked.

"Because I am more anxious to save time than a young widow," I answered.

"You may save a young widower before you return," M. Verne said with a smile.

I smiled with a superior knowledge, as women, fancy free, always will at such insinuations.

I looked at the watch on my wrist and saw that my time was getting short. There was only one train that I could take from here to Calais, and if I missed it I might just as well return to New York by the way I came, for the loss of that train meant one week's delay.

"If M. Verne would not consider it impertinent I should like to see his study before I go," I said at last.

He said he was only too happy to show it me, and even as my request was translated Mme. Verne sprang to her feet and lighted one of the tall wax candles.

She started with the quick, springy step of a girl to lead the way. M. Verne, who walks with a slight limp, the result of a wound, followed, and we brought up the rear. We went through the conservatory to a small room up through which was a winding stair, or, more properly speaking, a spiral stair-case. Mme. Verne paused at every curve to light the gas.

Up at the top of the house and along a hall that corresponded in shape to the conservatory below, M. Verne went, Mme. Verne stopping to light the gas in the hall. He opened a door that led off the hall and I stepped inside after him.

I was astonished. I had expected, judging from the rest of the house, that M. Verne's study would be a room of ample proportions and richly furnished. I had read so many descriptions of the studies of famous authors, and have dwelt with something akin to envy (our space is so limited and expensive in New York) on the ample room, the beautiful hand-carved desks filled with costly trinkets, the rare etchings and paintings that covered the walls, the rich hangings, and, I will confess it, I have thought it small wonder that amid such surroundings authors were able to dream fancies that brought them fame.

But when I stood in M. Verne's study I was speechless with surprise. He opened a latticed window, the only window in the room, and Mme. Verne, hurrying in after us, lighted the gas jet that was fastened above a low mantel.

The room was very small; even my little den at home was almost as large. It was also very modest and bare. Before the window was a flat-topped desk. The usual litter that accompanies and fills the desks of most literary persons was conspicuously absent, and the waste-basket that is usually filled to overflowing with what one very often considers their most brilliant productions, in this case held but a few little scraps.

On the desk was a neat little pile of white paper, probably 8x10 in size. It was part of the manuscript of a novel that M. Verne is engaged on at present. I eagerly accepted the manuscript when he handed it to me, and when I looked at the neat penmanship, so neat in fact that had I not known it was prose I should have thought it was the work of a poet, I was more impressed than ever with the extreme tidiness of this French author. In several places he had most effectually blotted out something that he had written, but there was no interlining, which gave me the idea that M. Verne always improved his work by taking out superfluous things and never by adding.

One bottle of ink and one penholder was all that shared the desk with the manuscript. There was but one chair in the room, and it stood before the desk. The only other piece of furniture was a broad, low couch in the corner, and here in this room with these meagre surroundings, Jules Verne has written the books that have brought him everlasting fame.

I leaned over the desk and looked out of the little latticed window which he had thrown open. I could see through the dusk the spire of a cathedral in the distance, while stretching down beneath me was a park, beyond which I saw the entrance to a railway tunnel that goes under M. Verne's house, and through which many Americans travel every year, on their way to Paris.

Leading off from the study, is an enormous library. The large room is completely lined with cases from ceiling to floor, and these glass-doored cases are packed with handsomely bound books which must be worth a fortune.

While we were examining the wealth of literature that was there before us, M. Verne got an idea. Taking up a candle and asking us to follow, he went out into the hall; stopping before a large map that hung there, holding up with one hand the candle, he pointed out to us several blue marks. Before his words were translated to me, I understood that on this map he had, with a blue pencil, traced out the course of his hero, Phileas Fogg, before he started him in fiction to travel around the world in eighty days. With a pencil he marked on the map, as we grouped about him, the places where my line of travel differed from that of Phileas Fogg.

Our steps lagged as we descended the winding stair again. It had come time to take farewell, and I felt as if I was separating from friends. Down in the room where we had been before, we found wine and biscuit on the little table, and M. Jules Verne explained that, contrary to his regular rules, he intended to take a glass of wine, that we might have the pleasure of drinking together to the success of my strange undertaking.

They clinked their glasses with wine, and wished me "God speed."

"If you do it in seventy-nine days, I shall applaud with both hands," Jules Verne said, and then I knew he doubted the possibility of my doing it in seventy-five, as I had promised. In compliment to me, he endeavored to speak to me in English, and did succeed in saying, as his glass tipped mine:

"Good luck, Nellie Bly."

Mme. Verne was not going to be outdone by her gallant husband in showing kindness to me. She told Mr. Sherard that she would like to kiss me good-bye, and when he translated her kind request, he added that it was a great honor in France, for a woman to ask to kiss a stranger.

I was little used to such formalities, or familiarities, as one may deem them, but still I had not one thought of refusing such delicate attention, so I gave her my hand and inclined my head, for I am taller than she, and she kissed me gently and affectionately on either check. Then she put up her pretty face for me to kiss. I stifled a strong inclination to kiss her on the lips, they were so sweet and red, and show her how we do it in America. My mischievousness often plays havoc with my dignity, but for once I was able to restrain myself, and kissed her softly after her own fashion.

With uncovered heads, and despite our protestations, they followed us out into the cold court-yard, and as far as I could see I saw them standing at the gate waving farewell to me, the brisk winds tossing their white hair.

Chapter 5: On to Brindisi

WHEN M. and Mme. Verne were no longer visible, my thoughts turned to my trip. I feared that the enjoyment of my visit to their home had jeopardized the success of my tour.

The driver had been told to make the best speed back to the station, but the carriage seemed to be rolling along so quietly that I could not rest until it was urged again upon the coachman to reach the station in the shortest possible time.

Some few moments after we reached there the train came in. Bidding a hearty good-bye to Mr. Sherard, I started again on my tour of the world, and the visit to Jules Verne was a thing of the past. I had gone without sleep and rest; I had traveled many miles out of my way for the privilege of meeting M. and Mme. Verne, and I felt that if I had gone around the world for that pleasure, I should not have considered the price too high.

The train which carried us to Calais is, I infer from what I have heard, the pride of France. It is called the Club train, and is built on the plan of the vestibule trains in America. The carriages are so narrow, that after having been accustomed to wide ones, the Club train seems like a toy.

I have been curious to know why this train is called the Club train. I had a foolish idea at first that it was the private property of some club, run for the special benefit of its members, and I felt some hesitancy about traveling on a train devoted to the use of men. However, the presence of a number of women put me at ease, and though I made many inquiries about the train, all I could learn was that it was considered quite the finest equipped train in Europe.

The car in which we sat, as I said before, contained some women, and was besides liberally filled with men passengers. Shortly after we left Amiens, a porter announced that dinner was served in a front car. Everybody at once filed out and into the dining car. I have thought since that probably the train carried two dining cars, because the dinner, and an excellent one it proved to be, was served *table d'hôte*, and there seemed to be accommodations for all.

After we had our cheese and salad, we returned to our drawing-room car, where we were served with coffee, the men having the privilege of smoking with it. I thought this manner of serving coffee a very pleasing one, quite an improvement on our own system, and quite worthy of adoption.

When I reached Calais, I found that I had two hours and more to spend in waiting. The train that I intended to take for Brindisi is a weekly mail train that runs to accommodate the mails and not passengers. It starts originally from London, at eight o'clock Friday evening of each week. The rule is that the persons desiring to travel on it must buy their tickets twenty-four hours in advance of the time of its departure. The mail and passengers are carried across the channel, and the train leaves Calais at 1.30 in the morning.

There are pleasanter places in the world to waste time in than Calais. I walked down along the pier and looked at the light-house, which I am told is one of the most perfect in the world, throwing its light farther away than any other. It is a revolving light, and it throws out long rays that seem so little above our heads that I found myself dodging to avoid being struck. Of course, that was purely imaginary on my part, for the rays are just the opposite to being near the ground, but they spread between the ground and the sky like the laths of an unfinished partition. I wonder if the people of Calais ever saw the moon and stars.

There is a very fine railway station built near the end of the pier. It is of generous size, but seemed, as far as I could judge, at this hour of the night, quite empty. There is a smoothly tiled enclosed promenade on the side of the station facing the pier that I should say would prove quite an attraction and comfort for passengers who were forced to wait in that place.

My escort took me into the restaurant where we found something to eat, which was served by a French waiter who could speak some English and understand more. When it was announced that the boat from England was in we went out and saw the be-bundled and be-baggaged passengers come ashore and go to the train which was waiting alongside. One thousand bags of mail were quickly transferred to the train, and then I bade my escort good-bye, and was shortly speeding away from Calais.

There is but one passenger coach on this train. It is a Pullman Palace sleeping-car with accommodations for twenty-two passengers, but it is the rule never to carry more than twenty-one, one berth being occupied by the guard.

The next morning, having nothing else to occupy my time, I thought that I would see what my traveling companions looked like. I had shared the stateroom at the extreme end of the car with a pretty English girl who had the rosiest cheeks and the greatest wealth of golden brown hair I ever saw. She was going with her father, an invalid, to Egypt, to spend the winter and spring months. She was an early riser, and before I was awake had gotten up and joined her father in the other part of the car.

When I went out so as to give the porter an opportunity to make up my stateroom, I was surprised at the strange appearance of the interior of the car. All the head and foot boards were left in place, giving the impression that the coach was divided into a series of small boxes. Some of the passengers were drinking, some were playing cards, and all were smoking until the air was stifling. I never object to cigar smoke when there is some little ventilation, but when it gets so thick that one feels as if it is molasses instead of air that one is inhaling, then I mildly protest. It was soon this occasion, and I wonder what would be the result in our land of boasted freedom if a Pullman car should be put to such purposes. I concluded it is due to this freedom that we do not suffer from such things. Women travelers in America command as much consideration as men.

I walked down the car looking in the "boxes" only to find them all occupied by unsocial looking men. When I reached the middle of the car my little English room-mate, who was sitting with her father, saw me and kindly asked me to sit down with them.

Her father I remember as a cultured, broad-minded man, with a sense of humor that helped me to hear with less dread the racking cough that frequently stopped all speech and shook his thin frame as though he had the ague.

"Father," the little English girl said in a clear, musical voice, "the clergyman sent you his large prayer-book just before our departure, and I put it in your bag."

"My daughter is very thoughtful," he said to me, then turning to her he added, with a smile in his eye, "Please take the first opportunity to return the prayer-book to the clergyman, and tell him, with my compliments, that he might have saved himself that trouble; that I was grieved to deprive him of his book for so long."

The young girl's face settled into a look that spoke disapproval of her father's words, and a determination not to return the prayer-book. She held, clasped to her breast. a large prayer-book, and when her father jokingly told her she had bought the largest one she could find, which he looked on as wasting valuable packing space, when she could have carried a small one that would have been of as much service, I was actually startled by the hard, determined light on her face. In everything else she was the sweetest, most gentle girl I ever met, but her religion was of the hard, uncompromising kind, that condemns everything, forgives nothing, and swears the heathen is forever damned because he was not born to know the religion of her belief.

She spent all the afternoon trying to implant the seeds of her faith in my mind, and I listened, thinking from her words that if she was not the original Catherine Elsmere, she at least could not be more like that interesting character.

For the first day food was taken on the train at different stations, and the conductor, or guard, as they called him, served it to the passengers. A dining car was attached in the evening but I was informed by the women that it was not exactly the thing for us to eat in a public car with men, so we continued to be served in our state rooms.

I might have seen more while traveling through France if the car windows had been clean. From their appearance I judged that they had never been washed. We did not make many stops. The only purpose of stopping was for coal or water, as passengers are not taken on or off this train between Calais and Brindisi.

In the course of the afternoon we passed some high and picturesque mountains that were covered with a white frost. I found that even wearing my ulster and wrapped in a rug I was none too warm. About eight o'clock in the morning we reached Modena. The baggage was examined there and all the passengers were notified in advance to be prepared to get out and unlock the boxes that belonged to them. The conductor asked me several times if I was quite certain that I had no more than the handbag with me, telling me at the same time if any boxes were found locked, with no owner to open them, they would be detained by the custom inspectors. When partly assured that I had no trunks he said that it was not necessary to get out with my hand-bag, as no one would think it necessary to examine it.

Half an hour later we were in Italy. I was anxiously waiting to see that balmy, sunny land, but though I pressed my face close to the frosty window pane bleak night denied me even one glimpse of sunny Italy and its dusky people. I went to bed early. It was so very cold that I could not keep warm out of bed, and I cannot say that I got much warmer in bed. The berths were provided with only one blanket each. I piled all my clothing on the berth and spent half the night lying awake thinking how fortunate the passengers were the week previous on this train. Just in the very same place that we were traveling through Italian bandits had attacked the train and I thought, with regretful envy, if the passengers then felt the scarcity of blankets they at least had some excitement to make their blood circulate.

When I got awake in the morning I hastily threw up the window shade and eagerly looked out. I fell back in surprise, wondering, if for once in my life I had made a mistake and waked up early. I could not see any more than I had the night before on account of a heavy gray fog that completely hid everything more than a yard away. Looking at the watch on my wrist I found that it was ten o'clock, so I dressed with some haste determined to find the guard and demand an explanation of him.

"It is a most extraordinary thing," he said to me; "I never saw such a fog in Italy before."

There was nothing for it except to sit quietly counting the days I had been away from New York; subtracting them from the number that must elapse before my return. When this grew monotonous I carefully thought over the advisability of trying to introduce brown uniforms for railroad employees in the United States. I thought with wearied frenzy of the universal employment of navy-blue uniforms in America, and I turned with rest to the neat brown uniforms brightened with a touching of gold braid on the collars and cuffs, that adorned the conductor and porter of the India mail.

But even this subject would not fill the day, so I began to notice the difference between the whistles employed on these engines and those at home. There was no deafening, ear-racking blast from these, but plaintive sounds, pitched in a high key that was very soprano indeed, compared with our bass whistles.

I noticed in Italy, as in all the other countries where I found railroads, that trains are started by a blast from a tin horn-horns such as those that take conspicuous places in political campaigns once every four years, succeeding, by the aid of enthusiastic campaigners, in making night hideous for several months preceding the election.

In most cases these horn-blowers seemed to be located at the station, but in France and Italy they occupied the front platform of a coach, and I noticed, with amusement, that the tin horns were chained to them.

All day I traveled through Italy-sunny Italy, along the Adriatic Sea. The fog still hung in a heavy cloud over the earth, and only once did I get a glimpse of the land I had heard so much about. It was evening, just at the hour of sunset, when we stopped at some station. I went out on the platform, and the fog seemed to lift for an instant, and I saw on one side a beautiful beach and a smooth bay dotted with boats bearing oddly-shaped and brightly-colored sails, which somehow looked to me like mammoth butterflies, dipping, dipping about in search of honey. Most of the sails were red, and as the sun kissed them with renewed warmth, just before leaving us in darkness, the sails looked as if they were composed of brilliant fire.

A high rugged mountain was on the other side of the train. It made me feel dizzy to look at the white buildings perched on the perpendicular side. I noticed the road that went in a winding line up the hill had been built with a wall on the ocean side; still I thought I would not care to travel up it.

I got out for a few minutes at the next station where we stopped to take our dinners. I walked into a restaurant to look about. It was very neat and attractive. Just as I stepped inside a little girl with wonderful large black eyes and enormous gold hoop-rings in her ears, ran forward to me with the fearless boldness of a child. I touched her pretty black hair, and then naturally felt in my pocket for something to give her. Just as I drew forth a large copper coin-the less the value of a coin generally, the larger its size-a small man with a delicately refined face, flashing black eyes, wide expanse of white shirt front, broken by a brilliant diamond, came up and spoke to the baby. In the way she drew back from me, although her little hand had been stretched out expectantly before, I knew he had told her not to accept anything from me.

I felt on first impulse like boxing his ears, he was so tiny and impudent. The guard coming in search of me, found us at this critical moment.

"You have insulted him," he said to me, as if I was not conscious of it! "The Italians are the poorest and proudest people on earth. They hate the English."

"I am an American," I said bluntly and abruptly. At this a waiter who had been standing close by apparently not listening, but catching every word just the same, came up and spoke to me in English. Then I determined to remedy the fault I had committed, but nevertheless I had a dogged determination that the child should yet take the coin.

"What a beautiful restaurant!" I exclaimed. "I am passing hurriedly through Italy and in my desire to see, judging from the samples of good cooking I have had *en route*, Italian eating houses are excellent. I hope I have not put you to any inconvenience. I almost forgot the restaurant when I saw that lovely baby. What exquisitely beautiful eyes! Exactly the same as her father's, at least I judge from the similarity of their eyes that he is her father, though he looks so young."

The waiter smiled and bowed and translated. I knew he would, and that is why I said it all. Then the little man's pride melted away, and a smile replaced the frown on his face. He spoke to the baby who came up and shook hands with me. I gave her the coin and our peace was sealed. Then the little father brought forth a bottle of wine, and with the most cordial smiles and friendliest words, begged me to accept it. I did not intend to be out-done, so I told the waiter that I must take some wine with me, insisted on paying for it, and with low bows and sweet smiles we took leave of one another, and I rushed after the guard to the train, boarding it just as the horn blew for it to continue on its way.

We arrived at Brindisi two hours late. When the train stopped, our car was surrounded with men wanting to carry us as well as our baggage to the boats. Their making no mention of hotels led me to wonder if people always passed through Brindisi without stopping. All these men spoke English very well, but the guard said he would get one omnibus and escort the English women, the invalid man and his daughter, and myself to our boats, and would see that we were not charged more than the right fare.

We drove first to the boat bound for Alexandria, where we took leave of my room-mate, and her father. Then we drove to the boat that we expected to sail on.

I alighted from the omnibus, and followed my companions up the gang plank. I dreaded meeting English people with their much-talked-of prejudices, as I knew I would shortly have to do. I was earnestly hoping that everybody would be in bed. As it was after one in the morning, I hardly expected the trial of facing them at once. The crowds of men on the deck dispelled my fond hope. I think every man on board that boat was up waiting to see the new passengers. They must have felt but illy paid for their loss of sleep, for besides the men who came on board, there were only the two large English women and my own plain, uninteresting self.

These women were more helpless than I. As they were among their own people, I waited for them to take the lead; but after we had stood at the foot of the stairs for some time, gazed at by the passengers, and no one came forward to attend to our wants, which were few and simple, I gently asked if that was the usual manner of receiving passengers on English boats.

"It is strange, very strange. A steward, or some one should come to our assistance," was all they could say.

At last a man came down below, and as he looked as if he was in some way connected with the boat, I ventured to stop him and inquire if it was expecting too much to ask if we might have a steward to show us to our cabins. He said there should be some about, and began lustily to call for one. Even this brought no one to us, and as he started to find one himself, I started in the opposite direction.

Among the crowd that stood about was but one man that dared to speak without waiting for an introduction before he could be commonly polite.

"You will find the purser in his office the first door to the left there," he said; and I went that way, followed by the guard from the train.

Sitting in the office was the purser and a man I supposed to be the doctor. I gave my ticket and a letter I had been given at the P. & O. office in London, to the purser. This letter requested that the commanders and pursers of all the P. & O. boats on which I traveled should give me all the care and attention it was in their power as such officers to bestow.

After leisurely reading the letter, the purser very carelessly turned around and told me the number of my cabin. I asked for a steward to show me the way, but he replied that there did not seen to be any about, that the cabin was on the port side, and with this meagre information, he impolitely turned his back and busied himself with some papers on the desk before him.

The train guard who still stood by my side, said he would help me find the cabin. After a little search, we did find it. I opened the door and stepped in, and the sight that met my eyes both amused me and dismayed me. At the opening of the door, two bushy heads were stuck out of the two lower berths, and two high pitched voices exclaimed simultaneously with a vexed intonation, "Oh!" I looked at the band-boxes, boots, hand bags, gowns and the upper berth that was also filled with clothes, and I echoed their "Oh!" in a little different tone and retired.

I returned to the purser and told him I could not sleep in an upper berth, and would not occupy a cabin with two other women. After looking again over the letter I had brought him, as if to see how much weight he should give it, he referred me to another cabin. This time a steward made his appearance and he took the part of an escort.

I found a pretty girl in that cabin, who lifted her head anxiously, and then gave me a friendly smile when I entered. I put my bag down and returned to the guard who was waiting to take me to the cable office. I stopped to ask the purser if I had time to make the trip, to which he replied in the affirmative, with the proviso, "If you hurry." The two women who had traveled with me from Calais, had by this time found their way to the purser's office, and I heard them telling that they had come away from home and left their purse and tickets lying on the table in the sitting-room, they had started in such a rush!

The guard took me down the gang plank, and along several dark streets. At last, coming to a building where a door stood open, he stopped and I followed him in. The room in which we stood was perfectly bare and lighted by a lamp whose chimney was badly smoked. The only things in the room were two stationary desks. On the one lay a piece of blank paper before an ancient ink well and a much used pen.

I thought that everybody had retired for the night, and the cable would have to wait until I reached the next port, until the guard explained to me that it was customary to ring for the operator, who would get up and attend to the message for me. Suiting the action to the words, the guard pulled at a knob near a small closed window, much like a postage stamp window. The bell made quite a clatter, still I had begun to think that hopeless, when the window opened with a clink, and a head appeared at the opening. The guard spoke in Italian, but hearing me speak English, the operator replied in the same language.

I told him I wanted to send a cable to New York. He asked me where New York was! I explained as best I could; then he brought out a lot of books, through which he searched first, to know by which line he could send the message; at least, so he explained; then what it would cost. The whole thing was so new and amusing to me that I forgot all about the departure of the boat until we had finished the business and stepped outside.

A whistle blew long and warningly. I looked at the guard, the guard looked at me. It was too dark to see each other, but I know our faces were the picture of dismay. My heart stopped beating and I thought with emotions akin to horror, "My boat was gone-and with it my limited wardrobe!"

"Can you run?" the guard asked in a husky voice. I said I could, and he taking a close grasp of my hand, we started down the dark street with a speed that would have startled a deer. Down the dark streets, past astonished watchmen and late pedestrians, until a sudden bend brought us in full view of my ship still in port. The boat for Alexandria had gone, but I was saved.

Chapter 6: An American Heiress

I had not been asleep long, it seemed to me, until I waked to find myself standing upright beside my berth. It required but a second, a glance at my drenched self, and the sounds of vigorous scrubbing on the deck above to explain the cause of my being out of bed before I knew it. I had gone to sleep with the port-hole open, and as my berth was just beneath it, I received the full force of the scrub-water as it came pouring over the sides. I managed to let the heavy window down and went back to bed, wet, but confident that I would not again be caught napping under such circumstances.

I had not been asleep many moments until I heard a voice call: "Miss, will you have your tea now?" I opened my eyes and saw a steward standing at the door awaiting a reply. I refused the tea, as did the English girl on the other side of my cabin, managing to answer her bright smile with a very tired one, and then I was off to sleep again.

"Miss, will you have your bath now?" a voice broke in on my slumbers shortly afterwards. I looked up in disgust at a little white-capped woman who was bending over me, tempted to say I had just had my bath, a shower-bath, but thought better of it before speaking. I know I said something about "in a few minutes," and then I was asleep again.

"Well, you are a lazy girl! You'll miss your bath and breakfast if you don't get up the instant," was my third greeting. My surprise at the familiarity of the remark got the better of my sleepiness, and I thought:

"Well, by all that is wonderful, where am I? Am I in school again that a woman dare assume such a tone to me?" I kept my thoughts to myself, and said stiffly:

"I generally get up when I feel so inclined."

I saw my room-mate was missing, but I felt like sleeping and I decided to sleep; whether it pleased the stewardess or not, it mattered little to me. The steward was the next one to put in an appearance.

"Miss, this ship is inspected every day and I must have this cabin made up before they come," he said complainingly. "The captain will be here presently."

There was nothing to do but to get up, which I did. I found my way to the bath-room, but soon saw that it was impossible for me to turn on the water, as I did not understand the mechanism of the faucet. I asked a steward I saw outside the door, the whereabouts of the stewardess, and was simply amazed to hear him reply:

"The stewardess is taking a rest and cannot be disturbed."

After dressing I wandered up on the next deck and was told that breakfast was over long ago. I went out on deck, and the very first glimpse of the lazy looking passengers in their summer garments, lounging about in comfortable positions, or slowly promenading the deck, which was sheltered from the heat of the sun by a long stretch of awnings, and the smooth, velvety looking water, the bluest I had ever seen, softly gurgling against the side of the ship as it almost imperceptibly steamed on its course, and the balmy air, soft as a rose leaf, and just as sweet, air such as one dreams about but seldom finds; standing there alone among strange people, on strange waters, I thought how sweet life is!

Before an hour had passed I was acquainted with several persons. I had thought and expected that the English passengers would hold themselves aloof from a girl who was traveling alone, but my cabin-companion saw me before I got away from the door, and came forward to ask me to join herself and friends. We first had an amusing search for the steamer-chair which I had told the guard to buy at Brindisi and send on before our departure. There were over three hundred passengers on the ship, and I suppose they averaged a chair apiece, so it can easily be pictured the trouble it would be to find a chair among that number. I asked where the deck-stewards were when at last I felt the search was useless, and was surprised to learn that a deck-steward was an unknown commodity on the P. and O. line.

"I presume the quarter-master has charge of the decks," my companion said in conclusion, "but we are expected to look after our own chairs and rugs, and if we don't it is useless to inquire for them if they disappear."

Shortly before noon I became acquainted with an Englishman who belongs to the Civil Service in Calcutta. He had been in India for the last twenty years, during which time he had repeatedly visited England, which made this trip an old story to him. He had made the same trip from Calais on the India express as I had, and said he noticed me on the train. Learning that I was traveling alone, he devoted most of his time looking out for my comfort and pleasure.

The bugle blew for luncheon, which is always called by the Indian title "tiffin" on ships traveling in Eastern seas. The Englishman asked if I would go with him to tiffin, and as I had gone without breakfast I was only too anxious to go at the first opportunity. The dining-hall is on the second deck. It is a small room nicely decorated with tropical foliage plants and looks quite cozy and pretty, but it was never intended to accommodate a ship carrying more than seven-five first-class passengers.

The head-waiter, who stood at the door, stared at us blankly as we went in. I hesitated, naturally thinking that he would show us to some table, but as he did not I suggested to the gentleman with me, that he ask before we take our places.

"Sit anywhere," was the polite reply we received, so we sat down at the table nearest.

We had just been served, when four women ranging from twenty-four to thirty-five came in, and with indignant snorts of surprise, seated themselves at the same table. They were followed by a short, fat woman with a sweeping walk and air of satisfied assurance, who eyed us in a supercilious way and then turned to the others with an air of injured dignity that was intensely amusing. They were followed by two men and as there were only places for seven at the table the elderly man went out. Two of the girls sat on a lounge at the end of the table, which made room for the young man. Then we were made to suffer. All kinds of rude remarks were made about us. "They did hate people coming to their table;" "Too bad papa was robbed of his place;" "Shame people had to be crowded from their own table," and similar pleasant speeches were hurled at us. The young woman who sat at my left was not content to confine her rudeness to her tongue, but repeatedly reached across my plate, brushing my food with her sleeves without one word of apology. I confess I never had a more disagreeable meal. I thought at first that this rudeness was due to my being an American and that they had taken this means of showing their hatred for all Americans. Still I could not understand why they should subject an Englishman to the same treatment unless it was because he was with me. After-experiences showed me that my first conclusion was wrong; that I was not insulted because I was an American, but because the people were simply ill-bred. When dinner came we found that we were debarred from the dining-room. Passengers who got on at London were given the preference, and as there was not accommodations for all, the passengers who boarded the ship at Brindisi had to wait for second dinner.

One never realizes, until they face such contingencies, what an important part dinner plays in one's life. It was nine o'clock when the dining-room was cleared that night, and the Brindisi passengers were allowed to take their places at the table. I hardly believe they took much else. Everything was brought to us as it was left from the first dinner-cold soup, the remnants of fish, cut up bits of beef and fowl-all down the miserable course until at last came cold coffee! I had thought the food on the India Express might have been better until after my experience on the P. & O. steamer Victoria, and then I decided it might have been worse.

Such a roar of complaint as went up from those late dinner passengers. They wanted to get up a protest to serve on the captain, but I refused to take any part in it, and several of the more conservative ones followed my example.

The two women I have already referred to as having traveled on the India Express to Brindisi, were treated even worse than I was. When we made inquiries, we were told that at dinner only were the places reserved, but that at breakfast and tiffin, first there were first served. Acting on this information they went in to early tiffin the following day, and a young man who sat at the head of an empty table said to them as they went to sit down:

"You can't sit there. I've reserved those places for some of my friends." They went to another table and after sitting down, were requested by some late comers to get up and give the places to them. The one woman cried bitterly over it.

"I am a grandmother, and this is the sixth trip I have made to Australia, and I was never treated so insultingly in my life."

There are circumstances under which a trip on the Mediterranean would be like a dream of Paradise. If one were in love, for instance; for they do say that people in love do not eat, and aside from the food, the trip is perfect. Probably it is a hope of finding the cure that will help them to forget a stomach void, that makes love the principal subject on the P. & O. boats. Travelers who care to be treated with courtesy, and furnished with palatable food, will never by any chance travel on the Victoria.

It is all rule and no practice on that ship. The impudence and rudeness of the servants in America is a standing joke, but if the servants on the Victoria are a sample of English servants, I am thankful to keep those we have, such as they are. I asked the stewardess to assist a woman who looked as if she was dying of consumption, to the deck with her rugs, only to be told in reply, that she would not help any one unless they came and requested her to do so.

I heard her tell a passenger one day, that she did not believe it was sickness, but laziness that ailed the woman. If complaints were made about the conduct of the servants, they were always met by the assertion that the servants had been for a long time in the company's employ, and would take privileges.

The commander of the ship set an example for rudeness. A Spanish gentleman of high position who was traveling to China, where he represented his country in the diplomatic service, also got on at Brindisi. He thought that his first duty was to pay his respects to the Captain in charge of the ship, so he asked some one to point the Captain out to him. This was done on deck. He walked up to the Captain, and with a profound bow, hat in hand, begged the Captain's pardon, and said that he was *chargé d'affaires* of China and Siam for the Spanish government, and he wished to pay his duty and respects to the Captain of the boat on which he was traveling. The Captain glared at him savagely for a moment after he had finished, and then asked rudely:

"Well, what of it?"

The Spaniard was speechless for a moment, but recovering, he said politely:

"I beg your pardon, I thought I was addressing a gentleman and the commander of this ship." Turning, he walked away, and they never spoke afterwards.

Although I had brought a letter to the Captain, he never noticed me in any way. A bright faced, jolly boy, who was going to Hong Kong to enter a banking house of his uncle's, brought a letter to the Captain. He presented himself one day on deck, stepping a foot or so away until the Captain should have time to read it and greet him. The Captain read the letter, folded it carefully, put it in his pocket, and walked away! He never spoke to the boy afterwards, and the boy was careful not to give him that trouble. The Captain had a tongue for gossip, too. Every time I heard a slighting story about any of the passengers, and would ask where it came from, the answer would always be the Captain had told it to somebody.

Notwithstanding all annoying trifles it was a very happy life we spent in those pleasant waters. The decks were filled all the day, and when the lights were put out at night the passengers reluctantly went to their cabins. The passengers formed two striking contrasts. There were some of the most refined and lovely people on board, and there were some of the most ill-bred and uncouth. Most of the women, whose acquaintance I formed, were very desirous of knowing all about American women, and frequently expressed their admiration for the free American woman, many going so far as to envy me, while admiring my unfettered happiness. Two clever Scotch women I met were traveling around the world, but are taking two years at it. One Irishwoman, with a laugh that rivaled her face in sweetness, was traveling alone to Australia. My cabin-mate was bound for New Zealand, but she was accompanied by her brother, a pleasant young Englishman, who insisted on relinquishing his place at first dinner in my favor, and who stayed away despite my protests and my determination not to deprive him of a warm dinner.

In the daytime the men played cricket and quoits. Sometimes, in the evenings, we had singing, and other times we went to the second-class deck and listened to better music given by second-class passengers. When there were no chairs we would all sit down on the deck, and I remember nothing that was more enjoyable than these little visits. There was one little girl with a pale, slender face, who was a great favorite with us all, though none of us ever spoke to her. She sang in a sweet, pathetic voice a little melody about "Who'll buy my silver herrings?" until, I know, if she had tried to sell any, we should all have bought. The best we could do was to join her in the refrain, which we did most heartily.

Better than all to me, it was to sit in a dark corner on deck, above where the sailors had their food, and listen to the sounds of a tom-tom and a weird musical chanting that always accompanied their evening meal. The sailors were Lascars. They were not interesting to look at, and doubtless, if I could have seen as well as heard them at their evening meal, it would have lost its charm for me. They were the most untidy looking lot of sailors I ever saw. Over a pair of white muslin drawers they wore a long muslin slip very like in shape to the old-time night-shirt. This was tied about the waist with a colored handkerchief, and on their heads they wore gayly colored turbans, which are really nothing but a crown of straw with a scarf-shaped piece of bright cloth, often six feet in length, wound about the head. Their brown feet are always bare. They chant, as all sailors do, when hoisting sails, but otherwise are a grim, surly looking set, climbing about over the ship like a pack of monkeys.

When I boarded the boat at Brindisi the purser gave me some cables that had been sent to me, care of the Victoria. After we had been out several days, a young woman came to me with an unsealed cable and asked if I was Nellie Bly. Upon telling her I was, she said that the purser had given the cable to some of the passengers the day before, as he did not know who Nellie Bly was, and after two days traveling among them it reached me. Occasionally we would have a dance on deck to the worst music it has ever been my misfortune to hear. The members of the band also washed the dishes, and though I could not blame the passengers who always disappeared at the appearance of the musicians (?) still I felt sorry for them; it was both ridiculous and pathetic that they should be required to cultivate two such inharmonious arts! One of the officers told me that the band they had before were compelled to scrub the decks, and their hands became so rough from the work that it was impossible for them longer to fill the role of musicians, so they were discharged and the new band were turned into dish-washers instead of deck-scrubbers.

I had not been on the Victoria many days until some one who had become friendly with me, told me it was rumored on board that I was an eccentric American heiress, traveling about with a hair brush and a bank book. I judged that some of the attention I was receiving was due to the story of my wealth. I found it convenient, later on, to correct the report when a young man came to me to say that I was the kind of a girl he liked, and as he was the second son and his brother would get both the money and the title, his sole ambition was to find a wife who would settle £1,000 a year on him.

There was another young man on board who was quite as unique a character and much more interesting to me. He told me that he had been traveling constantly since he was nine years old, and that he had always killed the desire to love and marry because he never expected to find a woman who could travel without a number of trunks, and bundles innumerable. I noticed that he dressed very exquisitely and changed his apparel at least three times a day, so my curiosity made me bold enough to ask how many trunks he carried with him.

"Nineteen," was the amazing reply. I no longer wondered at his fears of getting a wife who could not travel without trunks.

Chapter 7: "Two Beautiful Black Eyes"

IT was in the afternoon when the Victoria anchored at Port Said. We were all on deck eagerly watching for the first sight of land, and though that sight showed us a wide, sandy beach, and some uninteresting two-storied white houses with arcade fronts, still it did not lessen our desire to go ashore. I suppose that would have been the result under the circumstances had Port Said been the most desolate place on earth. I know everybody was experiencing a slight weariness, though we should all have stoutly denied such a reflection on our constant companions, and gladly welcomed the change of a few hours on shore, where at least we might see new faces. A more urgent reason still, for our going to land, was the fact that this was a coaling port for the Victoria, and I never knew of anything that would make one more quickly feel that there are things in life much worse than death, if I may use the expression, than to have to stay on board a ship during the coaling operation.

Before the boat anchored the men armed themselves with canes, to keep off the beggars they said; and the women carried parasols for the same purpose. I had neither stick nor umbrella with me, and refused all offers to accept one for this occasion, having an idea, probably a wrong one, that a stick beats more ugliness into a person than it ever beats out.

Hardly had the anchor dropped than the ship was surrounded with a fleet of small boats, steered by half-clad Arabs, fighting, grabbing, pulling, yelling in their mad haste to be first. I never in my life saw such an exhibition of hungry greed for the few pence they expected to earn by taking the passengers ashore. Some boatmen actually pulled others out of their boats into the water in their frantic endeavors to steal each other's places. When the ladder was lowered, numbers of them caught it and clung to it as if it meant life or death to them, and here they clung until the captain was compelled to order some sailors to beat the Arabs off, which they did with long poles, before the passengers dared venture forth. This dreadful exhibition made me feel that probably there was some justification in arming one's self with a club.

Our party were about the first to go down the ladder to the boats. It had been our desire and intention to go ashore together, but when we stepped into the first boat some were caught by rival boatmen and literally dragged across to other boats. The men in the party used their sticks quite vigorously; all to no avail, and although I thought the conduct of the Arabs justified this harsh course of treatment, still I felt sorry to see it administered so freely and lavishly to those black, half-clad wretches, and marveled at their stubborn persistence even while cringing under the blows. Having our party divided there was nothing to do under the circumstances but to land and reunite on shore, so we ordered the Arabs to pull away. Midway between the Victoria and the shore the boatmen stopped and demanded their money in very plain and forcible English. We were completely at their mercy, as they would not land us either way until we paid what they asked. One of the Arabs told me that they had many years' experience in dealing with the English and their sticks, and had learned by bitter lessons that if they landed an Englishman before he paid they would receive a stinging blow for their labor.

Walking up the beach, sinking ankle deep in the sand at every step, we came to the main street. Almost instantly we were surrounded by Arab boys who besought us to take a ride on the burros that stood patiently beside them. There were burros of all colors, sizes and shapes, and the boys would cry out, most beseechingly, "Here's Gladstone! Take a ride; see Gladstone with two beautiful black eyes."

This they would cry in such a soft plaintive way that one felt the "two beautiful black eyes" made the animals irresistible.

If one happened to be of a different political belief and objected to riding the Gladstone hobby, as it were, a choice could be made of almost any well-known, if not popular name. There were Mrs. Maybricks, Mary Andersons, Lillie Langtrys, and all the prominent men of the time.

I knew all about burros, having lived for some time in Mexico, but they proved to be quite a novelty to many of the passengers, almost all of whom were anxious to take a ride before returning to the boat. So, as many as could find animals to ride, mounted and went flying through that quaint, sleeping town, yelling with laughter, bouncing like rubber balls on their saddles, while half-naked Arab boys goaded the burros on by short, urgent hisses, and by prodding them from behind with a sharp stick.

After seeing about fifty of our passengers started off in this happy manner, a smaller number of us went to a gambling house, and in a short time were deep in the sport of placing our English gold on colors and numbers and waiting anxiously for the wheel to go 'round to see the money at last swept in by the man at the table. I do not think that any one of us knew anything about the game, but we recklessly put our money on the table and laughed to see it taken in by the man who gave the turn to the wheel.

There was another attraction in this place which helped to win a number of young men from that very expensive table. It was an orchestra composed of young women, some of whom were quite pleasing both in looks and manners.

The longer we remained at this gambling house the less money we had to spend in the shops. I went ashore with the determination not to buy anything as I was very anxious not to increase my baggage. I withstood the tempting laces which were offered at wonderfully low prices, the quaint Egyptian curios, and managed to content myself by buying a sun hat, as everybody else did; and a pugaree to wind about it, as is customary in the East.

Having bought a hat and seen all I cared to of the shops I went strolling about with some friends feasting my eyes on what were to me peculiarities of a peculiar people. I saw old houses with carved-wood fronts that would have been worth a fortune in America occupied by tenants that were unmistakably poor. The natives were apparently so accustomed to strangers that we attracted very little, if any attention, except from those who hoped to gain something from our visit. Unmolested we went about finding no occasion to use sticks on the natives. We saw a great number of beggars who, true to their trade, whined forth, with outstretched hands, their plaintive appeals, but they were not so intrusive or bothersome that they necessitated our giving them the cane instead of alms. The majority of these beggars presented such repulsive forms of misery that in place of appealing to my sympathetic nature, as is generally the case, they had a hardening effect on me. They seemed to thrust their deformities in our faces in order to compel us to give money to buy their absence from our sight.

While standing looking after a train of camels that had just come in loaded with firewood I saw some Egyptian women. They were small in stature and shapelessly clad in black. Over their faces, beginning just below the eyes, they wore black veils that fell almost to their knees. As if fearing that the veil alone would not destroy all semblance of features they wear a thing that spans the face between the hair and the veil down the line of their noses. In some cases this appears to be of gold, and in others it is composed of some black material. One Egyptian woman carried a little naked baby with her. She held it on her hips, its little black legs clinging to her waist much after the fashion of a boy climbing a pole.

Down at the beach we came upon a group of naked men clustered about an alligator that they had caught. It was securely fastened in some knotted rope, the end of which was held by some half dozen black fellows. The public water-carriers, with well filled goat-skins flung across their backs, we met making their way to the town for the last trip that day.

Darkness came on us very suddenly and sent us rushing off for our ship. This time we found the boatman would not permit us even to enter their boats until we paid them to take us across to the Victoria. Their price now was just double what they had charged to bring us to land. We protested, but they said it was the law to double the price after sunset.

They were just finishing the coaling when we reached the ship, but the sight we caught of the coal barges, lighted by some sputtering, dripping stuff, held in iron cages on the end of long poles, that showed the hurrying naked people rushing with sacks of coal up a steep gangplank, between the barges and the ship, was one long to be remembered. Nor were they working quietly. Judging from the noise, every one of them was yelling something that pleased his own fancy and humor.

The next morning I got up earlier than usual so anxious was I to see the famous Suez Canal. Rushing up on deck, I saw we were passing through what looked like an enormous ditch, enclosed on either side with high sand banks. We seemed to be hardly moving, which made us feel the heat very intensely. They tell me, that according to law, a ship must not travel through the canal at a speed exceeding five knots an hour, because a rapid passage of the ship would make a strong current that would wash in the sand banks. One gentleman, who had traveled all his life, helped us to pass some of the tedious, stifling hours in the canal by telling us the history of it.

It was begun in 1859 and took ten years to build. The work is estimated to have cost nearly £18,250,000, although the poor blacks that were employed to do the labor commanded the lowest possible wages. It is claimed that the lives of 100,000 laborers were sacrificed in the building of this canal, which is only 100 English miles, 88 geographical miles, 5 in length.

When first completed the width of the surface of the canal was three hundred and twenty-five feet, but the constant washing in of the banks has reduced it to one hundred and ninety-five feet. The bottom is said to be seventy-two feet wide and the depth is but twenty-six feet. The trip through the canal can be made in from twenty to twenty-four hours.

About noon of our first day in the canal we anchored in the bay fronting Ismailia. Here passengers were taken on, which gave us time to see the Khedive's palace, which is built a little way back from the beach in the heart of a beautiful green forest. Continuing the journey through the canal we saw little of interest. The signal stations were the only green spots that met the eye, but they were proof of what could be done, even in this sandy desert by the expenditure of time and energy.

The one thing that enlivened this trip was the appearance of naked Arabs, who would occasionally run along the banks of the canal, crying in pitiful tones, "bahkshish." This we understood meant money, which many of the kind hearted passengers would throw to them, but the beggars never seemed to find it, and would keep on after us, still crying, "bahkshish" until they were exhausted.

We passed several ships in the canal. Generally the passengers would call to the passengers on the other ships, but the conversation was confined mainly to inquiries as to what kind of a voyage had been theirs. We saw at one place in the canal, a lot of Arabs, both men and women, at work. Among them were a number of camels that were employed in carrying stone with which the laborers were endeavoring to strengthen the banks.

In the night the boat hung an electric light from the front, and by the aid of this light, moving it from side to side, were able to continue on their way. Before the introduction of electric head lights for this purpose, the vessels were always compelled to tie up in the canal over night, because of the great danger of running into the sand banks. In addition to making the trip longer, this stoppage added greatly to the discomfort of the passengers, who found that even the slow motion of the boat, helped, in a measure, to lessen the stifling heat that seemed to come from out the sand banks during the night as well as when the blazing sun was in the cloudless sky.

We saw, when near the end of the canal, several Arab encampments. They were both picturesque and interesting. First we would notice a small dull red fire, and between that fire and us we could see the outlines of people and resting camels. At one encampment we heard music, but at the others we saw the people either working over the fire, as if preparing their evening meal, or in sitting positions crouching about it in company with their camels.

Shortly after this we dropped anchor in the Bay of Suez. Hardly had we done so when the ship was surrounded by a number of small sail boats that, in the semi-darkness, with their white sails before the breeze, reminded me of moths flocking to a light, both from their white, winged-like appearance, and the rapid way in which numbers of them floated down on us. These sail boats were filled with men with native fruits, photographs and odd shells to sell. They all came on board, and among them were a number of jugglers. The passengers took very little interest in the venders, but all had a desire to see what was to be offered by the jugglers. There was one among them, a black man, who wore little else than a sash, a turban and a baggy pocket, in the lining of which he carried two lizards and a small rabbit. He was very anxious to show us his tricks and to get the money for them. He refused, however, to do anything with the rabbit and lizards until after he had shown us what he could do with a handkerchief and some bangles that he brought along for this purpose. He selected me from among the crowd, to hold the handkerchief, which he had first shaken as if to show us that it contained nothing. He then showed us a small brass bangle, and pretended to put the bangle in the handkerchief; he then placed the handkerchief in my hand, telling me to hold it tightly. I did so, feeling the presence of the bangle very plainly. He blew on it and jerking the handkerchief loose from my grasp, shook it. Much to the amazement of the crowd the bangle was gone. Some of the passengers in the mean time stole the juggler's rabbit, and one of the lizards had quietly taken itself off to some secluded spot. He was very much concerned about the loss of them and refused to perform any more tricks until they were restored to his keeping. At last one young man took the rabbit from his pocket and returned it to the juggler, much to his gratification. The lizard was not to be found, and as it was time for the ship to sail, the juggler was forced to return to his boat. After he had gone, several people came to know if I had any idea how the trick with the handkerchief had been done. I explained to them that it was an old and very uninteresting trick; that the man had one bangle sewn in the handkerchief, and the other bangle, which he showed to the people, he slipped quietly out of sight. Of course, the one who held the handkerchief held the bangle, but when the juggler would jerk the handkerchief from the hand, and shake it, in full view of his audience, the bangle being sewn to the handkerchief, would naturally not fall to the floor, and as he carefully kept the side to which the bangle was attached turned towards himself, he successfully duped his audience into thinking, that by his magic, he had made the bangle disappear. One of the men who listened to this explanation became very indignant, and wanted to know if I knew positively how this trick had been done, and why I had not exposed the man. I merely explained that I wanted to see the juggler get his money, much to the disgust of the Englishman.

Where we anchored at Suez some claim is the historic place where the Israelites crossed the Red Sea. Some people who bother themselves greatly about facts, figures and ancient history, bought views, which showed that at certain stages of the tide, people, in even this day, can wade around there without any risk of life or comfort. The next morning when we arose we were out of sight of land and well out on the Red Sea. The weather now was very hot, but still some of the passengers did their best to make things lively on board. One evening a number of young men gave a minstrel show. They displayed both energy and perseverance in preparing for it as well as in the execution of it. One end of the deck was set aside for the show. A stage was put up and the whole corner was enclosed by awnings, and the customary green curtain hung in place during service, as drop curtain between acts, as well appearing before and after the performance.

The young men filled their different roles in a very commendable manner, but as the night was so dreadfully warm, the passengers feeling the heat more than usual, owing to the deck being enclosed by awnings, it was difficult to awake any enthusiasm on the part of the audience. We had an intermission, when all retired to the dining room for punch and biscuits, and I know that no one appreciated the refreshments more than the actors, who joined us, their blackened faces streaked with perspiration.

Towards the last the passengers could find very little to do that proved interesting or in any way aided them to forget the heat. A few of those who could sing, or imagined they could, were persuaded to exercise their vocal organs for the benefit of those who could sing and would not, and those who realized they had no voice and knew enough to remain quiet. At other times many of us went to the deck reserved for the second-class passengers and enjoyed the concerts given by them. When there were no chairs for us on this deck we would sit on the floor, and we all acknowledged that the first-class passengers could not furnish music that was any better.

The days were spent mainly on deck lounging about in easy chairs. I found that no one enjoyed as much comfort as I did. I had changed my heavy waist for my silk bodice, and I felt cool and comfortable and lazily happy. When dinner hour approached we would see a few rush off to dress for dinner and later they would appear in full dress, low bodice and long train, much to the amusement of that class of passengers who maintained that it was decidedly not the thing to appear in full dress on an ocean steamer.

The evening dress, made of white linen, in which the young men in the East generally made their appearance at dinner, impressed me as being not only comfortable and appropriate, but decidedly becoming and elegant.

It is very seldom that men do not get more enjoyment out of life than women under like circumstances. Between cricket, to which they were passionately attached, and quoits and the smoking-room, which was the scene of many exciting games for large stakes and, later on, an hour or so spent in a dark corner of the deck pleasing and being pleased by some congenial companion of the opposite sex, the enforced rest was quite an agreeable one to the men.

We were all very much interested and concerned about a small bird that had traveled with us from Suez, sometimes flying along a little way and then resting on the rigging of the ship. It was a pretty bird with a slender gray tail and a silver breast and a black ring about its throat, its back being a modest drabish brown. At first it was easily frightened but after awhile it became very tame and would light on the deck among the passengers, picking up the crumbs they threw to it. Beside the bird as a topic of interest we had the lizard which was left behind by the juggler.

It was found in a quiet corner of the deck by the quarter-master the morning following our stop at Suez. A sympathizing young man took charge of it and endeavored to feed it, but after living in sullen quietness for a few days, it ceased to breathe and its death was solemnly announced to the passengers.

The Victoria is said to be the finest boat on the P. and O. Line, still it could not be more unsuited for the trip. It is very badly planned, being built so that a great number of cabins inside are absolutely cut off from light and air. It is a compliment to call them cabins as they are really nothing more than small, dark, disagreeable, and unventilated boxes. The passengers are charged all the same rate of fare, and if they are consigned to one of these undesirable boxes there is no redress; they must simply bow before the dictates of this company, who trade on the fact of their being an old established line, and a very desirable one in many respects, and passengers are treated–I judge only by what I saw and heard–as if they should consider that a favor had been conferred upon them when they were permitted to pay for tickets to travel on that line. The prices to ports that are touched at by rival steamship lines are rather reasonable, while to ports where they have the monopoly they charge exorbitant rates. I have stated that the conduct of the officers and servants, and the quality of the food left much to be desired by travelers.

The nights were so warm while on the Red Sea that the men left their cabins and spent their nights on deck. It is usually customary for the women to sleep on deck, one side of which, at such times, is reserved exclusively for them. During this trip none of the women had the courage to set the example, so the men had the decks to themselves.

Sleeping down below was all the more reason why women arising early would go on the decks before the sun began to boil in search of a refreshing spot where they could get a breath of cool air. At this hour the men were usually to be seen promenading about in their pajamas, but I heard no objections raised until much to the dismay of the women the Captain announced that the decks belonged to the men until after eight o'clock in the morning, and that the women were expected to remain below until after that hour.

Just before we came to Aden we passed in the sea a number of high brown mountains. They are known as the Twelve Apostles. Shortly after this we came in sight of Aden. It looked to us like a large, bare mountain of wonderful height, but even by the aid of glasses we were unable to tell that it was inhabited. Shortly after eleven o'clock in the morning we anchored in the bay. Our boat was soon surrounded by a number of small boats, which brought to us men who had things to sell, and the wonderful divers of the East.

The passengers had been warned by the officers on board not to go ashore at Aden because of the intense heat. So the women spent their time bargaining with the Jews who came to the ship to sell ostrich feathers and feather boas. The men helped them to close with the sellers always to the sellers' advantage, much as they might congratulate themselves to the contrary.

I, in company with a few of the more reckless ones, decided to brave the heat and go ashore and see what Aden had to offer.

Chapter 8: Aden to Colombo

HIRING a large boat, I went ashore with a half dozen acquaintances who felt they could risk the sun. The four oarsmen were black fellows, thin of limb, but possessed of much strength and tireless good humor. They have, as have all the inhabitants of Aden, the finest white teeth of any mortals. This may be due to the care they take of them and the manner of that care. From some place, I am unable to state where, as I failed to see one living thing growing at Aden, they get tree branches of a soft, fibrous wood which they cut into pieces three and four inches in length. With one end of this stick, scraped free of the bark, they rub and polish their teeth until they are perfect in their whiteness. The wood wears into a soft pulp, but as one can buy a dozen sticks for a penny one can well afford to throw the stick away after once using; although, if necessary, a stick can be used many times. I bought several sticks and found them the most efficient as well as pleasant tooth brush I had ever tried. I felt a regret that some enterprising firm had not thought of importing this useful bit of timber to replace the tooth-destroying brush used in America.

The man in charge of the boat that carried us to land was a small black fellow with the thinnest legs I ever saw. Somehow they reminded me of smoked herrings, they were so black, flat and dried looking. He was very gay notwithstanding his lack of weight. Around his neck and over his bare breast were twined strings of beads, black and gold and silver. Around his waist was a highly colored sash, and on his arms and ankles were heavy bracelets, while his fingers and toes seemed to be trying to outdo one another in the way of rings. He spoke English quite well, and to my rather impertinent question as to what number constituted his family told me that he had three wives and eleven children, which number, he added piously, by the grace of the power of his faith, he hoped to increase.

His hair was yellow which, added to his very light dress of jewelry and sash, gave him rather a strange look. The bright yellow hair and the black skin forming a contrast which was more startling than the black eyes and yellow hair that flashed upon the astonished vision of the American public some years ago, but has become since an old and tiresome sight. Some of the boatmen had their black wool pasted down and hidden under a coating of lime. I was very curious about it until the first man explained that they were merely bleaching their hair; that it was always done by covering the head with lime, which, being allowed to remain on for several days, exposed to the hot sun and the water, bleached the hair yellow or red at the expiration of that time. This bleaching craze, he also informed me, was confined to the men of Aden. So far, none of the women had tried to enhance their black beauty in that way, but it was considered very smart among the men.

While we were talking our men were vigorously pulling to the time of a rousing song, one line of which was sung by one man, the others joining in the refrain at the end. Their voices were not unpleasant, and the air had a monotonous rhythm that was very fascinating.

We landed at a well-built pier and walked up the finely-cut, white-stone steps from the boat to the land. Instantly we were surrounded by half-clad black people, all of whom, after the manner of hack-drivers at railway stations, were clamoring for our favor. They were not all drivers, however. Mingling with the drivers were merchants with jewelry, ostrich plumes and boas to sell, runners for hotels, beggars, cripples and guides. This conglomeration besought us to listen to every individual one of them until a native policeman, in the Queen's uniform, came forward and pushed the black fellows back with his hands, sometimes hastening their retreat with his boot.

A large board occupied a prominent position on the pier. On it was marked the prices that should be paid drivers, boatmen, and like people. It was, indeed, a praiseworthy thoughtfulness that caused the erection of that board, for it prevented tourists being robbed. I looked at it, and thought that even in that land there was more precaution taken to protect helpless and ignorant strangers than in New York city, where the usual custom of night hack-men is to demand exorbitant prices, and if they are not forthcoming, to pull off their coats and fight for it.

Perched on the side of this bleak, bare mountain is a majestic white building, reached by a fine road cut in the stone that forms the mountain. It is a club house, erected for the benefit of the English soldiers who are stationed on this barren spot. In the harbor lay an English man-of-war, and near a point where the land was most level, numbers of white tents were pitched for soldiers.

From the highest peak of the black, rocky mountain, probably 1700 feet above sea level, floated the English flag. As I traveled on and realized more than ever before how the English have stolen almost all, if not all, desirable sea-ports, I felt an increased respect for the level-headedness of the English government, and I cease to marvel at the pride with which Englishmen view their flag floating in so many different climes and over so many different nationalities.

Near the pier were shops run by Parsees. A hotel, post-office and telegraph office are located in the same place. The town of Aden is five miles distant. We hired a carriage and started at a good pace, on a wide, smooth road that took us along the beach for a way, passing low rows of houses, where we saw many miserable, dirty-looking natives; passed a large graveyard, liberally filled, which looked like the rest of that stony point, bleak, black and bare, the graves often being shaped by cobblestones.

The roads at Aden are a marvel of beauty. They are wide and as smooth as hardwood, and as they twist and wind in pleasing curves up the mountain, they are made secure by a high, smooth wall against mishap. Otherwise their steepness might result in giving tourists a serious roll down a rough mountain-side.

Just before we began to ascend we saw a black man at his devotions. He was kneeling in the centre of a little square formed by rocks. His face was turned heavenward, and he was oblivious to all else except the power before which he was laying bare his inmost soul, with a fervor and devotion that commanded respect, even from those who thought of him as a heathen. I inferred that he was a sun worshipper from the way in which he constantly had his face turned upward, except when he bent forward to kiss the ground on which he knelt.

On the road we saw black people of many different tribes. A number of women I noticed, who walked proudly along, their brown, bare feet stepping lightly on the smooth road. They had long purple-black hair, which was always adorned with a long, stiff feather, dyed of brilliant red, green, purple, and like striking shades. They wore no other ornament than the colored feather, which lent them an air of pride, when seen beside the much-bejeweled people of that quaint town. Many of the women, who seemed very poor indeed, were lavishly dressed in jewelry. They did not wear much else, it is true, but in a place as hot as Aden, jewelry must be as much as anyone would care to wear.

To me the sight of these perfect, bronze-like women, with a graceful drapery of thin silk wound about the waist, falling to the knees, and a corner taken up the back and brought across the bust, was most bewitching. On their bare, perfectly modeled arms were heavy bracelets, around the wrist and muscle, most times joined by chains. Bracelets were also worn about the ankles, and their fingers and toes were laden with rings. Sometimes large rings were suspended from the nose, and the ears were almost always outlined with hoop rings, that reached from the inmost edge of the lobe to the top of the ear joining the head. So closely were these rings placed that, at a distance, the ear had the appearance of being rimmed in gold. A more pleasing style of nose ornament was a large gold ornament set in the nostril and fastened there as screw rings fasten in the ear. Still, if that nose ornamentation was more pleasing than the other, the ear adornment that accompanied it was disgusting. The lobe of the ear was split from the ear, and pulled down to such length that it usually rested on the shoulder. The enormous loop of flesh was partially filled with large gold knobs.

At the top of the hill we came to a beautiful, majestic, stone double gate, the entrance to the English fort and also spanning the road that leads to the town. Sentinels were pacing to and fro but we drove past them without stopping or being stopped, through a strange, narrow cut in the mountain, that towered at the sides a hundred feet above the road bed. Both these narrow, perpendicular sides are strongly fortified. It needs but one glance at Aden, which is in itself a natural fort, to strengthen the assertion that Aden is the strongest gate to India.

The moment we emerged from the cut, which, besides being so narrow that two carriages pass with great difficulty, is made on a dangerous steep grade, we got a view of the white town of Aden, nestling in the very heart of what seems to be an extinct volcano. We were driven rapidly down the road, catching glimpses of gaudily attired mounted policemen, water-carriers from the bay, with their well-filled goat-skins flung across their backs, camels loaded with cut stone, and black people of every description.

When we drove into the town, which is composed of low adobe houses, our carriage was surrounded with beggars. We got out and walked through an unpaved street, looking at the dirty, uninviting shops and the dirty, uninviting people in and about them. Very often we were urged to buy, but more frequently the natives stared at us with quiet curiosity. In the heart of the town we found the camel market, but beyond a number of camels standing, lying, and kneeling about, the sight was nothing extraordinary. Near by was a goat market, but business seemed dull in both places.

Without buying anything we started to return to the ship. Little naked children ran after us for miles, touching their foreheads humbly and crying for money. They all knew enough English to be able to ask us for charity.

When we reached the pier, we found our driver had forgotten all the English he knew when we started out. He wanted one price for the carriage and we wanted to pay another. It resulted in our appealing to a native policeman, who took the right change from us, handed it to the driver, and gave him, in addition, a lusty kick for his dishonesty.

Our limited time prevented our going to see the water tanks, which are some miles distant from Aden. When we returned to the ship we found Jews there, selling ostrich eggs and plumes, shells, fruit, spears of sword-fish, and such things. In the water, on one side of the boat, were numbers of men, Somali boys, they called them, who were giving an exhibition of wonderful diving and swimming.

They would actually sit in the water looking like bronze statues, as the sun rested on their wet, black skins. They sat in a row, and turning their faces up towards the deck, would yell methodically, one after the other, down the entire line:

"Oh! Yo! Ho!"

It sounded very like a chorus of bull-frogs and was very amusing. After finishing this strange music they would give us a duet, half crying, persuasively, in a sing-song style:

"Have a dive! Have a dive! Have a dive!"

The other half, meanwhile, would put their hands before their widely opened mouths, yelling through their rapidly moving fingers with such energy that we gladly threw over silver to see them dive and stop the din.

The moment the silver flashed over the water all the bronze figures would disappear like flying fish, and looking down we would see a few ripples on the surface of the blue water-nothing more. After a time that seemed dangerously long to us, they would bob up through the water again. We could see them coming before they finally appeared on the surface, and one among the number would have the silver between his teeth, which would be most liberally displayed in a broad smile of satisfaction. Some of these divers were children not more than eight years old, and they ranged from that up to any age. Many of them had their hair bleached. As they were completely naked, excepting a small cloth twisted about the loins, they found it necessary to make a purse out of their cheeks, which they did with as much ease as a cow stows away grass to chew at her leisure.

I have often envied a cow this splendid gift. One wastes so much time eating, especially when traveling, and I could not help picturing the comfort it would be sometimes to dispose of our food wholesale and consume it at our leisure afterwards. I am certain there would be fewer dyspeptics then.

No animal, waterborn and bred, could frisk, more gracefully in the water than do these Somali boys. They swim about, using the legs alone, or the arms alone, on their backs, or sides, and, in most cases, with their faces under water. They never get out of the way of a boat. They merely sink and come up in the same spot when the boat passes. The bay at Aden is filled with sharks, but they never touch these black men, so they tell me, and the safety with which they spend their lives in the water proves the truth of the assertion. They claim that a shark will not attack a black man, and after I had caught the odor of the grease with which these men annoint their bodies, I did not blame the sharks.

After a seven hours stay at Aden we left for Colombo, being followed a long ways out from land by the divers. One little boy went out with us on the ship, and when he left us he merely took a plunge from the upper deck into the sea and went happily back towards Aden, on his side, waving a farewell to us with his free hand.

The passengers endeavored to make the time pass pleasantly between Aden and Colombo. The young women had some *tableaux vivants* one evening, and they were really very fine. In one they wished to represent the different countries. They asked me to represent America, but I refused, and then they asked me to tell them what the American flag looked like! They wanted to represent one as nearly as possible and to rise it to drape the young woman who was to represent America. Another evening we had a lantern slide exhibition that was very enjoyable.

The loyalty of the English to their Queen on all occasions, and at all times, had won my admiration. Though born and bred a staunch American, with the belief that a man is what he makes of himself, not what he was born, still I could not help admiring the undying respect the English have for their royal family. During the lantern slide exhibition, the Queen's picture was thrown on the white sheet, and evoked warmer applause than anything else that evening. We never had an evening's amusement that did not end by everybody rising to their feet and singing "God Save the Queen." I could not help but think how devoted that woman, for she is only a woman after all, should be to the interests of such faithful subjects.

With that thought came to me a shamed feeling that there I was, a free born American girl, the native of the grandest country on earth, forced to be silent because I could not in honesty speak proudly of the rulers of my land, unless I went back to those two kings of manhood, George Washington and Abraham Lincoln.

Chapter 9: Delayed Five Days

ABOUT nine o'clock in the morning we anchored in the bay at Colombo, Ceylon. The island, with its abundance of green trees, was very restful and pleasing to our eyes after the spell of heat we had passed through on the ocean coming from Aden.

Preparations had been made by the passengers before we anchored, to go ashore, and as we came slowly into the small harbor, where a number of vessels were lying, we all stood impatiently on deck waiting for the first opportunity to desert the ship.

With all our impatience we could not fail to be impressed with the beauties of Colombo and the view from the deck of our incoming steamer. As we moved in among the beautiful ships laying at anchor, we could see the green island dotted with low arcaded buildings which looked, in the glare of the sun, like marble palaces. In the rear of us was the blue, blue sea, jumping up into little hills that formed into snow drifts which softly sank into the blue again. Forming the background to the town was a high mountain, which they told us was known as Adam's Peak. The beach, with a forest of tropical trees, looked as if it started in a point away out in the sea, curving around until near the harbor it formed into a blunt point, the line of which was carried out to sea by a magnificent breakwater surmounted by a light-house. Then the land curved back again to a point where stood a signal station, and on beyond a wide road ran along the water's edge until it was lost at the base of a high green eminence that stood well out over the sea, crowned with a castle-like building glistening in the sunlight.

Little boats filled with black-men, we could see coming out towards us from the shore, but my eyes were fastened on a strangely shaped object, resting on the surface of the water in the bay. It seemed a living, feathered thing of so strange a shape that I watched it with feelings akin to horror. What horrible feathered monster could that lovely island produce, I wondered, noticing with dismay that the ship was heading for it. Just as we were upon it, there was a flutter of wings and a cloud of birds flew across and settled down upon the breakwater, where some fishermen, their feet overhanging the stony sides, were watching their lines. I looked back at what had raised so much consternation in my mind, and saw now that it was relieved of a feathered mass off birds,-a harmless red buoy!

Accompanied by a friend, I was the first to step ashore. Some passengers who started in advance of us, took a steam launch. My escort said that he would give me a novel experience, and also show me a small boat that traveled faster than a steam launch. The gentleman who had offered to be my escort during our jaunt on land, was a traveler of vast experience. He has averaged a yearly tour of the world for several years, and knows the eastern countries as he knows his home. Still, when I saw the boat in which he intended to take me ashore, I rather doubted his judgment, but I said nothing.

The boat was a rudely constructed thing. The boat proper was probably five feet in length and two feet in width across the top, narrowing down to the keel, so that it was not wide enough to allow one's feet to rest side by side in the bottom. There were two seats in the middle of the boat facing one another. They are shaded by a bit of coffee sack that must be removed to give room for passengers to get in. The two men sit at either end of this peculiar boat, and with one paddle each. The paddle is a straight pole, with a board the shape and size of a cheese-box head tied to the end of it, and with both those paddles on the same side they row us ashore. The boat is balanced by a log the length of the boat and fastened out by two curved poles, probably three feet from the boat. These boats are called by tourists, outriggers, but are called by the people of Ceylon, catamarans.

With but slight exertion the men sent the boat cutting through the water, and in a few moments we had distanced the steam launch and had accommodations engaged at the hotel before the launch had landed its passengers. It is said at Colombo that catamarans are used by the native fisherman, who go out to sea in them, and that they are so seaworthy and so secure against capsizing that no case of an accident to a catamaran has ever been reported.

A nearer view of the hotel, the Grand Oriental, did not tend to lessen its attractiveness-in fact it increased it. It was a fine, large hotel, with tiled arcades, corridors airy and comfortable, furnished with easy chairs and small marble topped tables which stood close enough to the broad arm-rests, for one to sip the cooling lime squashes or the exquisite native tea, or eat of the delicious fruit while resting in an attitude of ease and laziness. I found no place away from America where smoking was prohibited, and in this lovely promenade the men smoked, consumed gallons of whiskey and soda and perused the newspapers, while the women read their novels or bargained with the pretty little copper-colored women who came to sell dainty hand-made lace, or with the clever, high-turbaned merchants who would snap open little velvet boxes and expose, to the admiring gaze of the charmed tourists, the most bewildering gems. There were deeply-dark emeralds, fire-lit diamonds, exquisite pearls, rubies like pure drops of blood, the lucky cat's -eye with its moving line, and all set in such beautiful shapes that even the men, who would begin by saying, "I have been sold before by some of your kind," would end by laying down their cigars and papers and examining the glittering ornaments that tempt all alike. No woman who lands at Colombo ever leaves until she adds several rings to her jewel box, and these rings are so well known that the moment a traveler sees one, no difference in what part of the globe, he says to the wearer, inquiringly:

"Been to Colombo, eh?"

For the first time since leaving America I saw American money. It is very popular in Colombo and commands a high price-as jewelry! It goes for nothing as money. When I offered it in payment for my bills I was told it would be taken at sixty per cent discount. The Colombo diamond merchants are very glad to get American twenty dollar gold pieces and pay a high premium on them. The only use they make of the money is to put a ring through it and hang it on their watch chains for ornaments. The wealth of the merchant can be estimated by his watch chain, they tell me; the richer the merchant the more American gold dangles from his chain. I saw some men with as many as twenty pieces on one chain. Most of the jewelry bought and sold in Colombo is sold in the corridor of the Grand Oriental Hotel. Merchants bring their wares with them and tourists find it pleasanter than visiting the shops.

Leading off from this corridor, pleasant in its coolness, interesting in its peculiarities, is the dining-hall, matching the other parts of the hotel with its picturesque stateliness. The small tables are daintily set and are richly decorated daily with the native flowers of Colombo, rich in color, exquisite in form, but void of perfume. From the ceiling were suspended embroidered punkas, that invention of the East which brings comfort during the hottest part of the day. The punkas are long strips of cloth, fastened to bamboo poles that are suspended within a short distance of the tables. They are kept in motion by a rope pulley, worked by a man or boy. They send a lazy, cooling air through the building, contributing much to the ease and comfort of the guest. Punkas are also used on all the ships that travel in the East.

Very good food was served at the hotel-which was all the more palatable to the passengers from the Victoria after the trials they had had for the past fortnight in eating the same kind of food under daily different names. Singalese waiters were employed, and they were not only an improvement on the English stewards, to whose carelessness and impudence we had been forced to submit, but they were interesting to the Westerner.

They managed to speak English very well and understood everything that was said to them. They are not unpleasing people, being small of stature and fine of feature, some of them having very attractive, clean-cut faces, light bronze in color. They wore white linen apron-like skirts and white jackets. Noiselessly they move over the smooth tile floor, in their bare, brown feet. Their straight black hair is worn long, twisted in a Psyche knot at the back of the head. On the crown of the head, instead of circling it from ear to ear, is always set a tortoise shell comb, like those worn by American school children. It was some time before I could tell a Singalese man from a Singalese woman. It is not difficult to distinguish the different sexes after one knows that the Singalese men wear the comb, which is as distinct a feature of their dress as men's trousers in America. Singalese women would not think of donning this little comb any more than a sensitive American woman would think of wearing men's apparel.

I did not hear the term waiter, or *garcon*, after leaving America. After leaving the English ships I did not hear the word steward, but instead, in the hotels and ships in the East, all the servants were called "boy." We can call "steward!. . . . waiter!. . . . garcon!" until we are weary, without any result, but the moment we whisper "boy!" a pleasant black fellow says, "yes, sir," at our side, and is ready to do our bidding.

At tiffin I had some real curry, the famous native dish of India. I had been unable to eat it on the Victoria, but those who knew said it was a most delicious dish when prepared rightly and so I tested it on shore. First a divided dish containing shrimps and boiled rice was placed before me. I put two spoonfuls of rice on my plate, and on it put one spoonful of shrimps; there was also chicken and beef for the meat part of the curry, but I took shrimps only. Then was handed me a much divided plate containing different preserved fruits, chuddah and other things hot with pepper. As instructed, I partook of three of this variety and put it on top of what had been placed first on my plate. Last came little dried pieces of stuff that we heard before we saw, its odor was so loud and unmistakable. They called it Bombay duck. It is nothing more or less than a small fish, which is split open, and after being thoroughly dried, is used with the curry. One can learn to eat it.

After all this is on the plate it is thoroughly mixed, making a mess very unsightly, but very palatable, as I found. I became so given to curry that I only stopped eating it when I found, after a hearty meal, curry threatened to give me palpitation of the heart. A story is told concerning the Bombay duck that is very amusing.

The Shah of Persia was notified that some high official in India intended to send him a lot of very fine Bombay duck. The Shah was very much pleased and, in anticipation of their arrival, had some expensive ponds built to put the Bombay ducks in! Imagine his consternation when he received those ill-smelling, dried fish!

After tiffin we drove to mount Lavania. We went along the smoothest, most perfectly made roads I ever saw. They seemed to be made of red asphalt, and I was afterwards told that they are constructed by convicts. Many of these roads were picturesque bowers, the over-reaching branches of the trees that lined the waysides forming an arch of foliage above our heads, giving us charming telescopic views of people and conveyances along the road. Thatched huts of the natives and glimpses of the dwellers divided our attention with the people we passed on the road.

Mount Lavania we found to be the place we had noticed on entering the harbor. It is a fine hotel situated on an eminence overlooking the sea, and is a favorite resort during the hot seasons. It is surrounded by a smooth green lawn and faces the blue sea, whence it gets a refreshing breeze all the year through.

After dinner, everybody at the Grand Oriental Hotel went out for a drive, the women, and many of the men going bare-headed. Driving through the town, down the wide streets, past beautiful homes set well back in tropical gardens, to the Galle Face drive that runs along the beach just out of reach of the waves that break on the sandy banks with a more musical roar than I ever heard water produce before. The road lies very close to the water's edge, and by the soft rays of the moon its red surface was turned to silver, the deep blue of the sea was black, and the foamy breakers were snow drifts. In the soft, pure light we would see silent couples strolling along arm and arm, apparently so near the breakers that I felt apprehensive lest one, stronger than the others, should catch them unawares and wash them out to that unknown land where we all travel to rest. Lounging on the benches that face the sea were occasional soldiers in the Queen's uniform, whom I looked at anxiously, unable to tell whether their attitude of weariness bespoke a rest from labor or hungry home-sickness. One night I saw a native standing waist deep fishing in the roaring breakers. They tell me that many of the fish bite more freely after night, but I thought how easily the fisherman might be washed away, and no one would be the wiser until his absence was noticed by his friends.

Where the Galle Face drive merges into another road, stands the Galle Face Hotel surrounded by a forest of palm trees. Lounging on long-bottomed, easy chairs, on the stone-floored and stone-pillared verandah, one can see through the forest of tall palms where the ocean kisses the sandy beach, and while listening to the music of the wave, the deep, mellow roar, can drift-drift out on dreams that bring what life has failed to give; soothing pictures of the imagination that blot out for a moment the stern disappointment of reality. Or, when the dreams fade away, one can drown the sigh with the cooling lime squash which the noiseless, bare-footed, living bronze has placed on the white arm-rest, at the same time lazily watching the jinrickshas come silently in through the gas-lit gate, the naked black runners coming to a sudden stop, letting the shafts drop so the passenger can step out.

Lazily I sat there one sweet, dusky night, only half hearing my escort's words that came to me mingled with the sound of the ocean. A couple stood close together, face bending over a face up-turned, hand clasped in hand and held closely against a manly heart, standing, two dark figures, beneath an arch of the verandah, outlined against the gate lamp. I felt a little sympathy for them as wrapped in that delusion that makes life heaven or hell, that forms the foundation for every novel, play or story, they stood, until a noisy new arrival wakened her from blissful oblivion, and she rushed, scarcely waiting for him to kiss the hand he held, away into the darkness. I sighed again, and taking another sip of my lime squash, turned to answer my companion.

Early next morning I was awakened by a Singalese waiter placing coffee and toast on a small table which he drew up close to my curtained bed, after which he went out. I knew from the dim light that crept in through the open glass door which led to the balcony, that it was still early, and I soon went off to sleep. I was awakened shortly by a rattling of the dishes on the table, and opening my eyes I saw, standing on the table, quietly enjoying my toast, a crow!

I was not then used to having toast and tea before arising, as is the custom in Ceylon, so I let the crow satisfy his appetite and leisurely take his departure without a protest. I arose earlier than was my habit, because I had a desire to see what there might be to see while I had the opportunity.

After a cool, refreshing bath, I dressed hastily and went down below. I found almost all of my friends up, some having already started out to enjoy the early morning. I regretted my generosity to the crow when I learned that breakfast was never served until nine o'clock, and as everybody endeavored to have the benefit of the cool, sweet morning, toast and tea was very sustaining.

In a light wagon we again drove down Galle Face road, and out past a lake in which men, women, children, oxen, horses, buffalo and dogs were sporting. It was a strange sight. Off on a little green island we saw the laundry folk at work, beating, sousing and wringing the clothes, which they afterwards spread upon the grass to dry. Almost all of the roads through which we drove were perfect with their picturesque curves, and often bordered and arched with magnificent trees, many of which were burdened with beautiful brilliant blossoms.

Everybody seemed to be out. The white people were driving, riding, riding bicycles, or walking. The breakwater, which is a good half mile in length, is a favorite promenade for the citizens of Colombo. Morning and evening gaily dressed people can be seen walking back and forth between the light-house and the shore. When the stormy season comes the sea dashes full forty feet above this promenade, which must be cleansed of a green slime, after the storms are over, before it can be traveled with safety. The Prince of Wales laid the first stone of this beautiful breakwater in 1875, and ten years later it was finished.

It is considered one of the finest in existence.

Colombo reminded me of Newport, R. I. Possibly-in my eyes, at least–Colombo is more beautiful. The homes may not be as expensive, but they are more artistic and picturesque. The roads are wide and perfect; the view of the sea is grand, and while unlike in its tropical aspect, still there is something about Colombo that recalls Newport.

After breakfast, which usually leaves nothing to be desired, guests rest in the corridor of the hotel; the men who have business matters to attend to look after them and return to the hotel not later than eleven. About the hour of noon everybody takes a rest, and after luncheon they take a nap. While they sleep the hottest part of the day passes, and at four they are again ready for a drive or a walk, from which they return after sunset in time to dress for dinner. After dinner there are pleasant little rides in jinrickshas or visits to the native theaters.

I went one night to a Parsee theatre. At the entrance were groups of people, some of whom were selling fruits, and some were jinricksha men waiting to haul the people home after the performance. There was no floor in the building. The chairs were placed in rows on the ground. the house was quite well filled with native men, women and children who were deeply interested in the performance which had begun before we reached there.

The actors were all men; my escort had told me women never think of going on the stage in that country. The stage was not unlike any other stage, and the scenery, painted by native artists, was quite as good as is usually seen. On the left of the stage, close to the wing, was a man, sitting cross-legged on a raised platform, beating a tom-tom. A tom-tom was undoubtedly the mother to the drum. It is made on the same principle, but instead of being round is inclined to be long in shape, The player uses his hands instead of drum-sticks, and when one becomes accustomed to it I do not think the sound of a tom-tom can be called unmusical. The musician who presided over the tom-tom this night was dressed in a thin white material, and he wore a very large turban of the same stuff on his head. His copper-colored face was long and earnest, and he beat the tom-tom with a will that was simply amazing when one was informed that he had been constantly engaged at it since nine in the morning. If his hands did not tire his legs did. Several times I saw him move, as if to find ease by shifting his squatting position, and every time I saw his bare feet turn up, in full view of the audience, I felt an irresistible desire to laugh.

On the right, directly opposite to the tom-tom player, was a man, whose duty it was to play a strange looking organ. He only used one hand, the left, for playing, and with the right he held a book, which he steadily perused throughout the entire performance, reading and playing mechanically without once looking at the actors.

The actors were amusing, at least. The story of the opera was not unlike those in other countries. The basis or plot of the play was a tale of love and tragedy. A tall young man, with his face painted a death-like white, sang shrilly through his very high-arched nose to another young man, dressed in the costume of a native woman. The latter was the lady, and the heroine of the play, and he sang sharply through his nose like his, or her, lover. All the actors sang through their noses, and the thinner their voices and the more nasal sound they employed the more the audience applauded.

The heroine of the play was a maid-servant employed by a very wealthy tea planter, who was the father of the lover who sang through his nose. The lover, like all lovers urged the girl to be his in songs that were issued through his nose for fifteen minutes at a time. He, the heroine, would endeavor to look shy all through this unsufferably long song of nasal sound, and then she would take up the same refrain, and to the same tune sing back at him for the same length, and after his own style, while he would hang his head and listen. Their gestures were very few, and they usually stood in one spot on the stage. Sometimes they would embrace, but only to fall apart and sing at each other again.

The play goes on. A bold, bad robber, whose chalk-whitened face has a most Jewish cast, sees the maid-servant and falls in love with her. She repels his advances and goes into her master's house. Then the robber puts a cross on the house and vows that he will return with his men to kill the inhabitants, for the heroine, in her simplicity, confesses to the truth of his supposition that she loves another, and that other is her master's son, so the villain swears that he will return, kill the people of the house, and not only carry off the wealth but the maidservant as well.

After the robber departs, the heroine comes out, and spies the cross upon her house. With a crafty look upon her face, she picks up the chalk which the robber had dropped, and marks all the other houses in the street in just the same way, so that when the robber returns he is foiled in his bold, bad game, for he cannot tell which house holds his charmer, and her wealthy lover and master. He is a patient robber, and lies in wait until the lovers come forth to coo on the street. While they are busy, making love through their noses, the man plays the organ with energy, the turbaned musician beats the tom-tom as if his life depended upon it, and the bold, bad robber clutches at his stomach, twists his face into the most agonized expressions, and otherwise shows his agony to the audience. When they go into the house he is about to follow, when the master appears, and, as he is going in, the robber approaches and, saying that he is a wealthy tea-merchant, begs to be permitted to rest at his house that night. The master most cordially consents, just as the heroine appears, and she, having heard the conversation tells her master not to allow the man to stay. The master becomes very angry at her boldness and promises her a liberal punishment, to take effect later in the day.

The merchant begs to be permitted to have his cases of tea placed within the garden-walls of his host, that the tea may be safe through the night. Of course the host consents, and the next scene shows the chests of tea in the garden, and the bold robber puts out the light at the door and goes into the house to bide his time. Even that heroine dreams, and, like other heroines, selects the cool, sweet night and the garden to dream in. She is surprised to find the garden in darkness, and lays her finger to the side of her nose when she sees the lamp is not burning. As she skips about, smelling the artificial flowers, the lid of a tea-chest is raised slightly, and a man sings something through his nose. She starts back in surprise, but instead of screaming, she answers the inquiry in nasal tones, and she learns that the chests are not filled with tea, but with men who belong to the robber, for whom they mistook her. When the man closes the lid again to wait the bidding to come forth, she deftly locks all the cases, and then calls upon a man servant who helps her, the heroine, to carry these cases containing men into a house in which they are securely locked.

The next scene shows a room in which the people are gathered and making merry. They are all sitting on the floor, and among them is the chief robber. The heroine, and other maidservants are brought in to give a dagger dance. They have bracelets of bells around their wrists and ankles, and the dance is very pleasing. The heroine and another servant dance while battling with each other with their knives. Occasionally they break apart and encircle the room, and the heroine makes motions as if she intended to give the guests a playful thrust. She sees the robber slyly poison her master's wine, and so she dances around the robber's way, and sticks her dagger in his heart and goes on with her dance. The guests laugh until they see the robber rise to his feet and fall dead. They see then the thrust was not playful but real, and the girl is caught and the master says she shall die. Then she screeches out the story of the men in the tea-cases and tells about the poisoned wine, and the guests applaud her brave act, and she is told to ask for any favor she wishes. She asks for her master's son! She gets him, to the music of the tom-tom and the organ, and I suppose they live happy ever afterwards.

I rode home from the theatre in a bullock hackery. It was a very small springless cart on two wheels with a front seat for the driver, and on the back seat, with our backs to the driver and out feet hanging over, we drove to the hotel. The bullock is a strange, modest-looking little animal with a hump on its back and crooked horns on its head. I feared that it could not carry us all, but it traveled at a very good pace. There was a sound of grunt, grunt, grunting that concerned me very much until I found it was the driver and not the bullock that was responsible for the noise. With grunts he urged the bullock to greater speed.

The drive, along tree-roofed roads, was very quiet and lovely. The moonlight fell beautiful and soft over the land, and nothing disturbed the stillness except the sound of the sea and an occasional soldier we met staggering along towards the barracks. At one place we saw a mosque with low, dim lamps hanging about. We went in and found the priests lying about on the stone floor, some at the very foot of the altar. We talked with them in whispers and then returned to the cart, which soon carried us back to the hotel. Just as we turned a corner to go to the hotel, an officer rushed up and, catching hold of a wheel, tried to stop the hackery, telling the driver that we were all under arrest.

The candles in one of the lamps had burned out and we were arrested for driving with a dark side. My companion made it right with the policeman, and we went to the hotel instead of the jail.

Among the natives that haunt the hotel are the snake charmers. They are almost naked fellows, sometimes with ragged jackets on and sometimes turbans on their heads, but more often the head is bare. They execute a number of tricks in a very skillful manner. The most wonderful of these tricks, to me, was that of growing a tree. They would show a seed, then they would place the seed on the ground, cover it with a handful of earth, and cover this little mound with a handkerchief, which they first passed around to be examined, that we might be positive there was nothing wrong with it. Over this they would chant, and after a time the handkerchief is taken off and then up through the ground is a green sprout. We look at it incredulously, while the man says:

"Tree no good; tree too small," and covering it up again he renews his chanting. Once more he lifts the handkerchief and we see the sprout is larger, but still it does not please the trickster, for he repeats: "Tree no good; tree too small," and covers it up again. This is repeated until he has a tree from three to five feet in height. Then he pulls it up, shows us the seed and roots.

Although these men always asked us to "See the snake dance?" we always saw every other trick but the one that had caught us. One morning, when a man urged me to "See the snake dance?" I said that I would, but that I would pay to see the snake dance and for nothing else. Quite unwillingly the men lifted the lid of the basket, and the cobra crawled slowly out, curling itself up on the ground. The "charmer" began to play on a little fife, meanwhile waving a red cloth which attracted the cobra's attention. It rose up steadily, darting angrily at the red cloth, and rose higher at every motion until it seemed to stand on the tip end of its tail. Then it saw the charmer and it darted for him, but he cunningly caught it by the head and with such a grip that I saw the blood gush from the snake's mouth. He worked for some time, still firmly holding the snake by the head before he could get it into the basket, the reptile meanwhile lashing the ground furiously with its tail. When at last it was covered from sight, I drew a long breath, and the charmer said to me sadly:

"Cobra no dance, cobra too young, cobra too fresh!"

I thought quite right; the cobra was too fresh!

At Colombo I saw the jinricksha for the first time. The jinricksha is a small two-wheel wagon, much in shape like a sulky, except that it has a top which can be raised in rainy weather. It has long shafts joined at the end with a crossbar. The jinricksha men are black and wear little else than a sash. When the sun is hot they wear large hats that look like enormous mushrooms, but most of the time these hats are hanging to the back of the 'ricksha. There are stands at different places for these men as well as carriage stands. While waiting for patrons they let their 'rickshas rest on the shafts and they sit in the bottom, their feet on the ground. Besides dressing in a sash these men dress in an oil or grease, and when the day is hot and they run, one wishes they wore more clothing and less oil! The grease has an original odor that is entirely its own.

One day I was going out in a 'ricksha and an acquaintance was going with me. The man put his foot on the shaft when I got in, and as he raised it, ready to start, I saw my friend step into her 'ricksha. She sat down and instantly went out-the other way! The man did not have his foot on the shaft and she overbalanced.

I had a shamed feeling about going around the town drawn by a man, but after I had gone a short way, I decided it was a great improvement on modern means of travel; it was so comforting to have a horse that was able to take care of itself! When we went into the shops it was so agreeable not to have the worry of fearing the horses were not blanketed, and when we made them run we did not have to fear we might urge them into a damaging speed. It is a great relief to have a horse whose tongue can protest.

I have spoken about the perfect roads in Ceylon. I found the roads in the same state of perfection in almost all the Eastern ports at which I stopped. I could not decide, to my own satisfaction, whether the smoothness of the road was due to the entire and blessed absence of beer wagons, or to the absence of the New York street commissioners.

I visited at the temples in Colombo, finding little of interest, and always having to pay liberally for the privilege of looking about. One day I went to the Buddhist college, and while there I met the famous high priest of Ceylon. He was sitting on a verandah, that surrounded his low bungalow, writing on a table placed before him. His gown consisted of a straight piece of old gold silk wrapped deftly around the body and over the waist. The silk had fallen to his waist, but after he greeted us he pulled it up around his shoulders. He was a copper-colored old fellow, with gray hair that was shaved very close to the head. He spoke English quite well, and among other things told me he received hundreds of letters from the United States every year, and that they found more converts to the Buddhist religion in America than in any other land.

The two newspapers in Colombo are in charge of two young Englishmen who are very clever. They are very kind to strangers, and I am indebted to them for a great deal of pleasure during my stay in Ceylon. The hotel manager is a German of high birth. He is untiring in his efforts to make his guests comfortable. His wife is a very pretty little woman, with a beautiful voice. Through her kindness I learned of a tailor in Ceylon who makes gowns, that for style and fit are not excelled. I have seen gowns from Worth that could not equal them, and this man charges for making a gown, five rupees! Five rupees are about two dollars and a half. He will make a gown in two days.

The praises of Kandy had been sung to me, so one morning at seven o'clock I started for Kandy with the Spanish representative, who was going to Pekin, and a jolly Irish lad who was bound for Hong Kong, both of whom had traveled with me from Brindisi. We drove to the station and were passed with the people, through the gate to the train. English cars, and ones that leave everything to be desired, are used on this line. We got into a compartment where there was but one seat, which, luckily for us, happened to be facing the way we traveled. Our tickets were taken at the station, and then the doors were locked and the train started. Before the start, we had entered our names in a book which a guard brought to us with the information that we could have breakfast on the train if so desired. As it was too early for breakfast at the hotel, we were only too glad to get an opportunity to eat. At eight o'clock the train stopped and the guard unlocked our door, telling us to go front to the dining-car. It seemed strange to be compelled to get out of a train, instead of walking through it, in order to get to the other end of it.

The dining-car was fitted up with stationary tables which almost spanned the car, leaving a small space for people to walk along. There were more people than could be accommodated, but as the train had started, they were obliged to stand. Several persons had told me that the breakfast served on this train was considered remarkably good. I thought, on seeing the bill of fare, they had prepared a feast for a chicken hawk. First, there was fish dressed in vinegar and onions, followed by chicken soup, chicken aspic, grilled chicken, boned chicken, fried chicken, boiled chicken, cold chicken and chicken pie!

After we had finished our breakfast we were compelled to remain where we were until the train arrived at some station. Then the dining-car was unlocked and we returned to the other car, being again locked in until the end of our journey. The road to Kandy is spoken of as being very beautiful. It winds up the mountain side and is rather pretty, but nothing wonderful in that respect. It is a tropical land, but the foliage and flowers are very ordinary. About the prettiest things to be seen are the rice beds. They are built in terraces, and when one looks down into the deep valley, seeing terrace after terrace of the softest, lightest green, one is forced to cry: "How beautiful!"

Arriving at Kandy at last, we hired a carriage and went to see the lake, the public library and the temples. In one old temple, surrounded by a moat, we saw several altars, of little consequence, and a bit of ivory which they told us was the tooth of Buddha. Kandy is pretty, but far from what it is claimed to be. They said it was cool, but we found it so hot that we thought with regret of Colombo. Disgusted with all we found worth seeing we drove to Parathenia to see the great botanical garden. It well repaid us for the visit. That evening we returned to Colombo. I was tired and hungry and the extreme heat had given me a sick headache. On the way down, the Spanish gentlemen endeavored to keep our falling spirits up, but every word he said only helped to increase my bad temper, much to the amusement of the Irish boy. He was very polite and kind, the Spaniard, I mean, but he had an unhappy way of flatly contradicting one, that, to say the least, was very exasperating. It was to me, but it only made the Irish boy laugh. When we were going down the mountain side the Spaniard got up, and standing, put his head through the open window in the door to get a view of the country.

"We are going over," he said, with positive conviction, turning around to us. I was leaning up in a corner trying to sleep and the Irish boy, with his feet braced against the end of the compartment, was trying to do the same.

"We won't go over," I managed to say, while the Irish boy smiled.

"Yes, we will," the Spaniard shouted back, "Make your prayers!"

The Irish boy screamed with laughter, and I forgot my sickness as I held my sides and laughed. It was a little thing, but it is often little things that raise the loudest laughs. After that all I needed to say to upset the dignity of the Irish boy was: "Make your prayers!"

I went to bed that night too ill to eat my dinner. The next morning I had intended to go to the pearl market, but felt unequal to it, and when my acquaintances returned and told me that at the very end of the sale a man bought some left over oysters for one rupee and found in them five hundred dollars worth of pearls, I felt sorry that I had not gone, although there was great danger of getting cholera.

One day I heard a man ask another if he knew the meaning of the word "jinricksha." the first replied the word meant "Draw man power," and the second said, with innocent surprise, "I thought it was 'Pull man car!'" I heard a passenger who came ashore from an Australian boat ask Andrew, a clever native who stands at the hotel door, to get him one of those carts to take a ride.

Andrew did not know just what the man wanted as there were many different kinds of carts about.

"I don't recall the name of them," the passenger said, in a hesitating manner, "but I believe you call them Jim-Jams!"

He got a jinricksha.

Chapter 10: In the Pirate Seas

ONE night, after I had been five days in Colombo, the blackboard in the hotel corridor bore the information that the Oriental would sail for China the following morning, at eight o'clock. I was called at five o'clock and some time afterwards left for the ship. The "Spanish minister," as we called the Spaniard, wanted me to go to some of the shops with him until he should buy some jewelry, but I was so nervous and anxious to be on my way that I could not wait a moment longer than was necessary to reach the boat that was to carry me to China.

When farewells had been said, and I was on the Oriental, I found my patience had given way under the long delay. The ship seemed to be deserted when I went on deck, with the exception of a handsome, elderly man, accompanied by a young blonde man in a natty white linen suit, who slowly promenaded the deck, watching out to sea while they talked. I was trying to untie my steamer chair so as to have some place to sit, when the elderly man came up and politely offered to assist me.

"When will we sail," I asked shortly.

"As soon as the Nepaul comes in," the man replied. "She was to have been here at daybreak, but she hasn't been sighted yet. Waiting for the Nepaul has given us this five days' delay. She's a slow old boat."

"May she go to the bottom of the bay when she does get in!" I said savagely. "The old tub! I think it an outrage to be kept waiting five days for a tub like that."

"Colombo is a pleasant place to stay," the elderly man said with a twinkle in his eye.

"It may be, if staying there does not mean more than life to one. Really, it would afford me the most intense delight to see the Nepaul go the bottom of the sea."

Evidently my ill humor surprised them, and their surprise amused me, for I thought how little anyone could realize what this delay meant to me, and the mental picture of a forlorn little self creeping back to New York ten days behind time, with a shamed look on her face and afraid to hear her name spoken, made me laugh outright. They gazed at me in astonishment, while I laughed immoderately at my own unenviable position. My better nature surged up with the laugh, and I was able to say, once again: "Everything happens for the best."

"There is the Nepaul," I said, pointing out a line of smoke just visible above the horizon. They doubted it, but a few moments proved that I was correct. "I am very ill-natured," I said, glancing from the kindly blue eyes of the elderly man to the laughing blue eyes of the younger man; "but I could not help it. After being delayed for five days I was called at five o'clock because they said the ship was to sail at eight, and here it is nine o'clock and there's no sign of the ship sailing and–I am simply famished."

As they laughed at my woes the gong sounded for breakfast and they took me down. The Irish lad, with his sparkling eyes and jolly laugh, was there, as was a young Englishman who had also traveled on the ship Victoria to Colombo. I knew him by sight, but as he was a sworn woman-hater I did not dare to speak to him. There were no women on board. I was the only woman that morning, and a right jolly breakfast we had.

The captain, a most handsome man, and as polite and courteous as he was good looking, sat at the head of the table. Officers, that any ship might boast of, were gathered about him. Handsome, good natured, intelligent, polite, they were, every single one of them. I found the elderly man I had been talking to was the chief engineer, and the young man was the ship's doctor.

The dining-hall was very artistic and pleasant, and the food was good. The ship, although much smaller than the Victoria, was very much better in every way. The cabins were more comfortable, the ship was better ventilated, the food was vastly superior, the officers were polite and good natured, the captain was a gentleman in looks and manners, and everything was just as agreeable as it could be. For several days I let things go on and said nothing about myself, nor did I give them the letter which the London agent had kindly sent. It had brought me no attention or courtesy on the Victoria, and I decided to take my chances on the Oriental. When I saw that uniform kindness and politeness was the rule on this ship, I then gave them the letter, and though the captain was pleased to receive it, still, it could not have made his treatment of me any kinder than it was at first.

It was well on to one o'clock before the passengers were transferred from the Nepaul to the Oriental. In the meantime the ship was amply peopled with merchants from the shore, who were selling jewels and lace. How they did cheat the passengers! They would ask, and sometimes get, fabulous prices for things, and when the ship was ready to sail, they offered to sell at any price. They were quite saucy chaps, too. I heard a vender reply to a man who offered him a small price for some so-called precious stones:

"I am not charging you for looking at these."

In fact they grew so impudent and bold, that I am surprised that the steamship lines do not issue orders prohibiting their presence on board.

At one o'clock we sailed. The first day and the two days following were passed lazily on deck. I found it a great relief to be again on the sweet, blue sea, out of sight of land, and free from the tussle and worry and bustle for life which we are daily, hourly even, forced to gaze upon on land. Although the East is, in a very great measure, free from the dreadful crowding for life, still one is bound to see signs of it even among the most indolent of people. Only on the bounding blue, the grand, great sea, is one rocked into a peaceful rest at noon of day, at dusk of night, feeling that one is drifting, drifting, not seeing, or knowing, or caring, about fool mortals striving for life. True, the sailors do this and that, but it has an air far from that of elbowing each other for a living. To the lazy passengers it seems that they merely hoist a sail or pull it down, that they may drift-dream-sleep-talk-live for happiness and not for gain.

The fourth day out was Sunday. The afternoon was spent on deck looking at the most beautiful green islands which we slowly passed. Sometimes we would lazily conjecture as to whether they were inhabited or not.

The next day we anchored at Penang, or Prince of Wales Island, one of the Straits Settlements. As the ship had such a long delay at Colombo, it was said that we would have but six hours to spend on shore. With an acquaintance as escort, I made my preparations and was ready to go to land the moment we anchored. We went ashore in a Sampan, an oddly shaped flat boat with the oars, or rather paddles, fastened near the stern. The Malay oarsman rowed hand over hand, standing upright in the stern, his back turned towards us as well as the way we were going. Frequently he turned his head to see if the way was clear, plying his oars industriously all the while. Once landed he chased us to the end of the pier demanding more money, although we had paid him thirty cents, just twenty cents over and above the legal fare.

Hiring a carriage we drove to where a waterfall comes bounding down the side of a naturally verdant mountain which has been transformed, half way up, into a pleasing tropical garden. The picturesque waterfall is nothing marvelous. It only made me wonder from whence it procured its water supply, but after walking until I was much heated, and finding myself apparently just as far from the fount, I concluded the waterfall's secret was not worth the fatigue it would cost.

On the way to the town we visited a Hindoo temple. Scarcely had we entered when a number of half-clad, bare-footed priests rushed frantically upon us, demanding that we remove our shoes. The temple being built open, its curved roof and rafters had long been utilized by birds and pigeons as a bed-room. Doubtless ages had passed over the stone floor, but I could swear nothing else had, so I refused emphatically and unconditionally to un-boot myself. I saw enough of their idols to satisfy me. One was a black god in a gay dress, the other was a shapeless black stone hung with garlands of flowers, the filthy stone at its base being buried 'neath a profusion of rich blossoms.

English is spoken less in Penang than in any port I visited. A native photographer, when I questioned him about it, said:

"The Malays are proud, Miss. They have a language of their own and they are too proud to speak any other."

That photographer knew how to use his English to advantage. He showed me cabinet-sized proofs for which he asked one dollar each.

"One dollar!" I exclaimed in astonishment, "That is very high for a proof."

"If Miss thinks it is too much she does not need to buy. She is the best judge of how much she can afford to spend," he replied with cool impudence.

"Why are they so expensive?" I asked, nothing daunted by his impertinence.

"I presume because Penang is so far from England," he rejoined, carelessly.

I was told afterwards that a passenger from the Oriental pulled the photographer's long, thin, black nose for his impudence, and I was pleased to hear it.

A Chinese joss-house, the first I had seen, was very interesting. The pink and white roof, curved like a canoe, was ornamented with animals of the dragon tribe, with their mouths open and their tails in the air. The straggling worshippers could be plainly seen from the streets through the arcade sides of the temple. Chinese lanterns and gilt ornaments made gay the dark interior. Little josses, with usual rations of rice, roast pig and smouldering joss-sticks disbursing a strangely sweet perfume, were no more interesting than a dark corner in which the superstitious were trying their luck, a larger crowd of dusky people than were about the altars. In fact, the only devoutee was a waxed-haired Chinese woman, with a slit-eyed brown babe tied on her back, bowing meekly and lowly before a painted, be-bangled joss.

Some priests with shaven heads and old-gold silk garments, who were in a summer-house in the garden, saw us when we were looking at the gold-fish ponds. One came forth, and, taking me by the hand, gracefully led me to where they were gathered. They indicated their wish that we should sit with them and drink tea with them, milkless and sugarless, from child-like China cups, which they re-filled so often that I had reasons for feeling thankful the cups were so like unto play-dishes. We were unable to exchange words, but we smiled liberal smiles, at one another.

Mexican silver is used almost exclusively in Penang. American silver will be accepted at the same value, but American gold is refused and paper money is looked on with contempt. The Chinese jinricksha men in Penang, compared with those in Colombo, are like over-fed pet horses besides racers in trim. They were the plumpest Chinamen I ever saw; such round fat legs and arms!

When we started back to the ship the bay was very rough. Huge waves angrily tossed our small boat about in a way that blotted the red from my escort's checks and caused him to hang his head in a care-for-nothing way over the boat's side. I could not help liking the sea to a coquette, so indifferent and heedless is it to the strange emotions it raises in the breast of man. It was a reckless spring that landed us on the ship's ladder, the rolling of the coal barge helping to increase the swell which had threatened to engulf us. Hardly had we reached deck when the barge was ordered to cut loose; even as this was being done the ship hoisted anchor and started on its way. Almost immediately there was a great commotion on board. About fifty ragged black men rushed frantically on deck to find that while depositing their last sacks of coal in the regions below, their barge and companions had cast off and were rapidly nearing the shore. Then followed dire chattering, wringing of hands, pulling of locks and crying after the receding barge, all to no avail. The tide was coming in, a very strong tide it was, too, and despite the efforts of those on it the barge was steadily swept inland.

The captain appeased the coolies' fears by stating that they should go off in the pilot's boat. We all gathered to see the sight and a funny one it was! The tug being lashed to the ship they first tried to take the men off without slowing down but after one man got a dangerous plunge bath and the sea threatened to bury the tug then the ship was forced to slow down. Some coolies slid down a cable, their comrades grabbing and pulling them wet and frightened white on to the tug. Others went down the ladder which lacked five feet of touching the pilot boat. Those already on board would clutch the hanging man's bare legs, he meanwhile clinging despairingly to the ladder, fearing to loosen his grasp and only doing so when the ship officers would threaten to knock him off.

The pilot, a native, was the last to go down. Then the cable was cast off and we sailed away seeing the tug, so overloaded that the men were afraid to move even to bail it out, swept back by the tide towards the place where we had last seen the land.

I had a cabin down below at first and I found little rest owing to the close proximity of a nurse and two children whose wise parents selected a cabin on the other side of the ship. They could rest in peace. After I had been awakened several mornings at daybreak by the squabbling of the children I cherished a grudge against the parents. The mother made some show of being a beauty. She had a fine nose, everybody confessed that, and she had reduced her husband to such a state of servitude and subjection that she needed no maids.

I have always confessed that I like to sleep in the morning as well as I like to stay up at night, and to have my sleep disturbed makes me as ill-natured as a bad dinner makes a man. The fond father of these children had a habit of coming over early in the morning to see his cherubs, before he went to his bath. I know this from hearing him tell them so. He would open their cabin door and in the loudest, coldest, most unsympathetic voice in the world, would thoroughly arouse me from my slumbers by screaming:

"Good morning. How is papa's family this morning?"

A confused conglomeration of voices sounded in reply; then he would shout:

"What does baby say to mamma? Say; what does baby say to mamma?"

"Mamma!" baby would at length shout back in a coarse, unnatural baby voice.

"What does baby say to papa? Tell me, baby, what does baby say to papa?"

"Papa!" would answer back the shrill treble.

"What does the moo-moo cow say, my treasure; tell papa what the moo-moo cow says?"

To this the baby would make no reply and again he would shout:

"What does the moo-moo cow say, darling; tell papa what the moo-moo cow says?"

If it had been once, or twice even, I might have endured it with civilized forbearance but after it had been repeated, the very same identical word every morning for six long weary mornings, my temper gave way and when he said: "Tell papa what the moo-moo cow says?" I shouted frantically:

"For heaven's sake, baby, tell papa what the moo-moo cow says and let me go to sleep."

A heavy silence, a silence that was heavy with indignation and surprise, followed and I went off to sleep to dream of being chased down a muddy hill by babies sitting astride cows with crumpled horns, and straight horns and no horns at all, all singing in a melodious cow-like voice, moo! moo! moo!

The fond parents did not speak to me after that. They gazed on me in disdain and when the woman got sea-sick I persuaded an acquaintance of hers to go in and see her one day by telling her it was her Christian duty. The fond mother would not allow the ship doctor to see her although her husband had to relate her ills to the doctor and in that way get him to prescribe for them. I knew there was something she wished to keep secret. The woman, true to my counsel, knocked on the door; hearing no voice and thinking it lost in the roar of the ocean opened the door. The fond mother looked up, saw, and screaming buried her face in the pillows, She was toothless and hairless! The frightened Samaritan did not wait to see if she had a cork limb! I felt repentant afterwards and went to a deck cabin where I soon forgot the moo-moo cow and the fond parents. But the woman's fame as a beauty was irrevocably ruined on the ship.

It was so damply warm in the Straits of Malacca that for time first time during my trip I confessed myself uncomfortably hot. It was sultry and foggy and so damp that everything rusted, even the keys in one's pockets, and the mirrors were so sweaty that they ceased to reflect. The second day out from Penang we passed beautiful green islands. There were many stories told about the straits being once infested with pirates, and I regretted to hear that they had ceased to exist, I so longed for some new experience.

We expected to reach Singapore that night. I was anxious that we should, for the sooner we got in the sooner we should leave, and every hour lost meant so much to me. The pilot came on at six o'clock. I waited tremblingly for his verdict. A wave of despair swept over me when I heard that we should anchor outside until morning, because it was too dangerous to try to make the port after dark. And this was the result of slowing down to leave off the coolies at Penang. The mail contract made it compulsory for the ship to stay in port twenty-four hours, and while we might have been consuming our stay and so helping me on in my race against time I was wasting precious hours lying outside the gates of hope, as it were, merely because some black men had been too slow. Those few hours might mean time loss of my ship at Hong Kong; they might mean days to my record. What agony of suspense and impatience I suffered that night!

When I came on deck time next morning the ship lay along side the wharf, and naked Chinese coolies carrying, two by two, baskets of coal suspended between them on a pole, were constantly traversing the gang-plank between the ship and shore, while in little boats about were peddlers with silks, photographs, fruits, laces and monkeys to sell.

The doctor, a young Welshman, and I hired a gharry, a light wagon with latticed windows and comfortable seating room for four with the driver's seat on the same level outside. They are drawn by a pretty spotted Malay pony whose speed is marvelous compared with its diminutive size, and whose endurance is of such quality that the law confines their working hours to a certain limit.

Driving along a road as smooth as a ball-room floor, shaded by large trees, made picturesque by native houses built on pins in marshy land on either side, which tended to dampen our surprise at the great number of graveyards and the generous way in which they were filled, we drove to the town. The graves were odd, being round mounds with walls shaped like horse-shoes. A flat stone where the mound ends and the wall begins bears the inscriptions done in colored letters.

There are no sidewalks in Singapore, and blue and white in the painting of the houses largely predominate over other colors. Families seem to occupy the second story, the lower being generally devoted to business purposes. Through latticed windows we got occasional glimpses of peeping Chinese women in gay gowns, Chinese babies bundled in shapeless, wadded garments, while down below through widely opened fronts we could see people pursuing their trades. Barbering is the principal trade. A chair, a comb, a basin and a knife are all the tools a man needs to open shop, and he finds as many patrons if he sets up shop in the open street as he would under shelter. Sitting doubled over, Chinamen have their heads shaven back almost to the crown, when a spot about the size of a tiny saucer is left to bear the crop of hair which forms the pig-tail. When braided and finished with a silk tassel the Chinaman's hair is "done" for the next fortnight.

The people here, as at other ports where I stopped, constantly chew betel nut, and when they laugh one would suppose they had been drinking blood. The betel nut stains their teeth and mouthfuls blood-red. Many of the natives also fancy tinting their finger-nails with it.

Nothing is patronized more than the 'rickshas in Singapore, and while they are to be had for ten cents an hour it is no unusual sight to see four persons piled in one jinricksha and drawn by one man. We visited a most interesting museum, and saw along the suburban roads the beautiful bungalows of the European citizens. People in dog-carts and wheelmen on bicycles crowded the splendid drives.

We found the monkey-cage, of course. There was besides a number of small monkeys one enormous orang-outang. It was as large as a man and was covered with long red hair. While seeming to be very clever he had a way of gazing off in the distance with wide, unseeing eyes, meanwhile pulling his long red hair up over his head in an aimless, insane way that was very fetching. The doctor wanted to give him a nut, but feared to put his hand through the bars. The grating was too small for the old fellow to get his hand through, but he did not intend to be cheated of his rights, so he merely stuck his lips through the gratings until they extended fully four inches. I burst into laughter at the comical sight. I had heard of mouths, but that beat anything I ever saw, and I laughed until the old fellow actually smiled in sympathy. He got the nut!

The doctor offered him a cigar. He did not take it, but touched it with the back of his hand, afterwards smelling his hand, and then subsided into that dreamy state, aimlessly pulling his hair up over the back of his head.

At the cable office, in the second story of a building, I found the agents conversant with the English language. They would accept American silver at par, but they did not care to handle our other money. The bank and post-office are open places on the ground floor with about as much comfort and style as is found in ordinary wharf warehouses. Chinese and English are employed in both places.

We had dinner at the Hotel de l'Europe, a long, low, white building set back in a wide, green lawn, with a beautiful esplanade, faced by the sea, fronting it. Upon the verandah were long white tables where a fine dinner was served by Chinamen.

On our return from the Governor's House, I heard a strange, weird din as of many instruments in dire confusion and discord, very like in sound to a political procession the night after the presidential election.

"That's a funeral," my Malay driver announced.

"Indeed! If that is the way you have funerals here, I'll see one," I said. So he pulled the gharry to one side where we waited eagerly for a funeral that was heralded by a blast of trumpets. First came a number of Chinamen with black and white satin flags which, being flourished energetically, resulted in clearing the road of vehicles and pedestrians. They were followed by musicians on Malay ponies, blowing fifes, striking cymbals, beating tom-toms, hammering gongs, and pounding long pieces of iron, with all their might and main. Men followed carrying on long poles roast pigs and Chinese lanterns, great and small, while in their rear came banner-bearers. The men on foot wore white trousers and sandals, with blue top dress, while the pall-bearers wore black garments bound with blue braid. There were probably forty pall-bearers. The casket, which rested on long poles suspended on the shoulders of the men, was hidden beneath a white-spotted scarlet cloth with decorations of Chinese lanterns or inflated bladders on arches above it. The mourners followed in a long string of gharries, They were dressed in white satin from head to toe and were the happiest looking people at the funeral. We watched until the din died away in the distance when we returned to town as delighted as if we had seen a circus parade.

"I would not have missed that for anything," Doctor Brown said to me.

"You could not," I replied laughingly, "I know they got it up for our special benefit."

And so laughing and jesting about what had to us no suggestion of death, we drove back to see the temples. None of us were permitted to pass beneath the gate of the Mahommedan temple, so we went on to a Hindoo temple. It was a low stone building, enclosed by a high wall. At the gateway leading to it were a superfluity of beggars, large and small, lame and blind, who asked for alms, touching their foreheads respectfully. The temple was closed but some priests rushed forth to warn us not step on the sacred old dirty stone-passage leading to it with our shoes on. Its filth would have made it sacred to me with my shoes off! My comrades were told that removing their shoes would give them admission but I should be denied that privilege because I was a woman.

"Why?" I demanded, curious to know why my sex in heathen lands should exclude me from a temple, as in America it confines me to the side entrances of hotels and other strange and incommodious things.

"No, Señora, no mudder," the priest said with a positive shake of the head.

"I'm not a mother!" I cried so indignantly that my companions burst into laughter, which I joined after a while, but my denials had no effect on the priest. He would not allow me to enter.

In some sheds which lined the inner part of the high wall we saw a number of fantastically shaped carts of heavy build. Probably they were juggernauts. Near by we saw through the bars a wooden image of a woman. Her shape was neither fairy-like nor girlish; her features were fiendish in expression and from her mouth fell a long string of beads. As the mother of a poor man's family she would have been a great success. Instead of one pair of arms she had four. One pair was employed in holding a stiff wooden baby before her and the other three pairs were taking care of themselves much like the legs of a crab. They showed us a white wooden horse mounted on wheels, images of most horrible devils, in short, we saw so many images of such horrible shapes that it would be impossible to recall them all. I remember one head that I was very much interested in and the limited English of the priest failed to satisfy my curiosity as to who, what, and for what purpose the thing was invented.

It was only a head but must have been fully twelve feet high and wide in proportion. The face was a fiery scarlet and the eyes were tightly closed. On the lawn, fastened to a slight pin, was a white cow, the only presentable cow I saw during my trip.

I noticed the doctor gave her wide range keeping his eye on her as she playfully tossed her head.

"Be careful," he said nervously to me. "I believe that's the sacred white cow."

"She looks old enough-and tough enough-to make her sacred in the eye of a butcher!" I replied.

"If she is the sacred cow," he continued, despite my levity, "and went for us they would consider it their duty to let the old beast kill an infidel. That pin does not look very strong."

So to quiet the fears of the doctor we left the old cow and the gods behind.

The people in Singapore have ranks as have people in other lands. There they do not wait for one neighbor to tell another or for the newspapers to inform the public as to their standing but every man, woman, and child carries his mark in gray powder on the forehead so that all the world may look and read and know his caste.

We stopped at the driver's humble home on our way to the ship and I saw there on the ground floor, his pretty little Malay wife dressed in one wrapping of linen, and several little brown naked babies. The wife had a large gold ring in her nose, rings on her toes and several around the rim of her ears, and gold ornaments on her ankles. At the door of their home was a monkey. I did resist the temptation to buy a boy at Port Said and also smothered the desire to buy a Singalese girl at Colombo, but when I saw the monkey my will-power melted and I began straightway to bargain for it. I got it.

"Will the monkey bite?" I asked the driver, and he took it by the throat, holding it up for me to admire as he replied:

"Monkey no bite." But he could not under the circumstances.

Chapter 11: Against the Monsoon

THAT evening we sailed for Hong Kong. The next day the sea was rough and head winds made the run slower than we had hoped for. Towards noon almost all the passengers disappeared. The roughness increased and the cook enjoyed a holiday. There was some chaffing among the passengers who remained on deck. During dinner the chief officer began to relate the woes of people he had seen suffering from the dire disease that threatened now to even overpower the captain. I listened for quite a while, merely because I could not help hearing; and if there was anything the chief could do well it was relating anecdotes. At last one made me get up and run, it was so vivid, and the moment the doctor, who sat opposite, saw me go he got up and followed. I managed to overcome my faintness without really being sick, but the doctor gave way entirely. I went back to dinner to find the cause of our misery had disappeared. When I saw him later, his face was pale and he confessed contritely that his realistic joke had made even him seasick.

During the roughness that followed the doctor would always say to me pleadingly:

"Don't make a start, for if you do I will have to follow."

The terrible swell of the sea during the Monsoon was the most beautiful thing I ever saw. I would sit breathless on deck watching the bow of the ship standing upright on a wave then dash headlong down as if intending to carry us to the bottom. Some of the men made no secret of being seasick and were stretched out in their chairs on deck where they might hope to catch the first breath of air. Although there was a dreadful swell, still the atmosphere was heavy and close. Sometimes I felt as if I would smother. One man who had been quite attentive to me became seasick. I was relieved when I heard it, still I felt very cruel when I would see his pale face and hear him plead for sympathy. As heartless as I thought it was I could not sympathize with a seasick man. There was an effort on the part of others to tease the poor fellow. When I sat down on deck they would carefully take away all the chairs excepting those occupied by themselves, but it mattered little to the seasick man. He would quietly curl up on his rugs at my feet and there lie, in all his misery, gazing at me.

"You would not think that I am enjoying a vacation, but I am," he said plaintively to me one day.

"You don't know how nice I can look," he said pathetically at another time. "If you would only stay over at Hong Kong for a week you would see how pretty I can look."

"Indeed, such a phenomenon might induce me to remain there six weeks," I said coldly.

At last some one told him I was engaged to the chief officer, who did not approve of my talking to other men, thinking this would make him cease following me about, but it only served to increase his devotion. Finding me alone on deck one stormy evening he sat down at my feet and holding to the arms of my chair began to talk in a wild way.

"Do you think life is worth living?" he asked.

"Yes, life is very sweet. The thought of death is the only thing that causes me unhappiness," I answered truthfully.

"You cannot understand it or you would feel different. I could take you in my arms and jump overboard, and before they would know it we would be at rest," he said passionately.

"You can't tell. It might not be rest–" I began and he broke in hotly.

"I know, I know. I can show you. I will prove it to you. Death by drowning is a peaceful slumber, a quiet drifting away."

"Is it?" I said, with a pretense of eagerness. I feared to get up for I felt the first move might result in my burial beneath the angry sea.

"You know, tell me about it. Explain it to me," I gasped, a feeling of coldness creeping over me as I realized that I was alone with what for the time was a mad man. Just as he began to speak I saw the chief officer come on deck and slowly advance towards me. I dared not call. I dared not smile, lest he should notice. I feared the chief would go away, but no, he saw me, and with a desire to tease the man who had been so devoted he came up on tip-toe, then, clapping the poor fellow on the back, he said: "What a very pretty love scene!"

"Come," I shouted, breaking away before the startled man could understand. The chief, still in a spirit of fun, took my hand and we rushed down below. I told him and the captain what had occurred and the captain wanted to put the man in irons but I begged that he be left free. I was careful afterwards not to spend one moment alone and unprotected on deck.

The Parsees, traveling first class, were compelled to go below when a heavy swell was on. We welcomed the storm on that account if on no other, because they had a peculiar habit of dropping off their slippers when they sat down. As they wore no hose, this habit was annoying.

The doctor seriously affirmed that every time he sat down anywhere a Parsee was sure to squat alongside, drop his shoes and turn his bare, brown feet up to be gazed upon.

The monkey proved a good seaman. One day when I visited it I found the young men had been toasting its health. It was holding its aching head when I went in, and evidently thinking I was the cause of the swelling, it sprang at me, making me seek safety in flight.

The hurricane deck was a great resort for lovers, so Chief Officer Sleeman told me; and evidently he knew, for he talked a great deal about two American girls who had traveled to Egypt, I believe, on the Thames when he was first officer of it. He had lost their address but his heart was true, for he had lost a philopoena to one and though he did not know her habitation he bought the philopoena and put it in a bank in London where it awaits some farther knowledge of the fair young American's whereabouts.

Lovers were not plentiful on the Oriental, there were so few passengers. The "Spanish minister" had an eye for beauty and a heart for romance, though he led a most quiet life on shipboard, and was the very essence of gallantry.

"I was very much in love with a woman once. Traveling on the same ship with me was a woman, a beautiful woman, most beautiful, indeed. I watched her, she watched me, and my eyes told her I admired her and her eyes said back to me they were pleased that it should be so. Two men were traveling with her. One day I awkwardly knocked against her in a corridor and I said, 'I beg your pardon, Miss!' To which she answered lowly and sadly: 'I beg YOUR pardon, – Mrs!' When she came to dinner that night her eyes were red from weeping. I caught her glance; it spoke so sadly to me, her lips trembling like a grieved child's . She started in to drink a great deal of wine but one look from me made her push her glass away. Her husband, for she was married, was a very brutal fellow and my love for the beautiful woman almost made me forget my family and hers in my longing to claim her as my heart's companion. They left us at the first port. I stood on deck as they came up to go ashore. Her husband and his comrade went down the steps. Starting to follow she saw me, and stopped. Her eyes said to me as plain as speech, 'Say but the word and I am yours,' and although my feelings made me spring towards her, I paused before touching her and my aching eyes said: 'Go! be a good woman.' She went slowly down into the boat. Rising to her feet as it moved off, she held out her arms to me and with a great despairing cry fell back in the boat insensible! I never saw her since, I never knew her name, but I know as well as I know you are there that beautiful woman loved me!"

"And you?" I said inquiringly.

"I!" with a slight shrug of the shoulders, accompanied by a little cold laugh, which was not unpleasant to hear; it somehow reminded me of the sound of dripping water on a hot day. "Ah, she was a beautiful lady, very, ver-ry beautiful, most beautiful, indeed, but Señorita, I have a son older than you and I am devoted to my family."

Impatiently I turned to an Englishman who was sitting on the other side.

"Why do Englishmen always say 'Deah me!' " I lazily asked.

"Deah me! Do they? I can't sai, don't you know."

"Well, I can. It's because they think so wonderfully much of themselves," I said with a laugh.

"Deah me! Really?" was all he said in reply.

"You are so jolly clever, now; can you tell me why Eve did not take the measles?" he asked after a time.

"'Cause she'd 'ad 'em" (Adam), I said in a Bowery tone.

"I sai, now, you are jolly clever, but can you tell me why Cain did not take them? Hasten, now, I cannot dwell."

"Because he wasn't Abel. Now don't dwell, but move on and tell me what chestnuts are?" I said, teasingly.

"Oh come, now–"

"I'm here."

"I sai, really, you Americans have such a jolly queer language. Deah me, I can't tell."

"I thought you could, you have such a jolly supply of them, 'don't you know.' "

"Deah me!" he exclaimed, as he rushed down below to brace on a whiskey and soda.

It is wonderful the amount of whiskey and soda Englishmen consume. They drink it at all times and places. There was an Englishman on the Oriental who drank whiskey and soda all the day, half a dozen different wines at dinner, and then complained, as he invariably staggered away from the table, that the wine list had no variety!

Talk about cranks! One woman told the chief officer one day that she wanted a cabin just over the ship's screw so she could tell that the ship was going! She got it, and she was the worst sea-sick woman I ever saw. Another passenger complained because the berths had spring mattresses!

One night during the monsoon the sea washed over the ship in a frightful manner. I found my cabin filled with water, which, however, did not touch my berth. Escape to the lower deck was impossible, as I could not tell the deck from the angry, pitching sea. As I crawled back into my bunk a feeling of awe crept over me and with it a conscious feeling of satisfaction. I thought it very possible that I had spoken my last word to any mortal, that the ship would doubtless sink, and with it all I thought, if the ship did go down, no one would be able to tell whether I could have gone around the world in seventy-five days or not. The thought was very comforting at that time, for I felt then I might not get around in one hundred days.

I could have worried myself over my impending fate had I not been a great believer in letting unchangeable affairs go their way. "If the ship does go down," I thought, "there is time enough to worry when it's going. All the worry in the world cannot change it one way or the other, and if the ship does not go down, I only waste so much time." So I went to sleep and slumbered soundly until the breakfast hour.

The ship was making its way laboriously through a very frisky sea when I looked out, but the deck was drained, even if it was not dry.

When I went out, the jolly Irish lad, for whom I had a great fondness, was stretched out languidly in a willow chair with a bottle of champagne on one arm-rest and a glass on the other. Every little motion of the ship made him vow that when he reached Hong Kong he would stay there until he could return to England overland!

"You should have seen my cabin-mate last night," he said with a laugh when I sat down beside him. The man he spoke of, a very clever Englishman, was the man who posed as a woman-hater, and naturally we enjoyed any joke at his expense.

"Finding our cabin filling with water, he got out of bed, put on a life preserver and bailed out the cabin with a cigarette box!"

I laughed until my sides ached at the mental picture presented to me of the little chunky Englishman in an enormous life preserver, bailing out his cabin with a tiny cigarette box! Even the box of the deadly cigarette seems to have its christian mission to perform. While I was wiping away the tears brought there by the strength of my laughter, the Englishman came up, and hearing what had amused us, said: "While I was bailing out the cabin, 'the boy,' "as we fondly called him, "clung to the upper berth all the time groaning and praying! He was certain the ship would sink, and I could not persuade him to get out of the top berth to help bail. He would do nothing but groan and pray."

The boy answered with a laugh, "I did not want to sleep the rest of the night in wet pajamas," which caused the woman-hater to flee!

Later in the day the rolling was frightful. I was sitting on deck when all at once the ship went down at one side like a wagon in a deep rut. I was thrown in my chair clear across the deck. A young man endeavored to come to my assistance just as the ship went the other way in a still deeper sea-rut. It flung me back again, and only by catching hold of an iron bar did I save my neck at least, for in another moment I would have been dashed through the skylight into the dining hall on the deck below.

As I caught the bar, I saw the man who had rushed to my assistance turned upside down and land on his face. I began to laugh, his position was so ludicrous. When I saw he made no move to get up, I ran to his side, still convulsed with laughter. I found his nose was bleeding profusely, but I was such an idiot that the sight of the blood only served to make the scene to me the more ridiculous. Helping him to a chair, I ran for the doctor and from laughing could hardly tell him what I wanted. The man's nose was broken, and the doctor said he would be scarred for life. Even the others laughed when I described the accident, and, although I felt a great pity for the poor fellow, hurt as he was in my behalf, still an irresistible impulse to laugh would sweep over me every time I endeavored to express my appreciation of his attempt to assist me.

Our passengers were rather queer. I always enjoy the queerness of people. One day, when speaking about the boat, I said:

"Everything is such an improvement on the Victoria. The food is good, the passengers are refined, the officers are polite and the ship is comfortable and pleasant."

When I finished my complimentary remarks about the ship, a little bride who had been a source of interest to us looked up and said:

"Yes, everything is very nice; but the life preservers are not quite comfortable to sleep in."

Shocked amazement spread over the countenances of all the passengers, and then in one grand shout that dining-room resounded with laughter. The bride said that ever since they left home on their bridal tour they had been sleeping in the life preservers. They thought it was the thing to do on board a ship.

But I never knew how queer our passengers were until we reached Hong Kong, which we did two days ahead of time, although we had the monsoon against us. When we landed, a man sued the company for getting him in ahead of time. He said he bought his tickets to cover a certain length of time, and if the company got him in before it expired they were responsible for his expenses, and they had to pay his hotel bill.

The captain asked a minister who was on board to read the service one Sunday. He did so, and when he reached Hong Kong he put in a bill for two pounds! He said he was enjoying a vacation and did not propose to work during that time unless he was paid for it! The company paid, but warned the officers not to let ministers read the service thereafter until they knew their price.

The evening of December 22 we all sat on deck in a dark corner. The men were singing and telling stories. The only other woman who was able to be up and I were the interested and appreciative audience. We all felt an eagerness for morning and yet the eagerness was mingled with much that was sad. Knowing that early in the day we would reach Hong Kong, and while it would bring us new scenes and new acquaintances, it would take us from old friends.

Chapter 12: British China

WE first saw the city of Hong Kong in the early morning. Gleaming white were the castle-like homes on the tall mountain side. We fired a cannon as we entered the bay, the captain saying that this was the custom of mail ships. A beautiful bay was this magnificent basin, walled on every side by high mountains. Once within this natural fortified harbor we could discern, in different directions, only small outlets between the mountains, but so small, indeed, they appeared that one could hardly believe a ship would find space large enough for passage. In fact, these outlets are said to be dangerously narrow, the most vigilant care being necessary until the ship is safely beyond on the ocean blue. Mirror-like was the bay in the bright sun, dotted with strange craft from many countries. Heavy iron-clads, torpedo boats, mall steamers, Portuguese lorchas, Chinese junks and sampans. Even as we looked, a Chinese ship wended its way slowly out to sea. Its queer, broad stern hoisted high out of the water and the enormous eye gracing its bow, were to us most interesting. A graceful thing I thought it, but I heard an officer call it most ungraceful and unshapely.

Hong Kong is strangely picturesque. It is a terraced city, the terraces being formed by the castle-like, arcaded buildings perched tier after tier up the mountain's verdant side. The regularity with which the houses are built in rows made me wildly fancy them a gigantic staircase, each stair made in imitation of castles.

The doctor, another gentleman, and I left the boat, and walking to the pier's end selected sedan chairs, in which we were carried to the town. The carriers were as urgent as our hackmen around railway stations in America. There is a knack of getting into a chair properly. It is placed upon the ground, the carrier tilts the shafts down, and the patron steps inside, back towards the chair, and goes into it backward. Once seated, the carriers hoist the chair to their shoulders and start off with a monotonous trot, which gives the chair a motion not unlike that of a pacing saddle-horse.

We followed the road along the shore, passing warehouses of many kinds and tall balconied buildings filled with hundreds of Chinese families, on the flat-house plan. The balconies would have lent a pleasing appearance to the houses had the inhabitants not seemed to be enjoying a washing jubilee, using the balconies for clotheslines. Garments were stretched on poles, after the manner of hanging coats so they will not wrinkle, and those poles were fastened to the balconies until it looked as if every family in the street had placed their old clothing on exhibition.

The town seemed in a state of untidiness, the road was dirty, the mobs of natives we met were filthy, the houses were dirty, the numberless boats lying along the wharf, which invariably were crowded with dirty people, were dirty, our carriers were dirty fellows, their untidy pig-tails twisted around their half-shaven heads. They trotted steadily ahead, snorting at the crowds of natives we met to clear the way. A series of snorts or grunts would cause a scattering of natives more frightened than a tie-walker would be at the tooting of an engine's whistle.

Turning off the shore road our carriers started up one of the roads which wind about from tier to tier up the mountain.

My only wish and desire was to get as speedily as possible to the office of the Oriental and Occidental Steamship Company to learn the earliest possible time I could leave for Japan, to continue my race against time around the world. I had just marked off my thirty-ninth day. Only thirty-nine days since leaving New York and I was in China. I was leaving particularly elated, because the good ship Oriental not only made up the five days I had lost in Colombo, but reached Hong Kong two days before I was due, according to my schedule. And that with the northeast monsoon against her. It was the Oriental's maiden trip to China, and from Colombo to Hong Kong she had broken all previous records.

I went to the O. and O. office feeling very much elated over my good fortune, with never a doubt but that it would continue.

"Will you tell me the date of the first sailing for Japan?" I asked a man in the office.

"In one moment," he said, and going into an inner office he brought out a man who looked at me inquiringly, and when I repeated my question, said:

"What is your name?"

"Nellie Bly," I replied in some surprise.

"Come in, come in," he said nervously. We followed him in, and after we were seated he said:

"You are going to be beaten."

"What? I think not. I have made up my delay," I said, still surprised, wondering if the Pacific had sunk since my departure from New York, or if all the ships on that line had been destroyed.

"You are going to lose it," he said with an air of conviction.

"Lose it? I don't understand. What do you mean?" I demanded, beginning to think he was mad.

"Aren't you having a race around the world?" he asked, as if he thought I was not Nellie Bly.

"Yes; quite right. I am running a race with Time," I replied.

"Time? I don't think that's her name."

"Her! Her!!" I repeated, thinking, "Poor fellow, he is quite unbalanced," and wondering if I dared wink at the doctor to suggest to him the advisability of our making good our escape.

"Yes, the other woman; she is going to win. She left here three days ago."

I stared at him; I turned to the doctor; I wondered if I was awake; I concluded the man was quite mad, so I forced myself to laugh in an unconcerned manner, but I was only able to say stupidly:

"The other woman?"

"Yes," he continued briskly; "Did you not know? The day you left New York another woman started out to beat your time, and she's going to do it. She left here three days ago. You probably met somewhere near the Straits of Malacca. She says she has authority to pay any amount to get ships to leave in advance of their time. Her editor offered one or two thousand dollars to the O. and O. if they would have the Oceanic leave San Francisco two days ahead of time. They would not do it, but they did do their best to get her here in time to catch the English mail for Ceylon. If they had not arrived long before they were due, she would have missed that boat, and so have been delayed ten days. But she caught the boat and left three days ago, and you will be delayed here five days."

"That is rather hard, isn't it?" I said quietly, forcing a smile that was on the lips, but came from nowhere near the heart.

"I'm astonished you did not know anything about it," he said. "She led us to suppose that it was an arranged race."

"I do not believe my editor would arrange a race without advising me," I said stoutly. "Have you no cables or messages for me from New York?"

"Nothing," was his reply.

"Probably they do not know about her," I said more cheerfully.

"Yes they do. She worked for the same newspaper you do until the day she started."

"I do not understand it," I said quietly, too proud to show my ignorance on a subject of vital importance to my well-doing. "You say I cannot leave here for five days?"

"No, and I don't think you can get to New York in eighty days. She intends to do it in seventy. She has letters to steamship officials at every point requesting them to do all they can to get her on. Have you any letters?"

"Only one, from the agent of the P. and O., requesting the captains of their boats to be good to me because I am traveling alone. That is all," I said with a little smile.

"Well, it's too bad; but I think you have lost it. There is no chance for you. You will lose five days here and five in Yokohoma, and you are sure to have a slow trip across at this season."

Just then a young man, with the softest black eyes and a clear pale complexion, came into the office. The agent, Mr. Harmon, introduced him to me as Mr. Fuhrmann, the purser of the Oceanic, the ship on which I would eventually travel to Japan and America. The young man took my hand in a firm, strong clasp, and his soft black eyes gave me such a look of sympathy that it only needed his kind tone to cheer me into a happier state.

"I went down to the Oriental to meet you; Mr. Harmon thought it was better. We want to take good care of you now that you are in our charge, but, unfortunately, I missed you. I returned to the hotel, and as they knew nothing about you there I came here, fearing that you were lost."

"I have found kind friends everywhere," I said, with a slight motion towards the doctor, who was speechless over the ill-luck that had befallen me. "I am sorry to have been so much trouble to you."

"Trouble! You are with your own people now, and we are only too happy if we can be of service," he said kindly. "You must not mind about the possibility of some one getting around the world in less time than you may do it. You have had the worst connections it is possible to make, and everybody knows the idea originated with you, and that others are merely trying to steal the work of your brain, so, whether you get in before or later, people will give you the credit of having originated the idea."

"I promised my editor that I would go around the world in seventy-five days, and if I accomplish that I shall be satisfied," I stiffly explained. "I am not racing with anyone. I would not race. If someone else wants to do the trip in less time, that is their concern. If they take it upon themselves to race *against* me, it is their lookout that they succeed. I am not racing. I promised to do the trip in seventy-five days, and I will do it; although had I been permitted to make the trip when I first proposed it over a year ago, I should then have done it in sixty days."

We returned to the hotel, where a room had been secured for me, after arranging the transfer of my luggage and the monkey from the Oriental to the Oceanic. I met a number of people after tiffin, who were interested in my trip, and were ready and anxious to do anything they could to contribute to my pleasure during my enforced stay.

Having but the one dress I refused to attend any dinners or receptions that were proposed in my honor. During the afternoon the wife of a prominent Hong Kong gentleman waited upon me to place herself and her home at my disposal. She was anxious that I should make her home mine during my stay, but I told her I could not think of accepting her kindness, because I would wish to be out most of the time, and could not make my hours conform to the hours of the house, and still feel free to go, come and stay, as I pleased. Despite her pleadings I assured her I was not on pleasure bent, but business, and I considered it my duty to refrain from social pleasures, devoting myself to things that lay more in the line of work.

I had dinner on the Oriental. As I bade the captain and his officers farewell, remembering their kindness to me, I had a wild desire to cling to them, knowing that with the morning light the Oriental would sail, and I would be once again alone in strange lands with strange people.

That evening the purser of the Oceanic, another acquaintance and I were carried in chairs up a winding road, arched with green trees, on which the leaves hung motionless and still in the silent night.

Our lazy voices, as occasionally we spoke softly to each other, and the steady, monotonous slap-slap-slap of the bare-feet of our carriers made the only break in the slumbering stillness. All earth seemed to have gone to rest. Silently we went along, now getting, by dim gas lamps at garden gates, glimpses of comfortable homes in all their Eastern splendor, and then, for a moment emerging from beneath the over-lapping arch of verdant trees, we would get a faint glimmer of the quivering stars and cloudless heavens. The ascent was made at last. We were above the city, lying dark and quiet, but no nearer the glorious starlit sky. A little rush through a wide gate in a high wall, a sudden blindness in a road banked and roofed by foliage, a quick lowering to the ground at the foot of wide steps that led to an open door through which a welcoming light shed its soft, warm rays upon us and we had reached our journey's end.

Inside, where a cordial welcome awaited us, was a bright wood fire before which I longed to curl up on a rug and be left alone to dream-dream. But there were friends instead of dreams, and realities in the shape of a splendid dinner. A table, graced with a profusion of tropical blossoms-a man, handsomer than an ideal hero, at its head-a fine menu, guests, handsome, witty and just enough in number to suit my ideas, were the items of what made up an ideal evening.

It is said people do not grow old in Hong Kong. Their youthful looks bear ample testimony to the statement. I asked the reason why, and they said it is because they are compelled to invent amusements for themselves, and by inventing they find, not time to grow *blasé*, but youth and happiness.

The theatre in Hong Kong knows few professional troupes, but the amateur actors in the English colony leave little to be desired in the way of splendid entertainments. The very best people in the town take part, and I believe they all furnish their own stage costumes. The regiments stationed there turn out very creditable actors in the persons of the young officers. I went one night to see "Ali Baba and the Forty Thieves" as given by the Amateur Dramatic Club of Hong Kong. It was a new version of the old story filled with local hits arranged for the club by a military captain; the music was by the band-master of the Argyll and Sutherland Highlanders. The beautiful and artistic scenery was designed and executed by two army men, as were the lime-light effects. Spectators came to the theatre in their chairs instead of carriages.

Inside, the scene was bewitching. A rustling of soft gowns, the odor of flowers, the fluttering of fans, the sounds of soft, happy whispering, a maze of lovely women in evening gowns mingling with handsome men in the regulation evening dress-what could be prettier? If American women would only ape the English in going bonnetless to the theatres, we would forgive their little aping in other respects, and call it even. Upon the arrival of the Governor the band played "God Save the Queen," during which the audience stood. Happily, they made it short. The play was pleasantly presented, the actors filling their roles most creditably, especially the one taking the part of Alley Sloper.

Afterwards, the sight of handsomely dressed women stepping into their chairs, the daintily-colored Chinese lanterns, hanging fore and aft, marking the course the carriers took in the darkness, was very oriental and affective. It is a luxury to have a carriage, of course, but there is something even more luxurious in the thought of owning a chair and carriers. A fine chair with silver mounted poles and silk hangings can be bought, I should judge, for a little more than twenty dollars. Some women keep four and eight carriers; they are so cheap that one can afford to retain a number. Every member of a well established household in Hong Kong has his or her own private chair. Many men prefer a coverless willow chair with swinging step, while many women have chairs that close entirely, so they can be carried along the streets secure against the gaze of the public. Convenient pockets, umbrella stands and places for parcels are found in all well-appointed chairs.

At every port I touched I found so many bachelors, men of position, means and good appearance, that I naturally began to wonder why women do not flock that way. It was all very well some years ago to say, "Go West, young man;" but I would say, "Girls, go East!" There are bachelors enough and to spare! And a most happy time do these bachelors have in the East. They are handsome, jolly and good natured. They have their own fine homes with no one but the servants to look after them. Think of it, and let me whisper, "Girls, go East!"

The second day after my arrival, Captain Smith, of the Oceanic, called upon me. I expected to see a hard-faced old man; so, when I went into the drawing-room and a youthful, good-looking man, with the softest blue eyes that seemed to have caught a tinge of the ocean's blue on a bright day, smiled down at me, I imagine I must have looked very stupid indeed. I looked at the smooth, youthful face, with its light-brown moustache, and I felt inclined to laugh at the long iron-gray beard my imagination had put upon the Captain of the Oceanic. I caught a laughing gleam of the bluest of blue eyes, and I thought of imaginary stern ones, and had to smother another insane desire to laugh. I looked at the tall, slender, shapely body, and recalled the imaginary short legs, holding upright a wide circumference under an ample waistcoat, and I laughed audibly.

"You were so different to what I imagined you would be," I said afterwards, when we talked over our first meeting.

"And I could not believe you were the right girl, you were so unlike what I had been led to believe," he said, with a laugh, in a burst of confidence. "I was told that you were an old maid with a dreadful temper. Such horrible things were said about you that I was hoping you would miss our ship. I said if you did come I supposed you would expect to sit at my table, but I would arrange so you should be placed elsewhere."

The Captain took me out to see "Happy Valley" that day before we separated. In jinrickshas we rode by the parade and cricket grounds where some lively games are played, the city hall, and the solid, unornamented barracks; along smooth, tree-lined roads, out to where the mountains make a nest of one level, green space. This level has been converted into a race-course. The judges' stand was an ordinary, commonplace race-course stand, but the stands erected by and for private families, were built of palms and were more pleasing because they were out of the usual.

During the month of February races are held here annually. They last three days, and during that period everybody stops work, rich and poor alike flocking to the race-course. They race with native-bred Mongolian ponies, having no horses, and the racing is pronounced most exciting and interesting.

"Happy Valley" lines the hillside. There are congregated the graveyards of all the different sects and nationalities in Hong Kong. The Fire Worshipers lie in ground joining the Presbyterians, the Episcopalians, the Methodists and the Catholics, and Mahommedans are just as close by. That those of different faiths should consent to place their dead together in this lovely tropical valley is enough to give it the name of Happy Valley, if its beauty did not do as much. In my estimation it rivals in beauty the public gardens, and visitors use it as a park. One wanders along the walks looking at the beautiful shrubs and flowers, never heeding that they are in the valley of death, so thoroughly is it robbed of all that is horrible about graveyards. We rode back to town through the crowded districts, where the natives huddle together in all their filth. It is said that over 100,000 people live within a certain district in Hong Kong not exceeding one-half square mile, and they furthermore positively affirm, that sixteen hundred people live in the space of an acre. This is a sample of the manner in which the Chinese huddle together. They remind me of a crowd of ants on a lump of sugar. An effort is being made in Hong Kong to compel owners to build differently, so as to make the huddling and packing impossible, for the filth that goes with it invariably breeds disease.

Queen's road is interesting to all visitors. In it is the Hong Kong Club, where the bachelors are to be found, the post office, and greater than all, the Chinese shops. The shops are not large, but the walls are lined with black-wood cabinets, and one feels a little thrill of pleasure at the sight of the gold, the silver, ivory carvings, exquisite fans, painted scrolls and the odor of the lovely sandal-wood boxes, coming faintly to the visitor, creates a feeling of greed. One wants them all-everything.

The Chinese merchants cordially show their goods, or follow as one strolls around, never urging one to buy, but cunningly bringing to the front the most beautiful and expensive part of their stock.

"Chin chin," which means "good day," "good bye," "good night," "How are you?" or anything one may take from it, is the greeting of Chinamen. They all speak mongrel English, called "pidgin" or "pigeon" English. It is impossible to make them understand pure English, consequently Europeans, even housekeepers, use pidgin English when addressing the servants. The servants are men, with the exception of the nurses, and possibly the cooks. To the uninitiated it sounds absurd to hear men and women addressing servants and merchants in the same idiotic language with which fond parents usually cuddle their offspring; but even more laughable is it to hear men swear in "pigeon English," at an unkind or unruly servant. Picture a man with an expression of frenzied rage upon his countenance, saying:

"Go to hellee, savey?"

Pidgin or pigeon, is applied to everything. One will hear people say: " Hab got pigeon," which means they have business to look after; or if a Chinaman is requested to do some work which he thinks is the duty of another, he will say: "No belongee boy pigeon."

While strolling about the Chinese localities, seeing shops more worthy a visit, being more truly Chinese, I came upon an eating house, from which a conglomeration of strange odors strolled out and down the road. Built around a table in the middle of the room, was a circular bench. The diners perched on this bench like chickens on a fence, not letting their feet touch the floor, or hang over, nor "hunkering" down, nor squatting crossed-legged like a Turk or tailor, but sitting down with their knees drawn up until knees and chin met; they held large bowls against their chins, pushing the rice energetically with their chop-sticks into their mouths. Cup after cup of tea is consumed, not only at meals, but at all hours during the day. The cup is quite small and saucerless, and the tea is always drank minus sugar and cream.

Professional writers, found in nooks and recesses of prominent thoroughfares, are interesting personalities. Besides writing letters for people they tell fortunes, and their patrons never go away without having their fates foretold. I noticed when paying for articles, merchants invariably weigh the money. It is also customary for merchants to put their private stamp upon silver dollars as an assurance of its legality and worth. Much silver is beaten into such strange shapes by this queer practice that at first I was afraid to accept it in change.

I saw a marriage procession in Hong Kong. A large band of musicians, who succeeded in making themselves heard, were followed by coolies carrying curious looking objects in blue and gilt, which, I was told, represent mythical and historical scenes. A number of very elegant Chinese lanterns and gorgeous looking banners were also carried along. I was told that in such processions they carry roast pig to the temples of the josses, but it is afterwards very sensibly carried off by the participants.

It would be a hopeless thing for a man to go to Hong Kong in search of employment. The banking and shipping houses, controlled by Europeans, certainly employ numbers of men, but they are brought from England under three and five years' contracts. When a vacancy occurs from a death, or a transfer, the business house immediately consults its representatives in London, where another man signs an agreement, and comes out to Hong Kong to work.

One day I went up to Victoria Peak, named in honor of the Queen. It is said to be 1,800 feet high, the highest point on the island. An elevated tramway is built from the town to Victoria Gap, 1,100 feet above the sea. It was opened in 1887. Before that time people were carried up in sedans.

The first year after its completion 148,344 passengers were carried up the mountain side. The fare is thirty cents up and fifteen cents down. During the summer months Hong Kong is so hot that those who are in a position to do so seek the mountain top, where a breeze lives all the year round. Level places for buildings are obtained by blasting, and every brick, stone, and bit of household furniture is carried by coolies from the town up to the height of 1,600 feet.

At the Gap we secured sedan chairs, and were carried to the Hotel Craigiburn, which is managed by a colored man. The hotel–Oriental in style-is very liberally patronized by the citizens of Hong Kong, as well as visitors. After the proprietor had shown us over the hotel and given us a dinner that could not be surpassed we were carried to Victoria Peak. It required three men to a chair ascending the peak. At the Umbrella Seat, merely a bench with a peaked roof, everybody stops long enough to allow the coolies to rest, then we continue on our way, passing sight-seers and nurses with children. After a while they stop again, and we travel on foot to the signal station.

The view is superb. The bay, in a breastwork of mountains, lies calm and serene, dotted with hundreds of ships that seem like tiny toys. The palatial white houses come half way up the mountain side, beginning at the edge of the glassy bay. Every house we notice has a tennis-court blasted out of the mountain side. They say that after night the view from the peak is unsurpassed. One seems to be suspended between two heavens. Every one of the several thousand boats and sampans carries a light after dark. This, with the lights on the roads and in the houses, seems to be a sky more filled with stars than the one above.

Early one morning a gentleman, who was the proud possessor of a team of ponies, the finest in Hong Kong, called at the hotel to take me for a drive. In a low, easy phaeton behind the spirited ponies that seem like playthings in their smallness but giants in their strength, we whirled along through the town and were soon on the road edging the bay. We had a good view of the beautiful dry dock on the other side, which is constructed entirely of granite and is said to be of such size that it can take in the largest vessels afloat. I thought there were other things more interesting, so I refused to go over to it.

During our drive we visited two quaint and dirty temples. One was a plain little affair with a gaudy altar. The stone steps leading to it were filled with beggars of all sizes, shapes, diseases and conditions of filth. They were so repulsive that instead of appealing to one's sympathy they only succeed in arousing one's disgust.

At another temple, near by a public laundry where the washers stood in a shallow stream slapping the clothes on flat stones, was a quaint temple hewed, cave-like, in the side of an enormous rock. A selvage of rock formed the altar, and to that humble but picturesque temple Chinese women flock to pray for sons to be born unto them that they may have some one to support them in their old age.

After seeing everything of interest in Hong Kong I decided to go to a real Simon-pure Chinese city. I knew we were trying to keep the Chinamen out of America, so I decided to see all of them I could while in their land. Pay them a farewell visit, as it were! So, on Christmas eve, I started for the city of Canton.

Chapter 13: Christmas in Canton

THE O. and O. agent escorted me to the ship Powan, on which I was to travel to Canton. He gave me in charge of Captain Grogan, the Powan's commander, an American, who has lived for years in China. A very bashful man he was, but a most kindly, pleasant one. I never saw a fatter man, or a man so comically fattened. A wild inclination to laugh crept over me every time I caught a glimpse of his roly-poly body, his round red face embedded, as it were, in the fat of his shoulders and breast. The thoughts of how sensitive I am concerning remarks about my personal appearance, in a measure subdued my impulse to laugh. I have always said to critics, who mercilessly write about the shape of my chin, or the cut of my nose, or the size of my mouth, and such personal attributes that can no more be changed than death can be escaped:

"Criticise the style of my hat or my gown, I can change them, but spare my nose, it was born on me."

Remembering this, and how nonsensical it is to blame or criticise people for what they are powerless to change, I pocketed my merriment, letting a kindly feeling of sympathy take its place.

Soon after we left, night descended. I went on deck where everything was buried in darkness. Softly and steadily the boat swam on, the only sound-and the most refreshing and restful sound in the world-was the lapping of the water.

To sit on a quiet deck, to have a star-lit sky the only light above or about, to hear the water kissing the prow of the ship, is, to me, paradise. They can talk of the companionship of men, the splendor of the sun, the softness of moonlight, the beauty of music, but give me a willow chair on a quiet deck, the world with its worries and noise and prejudices lost in distance, the glare of the sun, the cold light of the moon blotted out by the dense blackness of night. Let me rest rocked gently by the rolling sea, in a nest of velvety darkness, my only light the soft twinkling of the myriads of stars in the quiet sky above; my music, the round of the kissing waters, cooling the brain and easing the pulse; my companionship, dreaming my own dreams. Give me that and I have happiness in its perfection.

But away with dreams. This is a work-a-day world and I am racing Time around it. After dinner, when the boat anchored, waiting for the tide which was to carry us safely over the bar, I went below to see the Chinese passengers. They were gambling, smoking opium, sleeping, cooking, eating, reading and talking, all huddled together on one deck, which was in one large room, not divided into cabins. They carry their own beds, a bit of matting, and their own food, little else than rice and tea.

Before daybreak we anchored at Canton. The Chinamen went ashore the moment we landed, but the other passengers remained for breakfast.

While we were having breakfast, the guide whom the captain had secured for us, came on board and quietly supervised the luncheon we were to take with us. A very clever fellow was that guide, Ah Cum. The first thing he said to us was "A Merry Christmas!" and as it had even slipped our minds, I know we all appreciated the polite thoughtfulness of our Chinese guide. Ah Cum told me later that he had been educated in an American mission located in Canton, but he assured me, with great earnestness, that English was all he learned. He would have none of the Christian religion. Ah Cum's son was also educated in an American mission, and, like his father, has put his learning to good account. Besides being paid as guide, Ah Cum collects a percentage from merchants for all the goods bought by tourists. Of course the tourists pay higher prices than they would otherwise, and Ah Cum sees they visit no shops where he is not paid his little fee.

Ah Cum is more comely in features than most Mongolians, his nose being more shapely and his eyes less slit-like than those of most of his race. He had on his feet beaded black shoes with white soles. His navy-blue trousers, or tights, more properly speaking, were tied around the ankle and fitted very tight over most of the leg. Over this he wore a blue, stiffly starched shirt-shaped garment, which reached his heels, while over this he wore a short padded and quilted silk jacket, somewhat similar to a smoking jacket. His long, coal-black queue, finished with a tassel of black silk, touched his heels, and on the spot where the queue began rested a round black turban.

Ah Cum had chairs ready for us. His chair was a neat arrangement in black, black silk hangings, tassels, fringe and black wood-poles finished with brass knobs. Once in it, he closed it, and was hidden from the gaze of the public. Our plain willow chairs had ordinary covers, which, to my mind, rather interfered with sightseeing. We had three coolies to each chair. Those with us were bare-footed, with tousled pig-tail and navy-blue shirts and trousers, much the worse for wear both in cleanliness and quality. Ah Cum's coolies wore white linen garments, gayly trimmed with broad bands of red cloth, looking very much like a circus clown's costume.

Ah Cum led the way, our coolies following. For a time I was only conscious of a confused mass of black faces and long pig tails, though shortly I became accustomed to it, and was able to distinguish different objects along the crowded thoroughfare; could note the different stands and the curious looks of the people. We were carried along dark and dirty narrow ways, in and about fish stands, whence odors drifted, filling me with disgust, until we crossed a bridge which spanned a dark and sluggish stream.

This little island, guarded at every entrance, is Shameen, or Sandy Face, the land set aside for the habitation of Europeans. An unchangeable law prohibits Celestials from crossing into this sacred precinct, because of the hatred they cherish for Europeans. Shameen is green and picturesque, with handsome houses of Oriental design, and grand shade trees, and wide, velvety green roads, broken only by a single path, made by the bare feet of the chair-carriers.

Here, for the first time since leaving New York, I saw the stars and stripes. It was floating over the gateway to the American Consulate. It is a strange fact that the further one goes from home the more loyal one becomes. I felt I was a long ways off from my own dear land; it was Christmas day, and I had seen many different flags since last I gazed upon our own. The moment I saw it floating there in the soft, lazy breeze I took off my cap and said: "That is the most beautiful flag in the world, and I am ready to whip anyone who says it isn't."

No one said a word. Everybody was afraid! I saw an Englishman in the party glance furtively towards the Union Jack, which was floating over the English Consulate, but in a hesitating manner, as if he feared to let me see.

Consul Seymour received our little party with a cheery welcome. He was anxious that we should partake of his hospitality, but we assured him our limited time only gave us a moment to pay our respects, and then we must be off again.

Mr. Seymour was an editor before he went to China with his wife and only daughter, to be consul. Since then he has conceived a hobby for embroideries and carved ivories, which he is able to ride to the top of his bent in Canton. When tourists go there he always knows some place where he can guide them to bargains. Mr. Seymour is a most pleasant, agreeable man, and a general favorite. It is to be hoped that he will long have a residence in Shameen, where he reflects credit upon the American Consulate.

What a different picture Canton presents to Shameen. They say there are millions of people in Canton. The streets, many of which are roughly paved with stone, seem little over a yard in width. The shops, with their gayly colored and handsomely carved signs, are all open, as if the whole end facing the street had been blown out. In the rear of every shop is an altar, gay in color and often expensive in adornment. As we were carried along the roads we could see not only the usually rich and enticing wares, but the sellers and buyers. Every shop has a book-keeper's desk near the entrance. The book-keepers all wear tortoise-shell rimmed glasses of an enormous size, which lend them a look of tremendous wisdom. I was inclined to think the glasses were a mark of office, for I never saw a man employed in clerical work without them.

I was warned not to be surprised if the Chinamen should stone me while I was in Canton. I was told that Chinese women usually spat in the faces of female tourists when the opportunity offered. However, I had no trouble. The Chinese are not pleasant appearing people; they usually look as if life had given them nothing but trouble; but as we were carried along the men in the stores would rush out to look at me. They did not take any interest in the men with me, but gazed at me as if I was something new. They showed no sign of animosity, but the few women I met looked as curiously at me, and less kindly.

The thing that seemed to interest the people most about me were my gloves. Sometimes they would make bold enough to touch them, and they would always gaze upon them with looks of wonder.

The streets are so narrow that I thought at first I was being carried through the aisles of some great market. It is impossible to see the sky, owing to the signs and other decorations, and the compactness of the buildings; and with the open shops, just like stands in a market, except that they are not even cut off from the passing crowd by a counter, the delusion is a very natural one. When Ah Cum told me that I was not in a market-house, but in the streets of the city of Canton, my astonishment knew no limit. Sometimes our little train would meet another train of chairs, and then we would stop for a moment and there would be great yelling and fussing until we had safely passed, the way being too narrow for both trains to move at once in safety.

Coolie number two of my chair was a source of great discomfort to me all the day. He had a strap spanning the poles by which he upheld his share of the chair. This band, or strap, crossed his shoulders, touching the neck just where the prominent bone is. The skin was worn white and hard-looking from the rubbing of the band; but still it worried me, and I watched all the day expecting to see it blister. His long pig-tail was twisted around his head, so I had an unobstructed view of the spot. He was not an easy traveler, this coolie, there being as much difference in the gait of carriers as there is in the gait of horses. Many times he shifted the strap, much to my misery, and then he would turn and, by motions, convey to me that I was sitting more to one side than to the other.

As a result, I made such an effort to sit straight and not to move that when we alighted at the shops I would be cramped almost into a paralytic state. Before the day was over I had a sick headache, all from thinking too much about the comfort of the Chinamen.

A disagreeable thing about the coolies is that they grunt like pigs when carrying one. I can't say whether the grunt has any special significance to them or not, but they will grunt one after the other along the train, and it is anything but pleasant.

I was very anxious to see the execution ground, so we were carried there. We went in through a gate where a stand erected for gambling was surrounded by a crowd of filthy people. Some few idle ones left it to saunter lazily after us. The place is very unlike what one would naturally suppose it to be. At first sight it looked like a crooked back alley in a country town. There were several rows of half dried pottery. A woman, who was moulding in a shed at one side, stopped her work to gossip about us with another female who had been arranging the pottery in rows. The place is probably seventy-five feet long by twenty-five wide at the front, and narrowing down at the other end. I noticed the ground in one place was very red, and when I asked Ah Cum about it he said indifferently, as he kicked the red-colored earth with his white-souled shoe:

"It's blood. Eleven men were beheaded here yesterday."

He added that it was an ordinary thing for ten to twenty criminals to be executed at one time. The average number per annum is something like 400. The guide also told us that in one year, 1855, over 50,000 rebels were beheaded in this narrow alley.

While he was talking I noticed some roughly fashioned wooden crosses leaned up against the high stone wall, and supposing they were used in some manner for religious purposes before and during the executions, I asked Ah Cum about them. A shiver waggled down my spinal cord when he answered:

"When women are condemned to death in China they are bound to wooden crosses and cut to pieces."

"Men are beheaded with one stroke unless they are the worst kind of criminals," the guide added, "then they are given the death of a woman to make it the more discreditable. They tie them to the crosses and strangle or cut them to pieces. When they are cut to bits, it is done so deftly that they are entirely dismembered and disemboweled before they are dead. Would you like to see some heads?"

I thought that Chinese guide could tell as large stories as any other guides; and who can equal a guide for highly-colored and exaggerated tales? So I said coldly:

"Certainly; bring on your heads!"

I tipped a man, as he told me, who, with the clay of the pottery on his hands, went to some barrels which stood near to the wooden crosses, put in his hand and pulled out a head!

Those barrels are filled with lime, and as the criminals are beheaded their heads are thrown into the barrels, and when the barrels become full they empty them out and get a fresh supply. If a man of wealth is condemned to death in China he can, with little effort, buy a substitute. Chinamen are very indifferent about death; it seems to have no terror for them.

I went to the jail and was surprised to see all the doors open. The doors were rather narrow, and when I got inside and saw all the prisoners with thick, heavy boards fastened about their necks, I no longer felt surprised at the doors being unbarred. There was no need of locking them.

I went to the court, a large, square, stone-paved building. In a small room off one side I was presented to some judges who were lounging about smoking opium! In still another room I met others playing fan tan! At the entrance I found a large gambling establishment! They took me into a room to see the instruments of punishment. Split bamboo to whip with, thumb screws, pulleys on which people are hanged by their thumbs, and such pleasant things. While I was there they brought in two men who had been caught stealing. The thieves were chained with their knees meeting their chins, and in that distressing position were carried in baskets suspended on a pole between two coolies. The judges explained to me that as these offenders had been caught in the very act of taking what belonged not to them, their hands would be spread upon flat stones and with smaller stones every bone in their hands would be broken. Afterwards they would be sent to the hospital to be cured. Prisoners dying in jail are always beheaded before burial.

An American who has lived many years near Canton told me there is a small bridge spanning a stream in the city where it is customary to hang criminals in a fine wire hammock, first removing all their clothing. A number of sharp knives are laid at the end of the bridge, and every one crossing while the man is there is compelled to take a knife and give a slash to the wire-imprisoned wretch. As I saw none of this myself, I only give these stories as they were given to me.

They tell me bamboo punishment (I cannot now recall the name they gave it) is not as uncommon in China as one would naturally suppose from its extreme brutality. For some crimes offenders are pinioned in standing position with their legs astride, fastened to stakes in the earth. This is done directly above a bamboo sprout. To realize this punishment in all its dreadfulness it is necessary to give a little explanation of the bamboo. A bamboo sprout looks not unlike the delicious asparagus, but is of a hardness and strength not equaled by iron. When it starts to come up, nothing can stop its progress. It is so hard that it will go through anything on its way up; let that anything be asphalt or what it will, the bamboo goes through it as readily as though the obstruction didn't exist. The bamboo grows with marvelous rapidity straight up into the air for thirty days, and then it stops. When its growth is finished it throws off a shell-like bark, its branches slowly unfolding and falling into place. They are covered with a soft airy foliage finer than the leafage of a willow. From a distance a bamboo forest is a most beautiful thing, exquisitely soft and fine in appearance, but adamant is not harder in reality. As I have said, nothing can stop a bamboo sprout when it intends to come up. Nothing ever equaled the rapidity of its growth, it being affirmed that it can really be seen growing! In the thirty days that it grows it may reach a height of seventy-five feet.

Picture then a convict pinioned above a bamboo sprout and in such a position that he cannot get away from it. It starts on its upward course never caring for what is in its way; on it goes through the man who stands there dying, dying, worse than by inches, conscious for a while, then fever mercifully kills knowledge, and at last, after days of suffering, his head drops forward, and he is dead. But that is not any worse than tying a man in the boiling sun to a stake, covering him with quick-lime and giving him nothing but water to quench hunger and thirst. He holds out and out, for it means life, but at last he takes the water that is always within his reach. He drinks, he perspires, and the lime begins to eat. They also have a habit of suspending a criminal by his arms, twisting them back of him. As long as a man keeps his muscles tense he can live, but the moment he relaxes and falls, it ruptures blood vessels and his life floats out on a crimson stream. The unfortunate is always suspended in a public place, where magistrates watch so that no one may release him. Friends of the condemned flock around the man of authority, bargaining for the man's life; if they can pay the price extorted by him the man is taken down and set free; if not, he merely hangs until the muscles give out and he drops to death. They also have a way of burying the whole of criminals except their heads. The eyelids are fastened back so that they cannot close them, and so facing the sun they are left to die. Sticking bamboo splints under the finger nails and then setting fire to them is another happy way of punishing wrongdoers.

I had no idea what I was to see when we mounted the filthy stone steps leading to the Temple of Horrors. I concluded it most be an exhibition of human monstrosities. The steps were filled with dirty Mongolians of all sizes, ages, shapes and afflictions. When they heard our steps, those who could see and walk, rushed up to us, crying for alms, and those who were blind and powerless raised their voices the louder because they could not move. Inside, a filthy stone court was crowded with a mass of humanity. There were lepers, peddlers, monstrosities, fortune tellers, gamblers, quacks, dentists with strings of horrid teeth, and even pastry cooks! It is said the Chinese worship here occasionally and consult idols. In little, dirty cells were dirty figures, representing the punishment of the Buddhists' hell. They were being whipped, ground to death, boiled in oil, beheaded, put under red hot bells, being sawed in twain, and undergoing similar agreeable things.

Canton is noted for its many curious and interesting temples. There are over eight hundred temples in the city. The most interesting one I saw during my flying trip was the Temple of the Five Hundred Gods. While there the guide asked me if I was superstitious, and upon my answering in the affirmative, he said he would show me how to try my luck. Placing some joss sticks in a copper jar before the luck-god, he took from the table two pieces of wood, worn smooth and dirty from frequent use, which, placed together, were not unlike a pear in shape. With this wood-he called it the "luck pigeon"-held with the flat sides together, he made circling motions over the smouldering joss sticks, once, twice, thrice, and dropped the luck pigeon to the floor. He explained if one side of the luck pigeon turned up and the other turned down it meant good luck, while if they both fell in the same position it meant bad luck. When he dropped it they both turned the one way, and he knew he would have bad luck.

I took the luck pigeon then, and I was so superstitious that my arm trembled and my heart beat in little palpitating jumps as I made the motions over the burning joss sticks. I dropped the wood to the floor, and one piece turned one way and one the other, and I was perfectly happy. I knew I was going to have good luck.

I saw the Examination Hall, where there are accommodations for the simultaneous examination of 11,616 celestial students, all male. We went to the entrance-gate through a dirty park-like space where a few stunted trees grew feebly and a number of thin, black pigs rooted energetically. Dirty children in large numbers followed us, demanding alms in boisterous tones, and a few women who, by the aid of canes, were hobbling about on their cramped small feet, stopped to look after us with grins of curiosity and amusement. The open space is the principal entrance, then we go through a small gate called the gate of Equity, and later still another called the Dragon gate, which leads into the great avenue. A most strange and curious sight this avenue gives. An open space with a tower on the end known as the watch tower, has a god of literature in the second story. On each side of the open green space are rows of whitewashed buildings, not unlike railway cattle yards in appearance. In these ranges of cells, cells that measure 5-1/2 by 3-2/3 feet, 11,616 pig-tailed students undergo their written examination. On the sides facing the avenue are Chinese inscriptions showing what study is examined in that range. In each cell is a board to sit on, and one a little higher for a desk. This roughly improvised desk must be slid out to allow the student to enter or depart unless he crawls under or jumps over. The same texts are given to all at daylight, and very often when essays are not finished at night the students are kept over night in their cells. The Hall is about 1,380 feet long by 650 feet wide, and is really a strangely interesting place well worth a visit. It is said the examinations are very severe, and from the large number of candidates examined, sometimes only one hundred and fifty will be passed. The place in which the essays are examined is called the Hall of Auspicious Stars, and the Chinese inscription over the avenue translated reads, "The opening heavens circulate literature."

I had a great curiosity to see the leper village, which is commonly supposed to contain hundreds of Chinese lepers. The village consists of numbers of bamboo huts, and the lepers present a sight appalling in its squalor and filth. Ah Cum told us to smoke cigarettes while in the village so that the frightful odors would be less perceptible. He set the example by lighting one, and we all followed his lead. The lepers were simply ghastly in their misery. There are men, women and children of all ages and conditions. The few filthy rags with which they endeavored to hide their nakedness presented no shape of any garment or any color, so dirty and ragged were they. On the ground floors of the bamboo huts were little else than a few old rags, dried grass and things of that kind. Furniture there was none. It is useless to attempt a description of the loathsome appearance of the lepers. Many were featureless, some were blind, some had lost fingers, others a foot, some a leg, but all were equally dirty, disgusting and miserable. Those able to work cultivate a really prosperous-looking garden, which is near their village. Ah Cum assured me they sold their vegetables in the city market! I felt glad to know we had brought our luncheon from the ship. Those lepers able to walk spend the day in Canton begging, but are always compelled to sleep in their village, still I could not help wondering what was the benefit of a leper village if the lepers are allowed to mingle with the other people. On my return to the city I met several lepers begging in the market. The sight of them among the food was enough to make me vow never to eat anything in Canton. The lepers are also permitted to marry, and a surprising number of diseased children are brought into a cursed and unhappy existence.

As we left the leper city I was conscious of an inward feeling of emptiness. It was Christmas day, and I thought with regret of dinner at home, although one of the men in the party said it was about midnight in New York. The guide said there was a building near by which he wanted to show us and then we would eat our luncheon. Once within a high wall we came upon a pretty scene. There was a mournful sheet of water undisturbed by a breath of wind. In the background the branches of low, overhanging trees kissed the still water just where stood some long-legged storks, made so familiar to us by pictures on Chinese fans.

Ah Cum led us to a room which was shut off from the court by a large carved gate. Inside were hard wood chairs and tables. While eating I heard chanting to the weird, plaintive sound of a tom-tom and a shrill pipe. When I had less appetite and more curiosity, I asked Ah Cum where we were, and he replied: "in the Temple of the Dead."

And in the Temple of the Dead I was eating my Christmas luncheon. But that did not interfere with the luncheon. Before we had finished a number of Chinaman crowded around the gate and looked curiously at me. They held up several children, well clad, cleanly children, to see me. Thinking to be agreeable, I went forward to shake hands with them, but they kicked and screamed, and getting down, rushed back in great fright, which amused us intensely. Their companions succeeded after awhile in quieting them and they were persuaded to take my hand. The ice once broken, they became so interested in me, my gloves, my bracelets and my dress, that I soon regretted my friendliness in the outset.

It is customary at the death of a person to build a bonfire after night, and cast into the fire household articles, such as money boxes, ladies' dressing cases, etc., composed of gilt paper, the priests meanwhile playing upon shrill pipes. They claim the devil which inhabits all bodies leaves the body to save the property of the dead, and once they play him out he can never re-enter, so souls are saved.

I climbed high and dirty stone steps to the water-clock, which, they say, is over five hundred years old, and has never run down or been repaired. In little niches in the stone walls were small gods, before them the smouldering joss sticks. The water-clock consists of four copper jars, about the size of wooden pails, placed on steps, one above the other. Each one has a spout from which comes a steady drop-drop. In the last and bottom jar is an indicator, very much like a foot rule, which rises with the water, showing the hour. On a blackboard hanging outside, they mark the time for the benefit of the town people. The upper jar is filled once every twenty-fear hours, and that is all the attention the clock requires.

On our return to the Powan I found some beautiful presents from Consul Seymour and the cards of a number of Europeans who had called to see me. Suffering from a sick-headache, I went to my cabin and shortly we were on our way to Hong Kong, my visit to Canton on Christmas day being of the past.

Chapter 14: To the Land of the Mikado

SHORTLY after my return to Hong Kong I sailed for Japan on the Oceanic. A number of friends, who had contributed so much towards my pleasure and comfort during my stay in British China, came to the ship to say farewell, and most regretfully did I take leave of them. Captain Smith took us into his cabin, where we all touched glasses and wished one another success, happiness and the other good things of this earth. The last moment having come, the final good-bye being said, we parted, and I was started on my way to the land of the Mikado.

The Oceanic, on which I traveled from Hong Kong to San Francisco, has quite a history. When it was designed and launched twenty years ago by Mr. Harland, of Belfast, it startled the shipping world. The designer was the first to introduce improvements for the comfort of passengers, such as the saloon amidships, avoiding the noise of the engines and especially the racing of the screw in rough weather. Before that time ships were gloomy and somber in appearance and constructed without a thought of the happiness of passengers. Mr. Harland, in the Oceanic, was the first to provide a promenade deck and to give the saloon and staterooms a light and cheerful appearance. In fact, the Oceanic was such a new departure that it aroused the jealousy of other ship companies, and was actually condemned by them as unseaworthy. It is said that so great was the outcry against the ship that sailors and firemen were given extra prices to induce them to make the first trip.

Instead of being the predicted failure, the Oceanic proved a great success. She became the greyhound of the Atlantic, afterwards being transferred to the Pacific in 1875. She is the favorite ship of the O. and O. line, making her voyages with speed and regularity. She retains a look of positive newness and seems to grow younger with years. In November, 1889, she made the fastest trip on record between Yokohama and San Francisco. No expense is spared to make this ship comfortable for the passengers. The catering would be hard to excel by even a first-class hotel. Passengers are accorded every liberty, and the officers do their utmost to make their guests feel at home, so that in the Orient the Oceanic is the favorite ship, and people wait for months so as to travel on her.

When I first went to the ship the monkey had been transferred from the Oriental. Meeting the stewardess I asked how the monkey was, to which she replied dryly:

"We have met."

She had her arm bandaged from the wrist to the shoulder!

"What did you do?" I asked in consternation.

"I did nothing but scream; the monkey did the rest!" she replied.

I spent New Year's eve between Hong Kong and Yokohama. The day had been so warm that we wore no wraps. In the forepart of the evening the passengers sat together in Social Hall talking, telling stories and laughing at them. The captain owned an organette which he brought into the hall, and he and the doctor took turns at grinding out the music. Later in the evening we went to the dining-hall where the purser had punch and champagne and oysters for us, a rare treat which he had prepared in America just for this occasion.

What children we all become on board a ship! After oysters we were up to all sorts of childish tricks. As we sat around the table the doctor gave us each a word to say, such as Ish! Ash! Osh! Then when we were sure of our word, it coming in rotation around the circle, he told us to shout the words in unison when he gave the signal. We did, and it made one great big sneeze-the most gigantic and absurd sneeze I ever heard in my life. Afterwards a jolly man from Yokohama, whose wife was equally jolly and lively-spirited, taught us a song consisting of one line to a melody quite simple and catching.

"Sweetly sings the donkey when he goes to grass, Sweetly sings the donkey when he goes to grass, Ec-ho! Ec-ho! Ec-ho!"

When eight bells rang we rose and sang Auld Lang Syne with glasses in hand, and on the last echo of the good old song toasted the death of the old year and the birth of the new. We shook hands around, each wishing the other a happy New Year. 1889 was ended, and 1890 with its pleasures and pains began. Shortly after, the women passengers retired. I went to sleep lulled by the sounds of familiar negro melodies sung by the men in the smoking-room beneath my cabin.

Chapter 15: One Hundred and Twenty Hours in Japan

AFTER seeing Hong Kong with its wharfs crowded with dirty boats manned by still dirtier people, and its streets packed with a filthy crowd, Yokohama has a cleaned-up Sunday appearance. Travelers are taken from the ships, which anchor some distance out in the bay, to the land in small steam launches. The first-class hotels in the different ports have their individual launches, but like American hotel omnibuses, while being run by the hotel to assist in procuring patrons, the traveler pays for them just the same.

An import as well as an export duty is charged in Japan, but we passed the custom inspectors unmolested. I found the Japanese jinricksha men a gratifying improvement upon those I seen from Ceylon to China. They presented no sight of filthy rags, nor naked bodies, nor smell of grease. Clad in neat navy-blue garments, their little pudgy legs encased in unwrinkled tights, the upper half of their bodies in short jackets with wide flowing sleeves; their clean, good-natured faces, peeping from beneath comical mushroom-shaped hats; their blue-black, wiry locks cropped just above the nape of the neck, they offered a striking contrast to the jinricksha men of other countries. Their crests were embroidered upon the back and sleeves of their top garment as are the crests of every man, woman and child in Japan.

Rain the night previous had left the streets muddy and the air cool and crisp, but the sun creeping through the mistiness of early morning, fell upon us with most gratifying warmth. Wrapping our knees with rugs the 'ricksha men started off in a lively trot to the Pacific Mail and O. and O. Companies' office, where I met discourteous people for the first time since I left the P. & O. "Victoria." And these were Americans, too. The most generous excuse that can be offered for them is that they have held their positions so long that they feel they are masters, instead of a steamship company's servants. A man going into the office to buy a ticket to America, was answered in the following manner by one of the head men:

"You'll have to come back later if you want a ticket. I'm going to lunch now."

I stayed at the Grand Hotel while in Japan. It is a large building, with long verandas, wide halls and airy rooms, commanding an exquisite view of the lake in front. Barring an enormous and monotonous collection of rats, the Grand would be considered a good hotel even in America. The food is splendid and the service excellent. The "Japs," noiseless, swift, anxious to please, stand at the head of all the servants I encountered from New York to New York; and then they look so neat in their blue tights and white linen jackets.

I always have an inclination to laugh when I look at the Japanese men in their native dress. Their legs are small and their trousers are skin tight. The upper garment, with its great wide sleeves, is as loose as the lower is tight. When they finish their "get up" by placing their dish-pan shaped hat upon their heads, the wonder grows how such small legs can carry it all! Stick two straws in one end of a potato, a mushroom in the other, set it up on the straws and you have a Japanese in outline. Talk about French heels! The Japanese sandal is a small board elevated on two pieces of thin wood fully five inches in height. They make the people look exactly as if they were on stilts. These queer shoes are fastened to the foot by a single strap running between toes number one and two, the wearer when walking necessarily maintaining a sliding instead of an up and down movement, in order to keep the shoe on.

On a cold day one would imagine the Japanese were a nation of armless people. They fold their arms up in their long, loose sleeves. A Japanese woman's sleeves are to her what a boy's pockets are to him. Her cards, money, combs, hair pins, ornaments and rice paper are carried in her sleeves. Her rice paper is her handkerchief, and she notes with horror and disgust that after using we return our handkerchiefs to our pockets. I think the Japanese women carry everything in their sleeves, even their hearts. Not that they are fickle-none are more true, more devoted, more loyal, more constant, than Japanese women-but they are so guileless and artless that almost any one, if opportunity offers, can pick at their trusting hearts.

If I loved and married, I would say to my mate: "Come, I know where Eden is," and like Edwin Arnold, desert the land of my birth for Japan, the land of love-beauty-poetry-cleanliness. I somehow always connected Japan and its people with China and its people, believing the one no improvement on the other. I could not have made a greater mistake. Japan is beautiful. Its women are charmingly sweet. I know little about the men except that they do not go far as we judge manly beauty, being undersized, dark, and far from prepossessing. They have the reputation of being extremely clever, so I do not speak of them as a whole, only of those I came in contact with. I saw one, a giant in frame, a god in features; but he was a public wrestler.

The Japanese are the direct opposite to the Chinese. The Japanese are the cleanliest people on earth, the Chinese are the filthiest; the Japanese are always happy and cheerful, the Chinese are always grumpy and morose; the Japanese are the most graceful of people, the Chinese the most awkward; the Japanese have few vices, the Chinese have all the vices in the world; in short, the Japanese are the most delightful of people, the Chinese the most disagreeable.

The majority of the Europeans live on the bluff in low white bungalows, with great rooms and breezy verandas, built in the hearts of Oriental gardens, where one can have an unsurpassed view of the Mississippi bay, or can play tennis or cricket, or loll in hammocks, guarded from public gaze by luxurious green hedges. The Japanese homes form a great contrast to the bungalows. They are daintily small, like play houses indeed, built of a thin shingle-like board, fine in texture. Chimneys and fireplaces are unknown. The first wall is set back, allowing the upper floor and side walls to extend over the lower flooring, making it a portico built in instead of on the house. Light window frames, with their minute openings covered with fine rice paper instead of glass, are the doors and windows in one. They do not swing open and shut as do our doors, nor do they move up and down like our windows, but slide like rolling doors. They form the partitions of the houses inside and can be removed at any time, throwing the floor into one room.

They have two very pretty customs in Japan. The one is decorating their houses in honor of the new year, and the other celebrating the blossoming of the cherry trees. Bamboo saplings covered with light airy foliage and pinioned so as to incline towards the middle of the street, where meeting they form an arch, make very effective decorations. Rice trimmings mixed with sea-weed, orange, lobster and ferns are hung over every door to insure a plentiful year, while as sentinels on either side are large tubs, in which are three thick bamboo stalks, with small evergreen trees for background.

In the cool of the evening we went to a house that had been specially engaged to see the dancing, or *geisha*, girls. At the door we saw all the wooden shoes of the household, and we were asked to take off our shoes before entering, a proceeding rather disliked by some of the party, who refused absolutely to do as requested. We effected a compromise, however, by putting cloth slippers over our shoes. The second floor had been converted into one room, with nothing in it except the matting covering the floor and a Japanese screen here and there. We sat upon the floor, for chairs there are none in Japan, but the exquisite matting is padded until it is as soft as velvet. It was laughable to see us trying to sit down, and yet more so to see us endeavor to find a posture of ease for our limbs. We were about as graceful as an elephant dancing. A smiling woman in a black kimono set several round and square charcoal boxes containing burning charcoal before us. These are the only Japanese stove. Afterwards she brought a tray containing a number of long-stemmed pipes–Japanese women smoke constantly–a pot of tea and several small cups.

Impatiently I awaited the *geisha* girls. In the tiny maidens glided at last, clad in exquisite trailing, angel-sleeved kimonos. The girls bow gracefully, bending down until their heads touch their knees, then kneeling before us murmur gently a greeting which sounds like "Koinbanwa!"

drawing in their breath with a long, hissing suction, which is a token of great honor. The musicians sat down on the floor and began an alarming din upon *samisens*, drums and gongs, singing meanwhile through their pretty noses. If the noses were not so pretty I am sure the music would be unbearable to one who has ever heard a chest note. The *geisha* girls stand posed with open fan in hand above their heads, ready to begin the dance. They are very short with the slenderest of slender waists. Their soft and tender eyes are made blacker by painted lashes and brows; their midnight hair, stiffened with a gummy wash, is most wonderfully dressed in large coils and ornamented with gold and silver flowers and gilt paper pom-pons. The younger the girl the more gay is her hair. Their kimonos, of the most exquisite material, trail all around them, and are loosely held together at the waist with an obi-sash; their long flowing sleeves fall back, showing their dimpled arms and baby hands. Upon their tiny feet they wear cunning white linen socks cut with a place for the great toe. When they go out they wear wooden sandals. The Japanese are the only women I ever saw who could rouge and powder and be not repulsive, but the more charming because of it. They powder their faces and have a way of reddening their under lip just at the tip that gives them a most tempting look. The lips look like two luxurious cherries. The musicians begin a long chanting strain, and these bits of beauty begin the dance. With a grace, simply enchanting, they twirl their little fans, sway their dainty bodies in a hundred different poses, each one more intoxicating than the other, all the while looking so childish and shy, with an innocent smile lurking about their lips, dimpling their soft cheeks, and their black eyes twinkling with the pleasure of the dance. After the dance the *geisha* girls made friends with me, examining, with surprised delight, my dress, my bracelets, my rings, my boots-to them the most wonderful and extraordinary things,-my hair, my gloves, indeed they missed very little, and they approved of all. They said I was very sweet, and urged me to come again, and in honor of the custom of my land-the Japanese never kiss-they pressed their soft, pouting lips to mine in parting.

Japanese women know nothing whatever of bonnets, and may they never! On rainy days they tie white scarfs over their wonderful hair-dressing, but at other times they waddle bareheaded, with fan and umbrella, along the streets on their wooden clogs. They have absolutely no furniture. Their bed is a piece of matting, their pillows, narrow blocks of wood, probably six inches in length, two wide and six high. They rest the back of the neck on the velvet covered top, so their wonderful hair remains dressed for weeks at a time. Their tea and pipe always stand beside them, so they can partake of their comforts the last thing before sleep and the first thing after.

A Japanese reporter from Tokyo came to interview me, his newspaper having translated and published the story of my visit to Jules Verne. Carefully he read the questions which he wished to ask me. They were written at intervals on long rolls of foolscap, the space to be filled in as I answered. I thought it ridiculous until I returned and became an interviewee. Then I concluded it would be humane for us to adopt the Japanese system of interviewing.

I went to Kamakura to see the great bronze god, the image of Buddha, familiarly called Diabutsu. It stands in a verdant valley at the foot of two mountains. It was built in 1250 by Ono Goroyemon, a famous bronze caster, and is fifty feet in height; it is sitting Japanese style, ninety-eight feet being its waist circumference; the face is eight feet long, the eye is four feet, the ear six feet six and one-half inches, the nose three feet eight and one-half inches, the mouth is three feet two and one-half inches, the diameter of the lap is thirty-six feet, and the circumference of the thumb is over three feet. I had my photograph taken sitting on its thumb with two friends, one of whom offered $50,000 for the god. Years ago at the feast of the god sacrifices were made to Diabutsu. Quite frequently the hollow interior would be heated to a white heat, and hundreds of victims were cast into the seething furnace in honor of the god. It is different now, sacrifices being not the custom, and the hollow interior is harmlessly fitted up with tiny altars and a ladder stairway by which visitors can climb up into Diabutsu's eye, and from that height view the surrounding lovely country. We also visited a very pretty temple near by, saw a famous fan tree and a lotus-pond, and spent some time at a most delightful tea-house, where two little "Jap" girls served us with tea and sweets. I also spent one day at Tokio, where I saw the Mikado's Japanese and European castles, which are enclosed by a fifty foot stone wall and three wide moats. The people in Tokio are trying to ape the style of the Europeans. I saw several men in native costume riding bicycles. Their roads are superb. There is a street car line in Tokio, a novelty in the East, and carriages of all descriptions. The European clothing sent to Japan is at least ready-made, if not second hand. One woman I saw was considered very stylish. The bodice of a European dress she wore had been cut to fit a slender, tapering waist. The Japanese never saw a corset and their waists are enormous. The woman was able to fasten one button at the neck, and from that point the bodice was permitted to spread. She was considered very swell. At dinner one night I saw a "Jap" woman in a low cut evening dress, with nothing but white socks on her feet.

It would fill a large book if I attempted to describe all I saw during my stay in Japan. Going to the great Shiba temple, I saw a forest of superb trees. At the carved gate leading to the temple were hundreds of stone and bronze lanterns, which alone were worth a fortune. On either side of the gate were gigantic carved images of ferocious aspect. They were covered with wads of chewed paper. When I remarked that the school children must make very free with the images, a gentleman explained that the Japanese believed if they chewed paper and threw it at these gods and it stuck their prayers would be answered, if not, their prayers would pass unheeded. A great many prayers must have been answered. At another gate I saw the most disreputable looking god. It had no nose. The Japanese believe if they have a pain or ache and they rub their hands over the face of that god, and then where the pain is located, they will straightway be cured. I can't say whether it cured them or not, but I know they rubbed away the nose of the god.

The Japanese are very progressive people. They cling to their religion and their modes of life, which in many ways are superior to ours, but they readily adopt any trade or habit that is an improvement upon their own. Finding the European male attire more serviceable than their native dress for some trades they promptly adopted it. The women tested the European dress, and finding it barbarously uncomfortable and inartistic went back to their exquisite kimonos, retaining the use of European underwear, which they found more healthful and comfortable than the utter absence of it, to which they had been accustomed. The best proof of the comfort of kimonos lies in the fact that the European residents have adopted them entirely for indoor wear. Only their long subjection to fashion prevents their wearing them in public. Japanese patriotism should serve as a model for us careless Americans. No foreigner can go to Japan and monopolize a trade. It is true that a little while ago they were totally ignorant of modern conveniences. They knew nothing of railroads, or street cars, or engines, or electric lighting. They were too clever though to waste their wits in efforts to rediscover inventions known to other nations, but they had to have them. Straightway they sent to other countries for men who understood the secret of such things, and at fabulous prices and under contracts of three, five and occasionally ten years duration, brought them to their land. They were set to work, the work they had been hired to do, and with them toiled steadily and watchfully the cleverest of Japanese. When the contract is up it is no longer necessary to fill the coffers of a foreigner. The employé was released, and their own man, fully qualified for the work, stepped into the position. And so in this way they command all business in their country.

Kimonos are made in three parts, each part an inch or so longer than the other. I saw a kimono a Japanese woman bought for the holidays. It was a suit, gray silk crepe, with pink peach blossoms dotting it here and there. The whole was lined with the softest pink silk, and the hem, which trails, was thickly padded with a delicate perfume sachet. The underclothing was of the flimsiest white silk. The whole thing cost sixty dollars, a dollar and a half of which paid for the making. Japanese clothing is sewed with what we call a basting stitch, but it is as durable as it could be if sewed with the smallest of stitches. Japanese women have mirrors in which they view their numerous charms. Their mirrors are round, highly polished steel plates, and they know nothing whatever of glass mirrors. All the women carry silk card cases in their long sleeves, in which are their own diminutive cards.

English is taught in the Japan schools and so is gracefulness. The girls are taught graceful movements, how to receive, entertain and part with visitors, how to serve tea and sweets gracefully, and the proper and graceful way to use chopsticks. It is a pretty sight to see a lovely woman use chopsticks. At a tea-house or at an ordinary dinner a long paper laid at one's place contains a pair of chopsticks, probably twelve inches in length, but no thicker than the thinner size of lead pencils. The sticks are usually whittled in one piece and split only half apart to prove that they have never been used. Every one breaks the sticks apart before eating, and after the meal they are destroyed.

An American resident of Japan told me of his going to see a cremation. The Japanese graveyard is a strange affair, with headstones set close together, leaving the space for the graves less than the size of a baby's grave in America. As soon as the breath has left a body it is undressed and doubled up, head to feet, and is made to go in a very small bamboo box built in imitation of a Japanese house. This house may cost a great deal of money. It is carried along the streets on two poles to the place where it is to be cremated where it is given in charge of the cremator, and the friends go back to their homes until the following day, when they return for the ashes, which are generally placed in an urn and buried. The American, of whom I spoke, made arrangements with a cremator, and, accompanied by a friend, walked to the place in the country and waited out of sight until the mourners had vanished before they dared to draw near enough to see the cremation. They had walked quite a distance, dinnerless, and said, naively, that the odor was like that of veal, and it made him ravenously hungry.

A small hole about three feet long is made in the earth and in it the fire is built. When it was the proper heat the box was set over it, and in an instant it was consumed. The body released from its doubled position straightened out. The lower half being over the fire was soon cremated, excepting the feet and knee joints. The man in charge carefully pulled the upper part of the body over the fire, and with the same large fork put the half-consumed feet and knee-joints under the arms. In less than an hour all that remained of the body was a few ashes in the bottom of the pit. While the cremator was explaining it all to the gentleman he repeatedly filled his little pipe and lit it with the fire from the burning body. At his urgent request the gentleman consented to take tea with him when his task was done. They entered his neat little home while he jumped into a boiling bath in the open garden, from which he emerged later as red as a lobster. Meanwhile his charming and pretty daughters were dispensing the hospitalities of their home to their guests, and the father, desirous of enjoying their society, came and stood in the doorway, talking to them and watching them eat while he wiped his naked body with a towel!

The prettiest sight in Japan, I think, is the native streets in the afternoons. Men, women and children turn out to play shuttle-cock and fly kites. Can you imagine what an enchanting sight it is to see pretty women with cherry lips, black bright eyes, ornamented, glistening hair, exquisitely graceful gowns, tidy white-stockinged feet thrust into wooden sandals, dimpled cheeks, dimpled arms, dimpled baby hands, lovely, innocent, artless, happy, playing shuttlecock in the streets of Yokohama?

Japanese children are unlike any other children I ever saw at play. They always look happy and never seem to quarrel or cry. Little Japanese girls, elevated on wooden sandals and with babies almost as large as themselves tied on their backs, play shuttle-cock with an abandon that is terrifying until one grows confident of the fact that they move with as much agility as they could if their little backs were free from nursemaid burdens. Japanese babies are such comical little fellows. They wear such wonderfully padded clothing that they are as shapeless as a feather pillow. Others may think, as I did, that the funny little shaven spots on their heads was a queer style of ornamentation, but it is not. I am assured the spots are shaven to keep their baby heads cool.

The Japanese are not only pretty and artistic but most obliging. A friend of mine who guided us in Japan had a Kodak, and whenever we came upon an interesting group he was always taking snap shots. No one objected, and especially were the children pleasant about being photographed. When he placed them in position, or asked them to stand as they were, they would pose like little drum-majors until he gave them permission to move.

The only regret of my trip, and one I can never cease to deplore, was that in my hasty departure I forgot to take a Kodak. On every ship and at every port I met others-and envied them-with Kodaks. They could photograph everything that pleased them; the light in those lands is excellent, and many were the pleasant mementos of their acquaintances and themselves they carried home on their plates. I met a German who was spending two years going around the world and he carried two Kodaks, a large and a small size, and his collection of photographs was the most interesting I ever saw. At the different ports he had professional photographers develop his plates.

The Japanese thoughtfully reserve a trade for their blind. They are all taught massage bathing, and none but the blind are allowed to follow this calling. These people go through the streets uttering to a plaintive melody these words:

"I'll give you a bath from head to toe for two cents."

At Uyeno park, where they point out a tree planted by General Grant when on his tour around the world, I saw a most amusing monkey which belonged to the very interesting menagerie. It was very large and had a scarlet face and gray fur. It was chained to the fence, and when one of the young men in our party went up and talked to him the monkey looked very sagacious and wise. In the little crowd that gathered around, quite out of the monkey's reach, was a young Jap, who, in a spirit of mischief, tossed a pebble at the red-faced mystery, who turned with a grieved and inquiring air to my friend.

"Go for him," my friend responded, sympathetically, to the look, and the monkey turned and with its utmost strength endeavored to free itself so it could obey the bidding. The Jap made his escape and the monkey quieted down, looking expressively at the place where the Jap had stood and then at my friend for approval, which he obtained. The keeper gave the monkey its dinner, which consisted of two large boiled sweet potatoes. My friend broke one in two and the monkey greedily ate the inside, placing the remainder with the other potato on the fence between his feet. Suddenly he looked up, and as quick as a flash he flung, with his entire force, which was something terrific, the remaining potato at the head of some one in the crowd. There was some loud screaming and a scattering, but the potato missing all heads, went crashing with such force against a board fence that every particle of it remained sticking there in one shapeless splotch. The Jap who had tossed the pebble at the monkey, and so earned his enmity, quietly shrunk away with a whitened face. He had returned unnoticed by all except the monkey, who tried to revenge himself with the potato. I admired the monkey's cleverness so much that I would have tried to buy him if I had not already owned one.

In Yokohama, I went to Hundred Steps, at the top of which lives a Japanese belle, Oyuchisan, who is the theme for artist and poet, and the admiration of tourists. One of the pleasant events of my stay was the luncheon given for me on the Omaha, the American war vessel lying at Yokohama. I took several drives, enjoying the novelty of having a Japanese running by the horses' heads all the while. I ate rice and eel. I visited the curio shops, one of which is built in imitation of a Japanese house, and was charmed with the exquisite art I saw there; in short, I found nothing but what delighted the finer senses while in Japan.

Chapter 16: Across the Pacific

IT was a bright sunny morning when I left Yokohama. A number of new friends in launches escorted me to the Oceanic, and when we hoisted anchor the steam launches blew loud blasts upon their whistles in farewell to me, and the band upon the Omaha played "Home, Sweet Home," "Hail Columbia," and "The Girl I Left Behind Me," in my honor; and I waved my handkerchief so long after they were out of sight that my arms were sore for days. My feverish eagerness to be off again on my race around the world was strongly mingled with regret at leaving such charming friends and such a lovely land.

Everything promised well for a pleasant and rapid voyage. Anticipating this, Chief-engineer Allen caused to be written over the engines and throughout the engine room, this date and couplet:

"For   Nellie   Bly,
We'll   win   or   die.
January 20, 1890."

It was their motto and was all very sweet to me. The runs were marvelous until the third day out, and then a storm came upon us. They tried to cheer me, saying it would only last that day, but the next day found it worse, and it continued, never abating a moment; head winds, head sea, wild rolling, frightful pitching, until I fretfully waited for noon when I would slip off to the dining-room to see the run, hoping that it would have gained a few miles on the day before, and always being disappointed. And they were all so good to me! Bless them for it! If possible, they suffered more over the prospect of my failure than I did.

"If I fail, I will never return to New York," I would say despondently; "I would rather go in dead and successful than alive and behind time."

"Don't talk that way, child," Chief Allen would plead, "I would do anything for you in my power. I have worked the engines as they never were worked before; I have sworn at this storm until I have no words left; I have even prayed–I haven't prayed before for years–but I prayed that this storm may pass over and that we may get you in on time."

"I know that I am not a sinner," I laughed hysterically. "Day and night my plea has been, 'Be merciful to me a sinner,' and as the mercy has not been forthcoming, the natural conclusion is that I'm not a sinner. It's hopeless, it's hopeless!"

"Don't think so," the purser would beg; "don't be so disheartened; why, child, if by jumping overboard I could bring you happiness and success, I should do so in a moment."

"Never mind, little girl, you're all right," the jolly, happy-hearted captain would laugh. "I've bet every cent I have in the bank that you'll get in before you are due. Just take my word for it, you'll be in New York at least three days ahead of time."

"Why do you try to cheat me? You know we are way behind time now," I urged, longing to be still farther cheated into fresh hope, to which the doctor would say, dryly:

"Look here, Nellie Bly, if you don't stop talking so I'll make you take some pills for your liver."

"You mean wretch, you know I can't help being blue. It's head sea, and head winds, and low runs–not liver!"

And then I would laugh, and so would they; and Mr. Allen, who had been pleading for me to "smile just once, give them but one glimpse of my old, jolly smile," would go away content. This is but a repetition of the way in which I was coaxed out of my unhappiness every day, by those great-hearted, strong, tender men.

At last a rumor became current that there was a Jonah on board the ship. It was thought over and talked over and, much to my dismay, I was told that the sailors said monkeys were Jonahs. Monkeys brought bad weather to ships, and as long as the monkey was on board we would have storms. Some one asked if I would consent to the monkey being thrown overboard. A little struggle between superstition and a feeling of justice for the monkey followed. Chief Allen, when I spoke to him on the subject, told me not to do it. He said the monkey had just gotten outside of a hundred weight of cement, and had washed it down with a quart of lamp oil, and he, for one, did not want to interfere with the monkey's happiness and digestion! Just then some one told me that ministers were Jonahs; they always brought bad weather to ships. We had two ministers on board! So I said quietly, if the ministers were thrown overboard I'd say nothing about the monkey. Thus the monkey's life was saved.

Mr. Allen had a boy, Walter, who was very clever at tricks. One day Walter said he would show that he could lift a bottle merely by placing his open hand to the side of the bottle. He put everybody out of the cabin, as he said if they remained in it broke the influence. They watched intently through the open door as he rolled up his sleeve and rubbed his arm downward, quite vigorously, as if trying to get all the blood in his hand. Catching the wrist with the other hand, as if to hold all the blood there, he placed his open hand to the side of [the] bottle and, much to the amazement of his audience, the bottle went up with his hand. When urged to tell how to do the wonderful trick, he said:

"It's all very easy; all you do is to rub your arm, that's just for show; then you lay hold of your wrist just as if you wanted to keep all the blood in your hand; you keep one finger free-no one notices that-and you take the neck of the bottle between the hand and the finger, and the bottle goes up with the hand. See?"

One evening, when the ship was rolling frightfully, everybody was gathered in the dining-hall; an Englishman urged Walter to do some tricks, but Walter did not want to be bothered then, so he said: "Yes, sir; in a moment, sir," and went on putting the things upon the table. He had put down the mustard pot, the salt cellar and various things, and was wiping a plate. As he went to put the plate down the ship gave a great roll, the plate knocked against the mustard pot and the mustard flew all over the Englishman, much to the horror of the others. Sitting up stiffly, the mustard dotting him from head to knees, he said sternly:

"Walter! What is this?"

"That, sir, is the first trick," Walter replied softly, and he glided silently and swiftly off to the regions of the cook.

But Walter was caught one day. A sailor told him that he could hide an egg on him so no one would be able to find it. Walter had his doubts, but he willingly gave the sailor a test. The egg was hidden and a man called in to find it. He searched Walter all over without once coming upon the egg. The sailor suggested another trial to which Walter, now an interested and firm believer in the sailor's ability, gladly consented. The sailor opened Walter's shirt and placed the egg next to the skin in the region of his heart, carefully buttoning the shirt afterwards. The man was called in, he went up to Walter and hit him a resounding smack where Sullivan hit Kilrain. He found the egg and so did Walter!

Japanese "boys" serve in the dining-hall on the Oceanic, but the sailors are Chinese. They chant in a musical manner when hoisting sails. It sounds as if they say "Ah-Oh-Eh-Oh! Ah-Oh-Eh-Ah-Oh!" The "boys" shake the tablecloths into a plate. They put a plate in the tablecloth which two of them shake once or twice and then slide the plate to the floor. The plate will be seen to have gathered all the crumbs.

One Chinaman and one Japanese traveled first-class coming over. The Chinaman was confined to his cabin with sea-sickness all the time, so we saw very little of him. The Japanese wore European dress and endeavored to ape the manners of the Europeans. Evidently he thought it the custom to use tooth-picks. It is-with some people. After every meal he used a tooth-pick so that the whole table might see, as if wishing to show he was civilized! Then after a great amount of gorging he always placed the tooth-pick pen-like behind his ear where it stayed until the next meal.

But even with low runs our trip was bound to come to an end. One night it was announced that the next day we would be in San Francisco. I felt a feverish excitement, and many were the speculations as to whether there would be a snow blockade to hinder my trip across the Continent. A hopefulness that had not known me for many days came back, when in rushed the purser, his face a snow-white, crying:

"My God, the bill of health was left behind in Yokohama."

"Well-well-what does that mean?" I demanded, fearing some misfortune, I knew not what.

"It means," he said, dropping nerveless into a chair, "that no one will be permitted to land until the next ship arrives from Japan. That will be two weeks."

The thought of being held two weeks in sight of San Francisco, in sight of New York almost, and the goal for which I had been striving and powerless to move, was maddening.

"I would cut my throat, for I could not live and endure it," I said quietly, and that spurred him on to make another search, which resulted in finding the report safely lodged in the doctor's desk.

Later came a scare about a small-pox case on board, but it proved to be only a rumor, and early in the morning the revenue officers came aboard bringing the newspapers. I read of the impassable snow blockade which for a week had put a stop to all railroad traffic, and my despair knew no bounds. While the Oceanic was waiting for the quarantine doctor, some men came out on a tug to take me ashore. There was no time for farewells. The monkey was taken on the tug with me, and my baggage, which had increased by gifts from friends, was thrown after me. Just as the tug steamed off the quarantine doctor called to me that he had forgotten to examine my tongue, and I could not land until he did. I stuck it out, he called out "all right;" the others laugh, I wave farewell, and in another moment I was parted from my good friends on the Oceanic.

Chapter 17: Across the Continent

I ONLY remember my trip across the continent as one maze of happy greetings, happy wishes, congratulating telegrams, fruit, flowers, loud cheers, wild hurrahs, rapid hand-shaking and a beautiful car filled with fragrant flowers attached to a swift engine that was tearing like mad through flower-dotted valley and over snow-tipped mountain, on-on-on! It was glorious! A ride worthy a queen. They say no man or woman in America ever received ovations like those given me during my flying trip across the continent. The Americans turned out to do honor to an American girl who had been the first to make a record of a flying trip around the world, and I rejoiced with them that it was an American girl who had done it. It seemed as if my greatest success was the personal interest of every one who greeted me. They were all so kind and as anxious that I should finish the trip in time as if their personal reputations were at stake. The special train had been waiting for my arrival in readiness to start the moment I boarded it. The

Deputy Collector of the port of San Francisco, the Inspector of Customs, the Quarantine Officer and the Superintendent of the O. and O. steamers sat up all the night preceding my arrival, so there should be no delay in my transfer from the Oceanic to the special train. Nor were they the only ones to wait for me. One poor little newspaper woman did not see bed that night so anxious was she for an interview which she did not get. I was so entirely ignorant about what was to be done with me on landing, that I thought I was someone's guest until I was many miles away from San Francisco. Had I known in advance the special train was mine, every newspaper man and woman who cared to should have been my guest.

My train consisted of one handsome sleeping-car, the San Lorenzo, and the engine, The Queen, was one of the fastest on the Southern Pacific.

"What time do you want to reach New York, Miss Bly?" Mr. Bissell, General Passenger Agent of the Atlantic and Pacific system, asked me.

"Not later than Saturday evening," I said, never thinking they could get me there in that time.

"Very well, we will put you there on time," he said quietly, and I rested satisfied that he would keep his word.

It did not seem long after we left Oakland Mole until we reached the great San Joaquin valley, a level green plain through which the railroad track ran for probably three hundred miles as straight as a sunbeam. The road-bed was so perfect that though we were traveling a mile a minute the car was as easy as if it were traveling over a bed of velvet.

At Merced, our second stop, I saw a great crowd of people dressed in their best Sunday clothes gathered about the station. I supposed they were having a picnic and made some such remark, to be told in reply that the people had come there to see me. Amazed at this information I got up, in answer to calls for me, and went out on the back platform. A loud cheer, which almost frightened me to death, greeted my appearance and the band began to play "By Nellie's Blue Eyes." A large tray of fruit and candy and nuts, the tribute of a dear little newsboy, was passed to me, for which I was more grateful than had it been the gift of a king.

We started on again, and the three of us on the train had nothing to do but admire the beautiful country through which we were passing as swiftly as cloud along the sky, to read, or count telegraph poles, or pamper and pet the monkey. I felt little inclination to do anything but to sit quietly and rest, bodily and mentally. There was nothing left for me to do now. I could hurry nothing, I could change nothing; I could only sit and wait until the train landed me at the end of my journey. I enjoyed the rapid motion of the train so much that I dreaded to think of the end. At Fresno, the next station, the town turned out to do me honor, and I was the happy recipient of exquisite fruits, wines and flowers, all the product of Fresno County, California.

The men who spoke to me were interested in my sun-burnt nose, the delays I had experienced, the number of miles I had traveled. The women wanted to examine my one dress in which I had traveled around, the cloak and cap I had worn, were anxious to know what was in the bag, and all about the monkey.

While we were doing some fine running the first day, I heard the whistle blow wildly, and then I felt the train strike something. Brakes were put on, and we went out to see what had occurred. It was hailing just then, and we saw two men coming up the track. The conductor came back to tell us that we had struck a hand-car, and pointed to a piece of twisted iron and a bit of splintered board-all that remained of it-laying alongside. When the men came up, one remarked, with a mingled expression of wonder and disgust upon his face:

"Well, you ARE running like h–!"

"Thank you; I am glad to hear it," I said, and then we all laughed. I inquired if they had been hurt; they assured me not, and good humor being restored all around, we said good-bye, the engineer pulled the lever, and we were off again. At one station where we stopped there was a large crowd, and when I appeared on the platform, one yell went up from them. There was one man on the outskirts of the crowd who shouted:

"Nellie Bly, I must get up close to you!"

The crowd evidently felt as much curiosity as I did about the man's object, for they made a way and he came up to the platform.

"Nellie Bly, you must touch my hand," he said, excitedly. Anything to please the man. I reached over and touched his hand, and then he shouted:

"Now you will be successful. I have in my hand the left hind foot of a rabbit!"

Well, I don't know anything about the left hind foot of a rabbit, but when I knew that my train had run safely across a bridge which was held in place only by jack-screws, and which fell the moment we were across; and when I heard that in another place the engine had just switched off from us when it lost a wheel, then I thought of the left hind foot of a rabbit, and wondered if there was anything in it.

One place, where a large crowd greeted me, a man on the limits of it yelled:

"Did you ride on an elephant, Nellie?" and when I said I had not, he dropped his head and went away. At another place the policemen fought to keep the crowd back; everybody was wanting to shake hands with me, but at last one officer was shoved aside, and the other seeing the fate of his comrade, turned to me, saying: "I guess I'll give up and take a shake," and while reaching for my hand was swept on with the crowd. I leaned over the platform and shook hands with both hands at every station, and when the train pulled out crowds would run after, grabbing for my hands as long as they could. My arms ached for almost a month afterwards, but I did not mind the ache if by such little acts I could give pleasure to my own people, whom I was so glad to be among once more.

"Come out here and we'll elect you governor," a Kansas man said, and I believe they would have done it, if the splendid welcomes they gave me are any criterion. Telegrams addressed merely to "Nellie Bly, Nellie Bly's Train," came from all parts of the country filled with words of cheer and praise at all hours of the day and night. I could not mention one place that was kinder than another. Over ten thousand people greeted me at Topeka. The mayor of Dodge City presented me, in behalf of the citizens, with resolutions of praise. I was very anxious to go to Kansas City, but we only went to the station outside of the limits, in order to save thirty minutes. At Hutchinson a large crowd and the Ringgold Cornet Band greeted me, and at another place the mayor assured me that the band had been brought down, but they forgot to play. They merely shouted like the rest, forgetting in the excitement all about their music.

I was up until four o'clock, talking first with a little newspaper girl from Kearney, Nebraska, who had traveled six hundred miles to meet and interview me, and later dictating an account of my trip to a stenographer, who was sea-sick from the motion of the train. I had probably slept two hours when the porter called me, saying we would soon be in Chicago. I dressed myself leisurely and drank the last drop of coffee there was left on our train, for we had been liberally entertaining everybody who cared to travel any distance with us. I was surprised, on opening the door of my state-room, to see the car quite filled with good-looking men. They were newspaper men, members of the Chicago Press Club, I found a moment later, who had come out to Joliet to meet me and to escort me to their city. Mr. Cornelius Gardener, the vice-president of the club, in the absence of the president, took charge of our little party. Before we were in I had answered all their questions, and we joked about my sun-burnt nose and discussed the merits of my one dress, the cleverness of the monkey, and I was feeling happy and at home and wishing I could stay all day in Chicago.

Carriages were waiting to take us to the rooms of the Press Club. I went there in a coupe with Vice-President Gardener who said, in a published narration of my visit afterwards, that he was strongly tempted to steal me, which clever idea so amused me that had the case been reversed, I know I should have acted on it, much to the confusion of a waiting public in New York. In the beautiful rooms of the Press Club I met the president, Stanley Waterloo, and a number of clever newspaper men. I had not been expected in Chicago until noon, and the club had arranged an informal reception for me, and when they were notified of my speedy trip and consequently earlier arrival, it was too late to notify the members. After a most delightfully informal reception I was escorted to Kinsley's, where the club had a breakfast prepared. And then I learned that, owing to some misunderstanding, none of the men had had anything to eat since the night before. After breakfast the members of the Press Club, acting as my escort, took me to visit the Chicago Board of Trade. When we went in, the pandemonium which seems to reign during business hours was at its height. My escorts took me to the gallery, and just as we got there a man raised his arm to yell something to the roaring crowd, when he saw me, and yelled instead:

"There's Nellie Bly!"

In one instant the crowd that had been yelling like mad became so silent that a pin could have been heard fall to the floor. Every face, bright and eager, was turned up towards us, instantly every hat came off, and then a burst of applause resounded through the immense hall. People can say what they please about Chicago, but I do not believe that anywhere else in the United States a woman can get a greeting which will equal that given by the Chicago Board of Trade. The applause was followed by cheer after cheer and cries of "Speech!" but I took off my little cap and shook my head at them, which only served to increase their cheers.

Shortly afterwards the Press Club escorted me to the Pennsylvania Station, where I reluctantly bade them good-bye, unable to thank them heartily enough for the royal manner in which they had treated a little sun-burnt stranger.

Now I was on a regular train which seemed to creep, so noticeable was the difference in the speed of traveling. Instead of a fine sleeping-car at my disposal, I had but a state-room, and my space was so limited that floral and fruit offerings had to be left behind. In Chicago, a cable which afforded me much pleasure reached me, having missed me at San Francisco.

"Mr. Verne wishes the following message to be handed to Nellie Bly the moment she touches American soil: M. and Mme. Jules Verne address their sincere felicitations to Miss Nellie Bly at the moment when that intrepid young lady sets foot on the soil of America."

The train was rather poorly appointed, and it was necessary for us to get off for our meals. When we stopped at Logansport for dinner, I being the last in the car, was the last to get off. When I reached the platform a young man, whom I never saw before or since, sprang upon the other platform, and waving his hat, shouted:

"Hurrah for Nellie Bly!"

The crowd clapped hands and cheered, and after making way for me to pass to the dining-room, pressed forward and cheered again, crowding to the windows at last to watch me eat. When I sat down, several dishes were put before me bearing the inscription, "Success, Nellie Bly."

It was after dark when we reached Columbus, where the depot was packed with men and women waiting for me. A delegation of railroad men waited upon me and presented me with beautiful flowers and candy, as did a number of private people. I did not go to bed until after we had passed Pittsburgh, and only got up in the morning in time to greet the thousands of good people who welcomed me at Harrisburg, where the Harrisburg Wheelman's Club sent a floral offering in remembrance of my being a wheelman. A number of Philadelphia newspaper men joined me there, and at Lancaster I received an enthusiastic reception.

Almost before I knew it I was at Philadelphia, and all too soon to please me, for my trip was so pleasant I dreaded the finish of it. A number of newspaper men and a few friends joined me at Philadelphia to escort me to New York. Speech-making was the order from Philadelphia on to Jersey City. I was told when we were almost home to jump to the platform the moment the train stopped at Jersey City, for that made my time around the world. The station was packed with thousands of people, and the moment I landed on the platform, one yell went up from them, and the cannons at the Battery and Fort Greene boomed out the news of my arrival. I took off my cap and wanted to yell with the crowd, not because I had gone around the world in seventy-two days, but because I was home again.

Chapter 18: The Record

I STARTED from Hoboken, on my trip, around the world, November 14, 1889. I finished it in Jersey, January 25, 1890. The itinerary of my trip, published the morning I started, and the itinerary as I found it, were as follows:

Nov. 14–Leave New York by Augusta Victoria, 9.30 a.m.	Nov. 14–Left New York via Augusta Victoria.

" 21–Due Southampton. London by rail in three hours.	
" 22–Leave Victoria Station, London, 8 p.m., on India Mail	" 22–2.30 a.m. Arrived Southhampton-London " 22–10.00 a.m. Left London, Charing Cross Station
" 23–Calais, Paris and Turin	" 23–1.30 a.m. Left Calais
" 24–Brindisi at 10.14 p.m.	
" 25–Leave Brindisi, steamship Cathay, 9 a.m.	" 25–1.30 a.m. Arrived Brindisi. 3.00 a.m. Left Brindisi, steamship Victoria
" 27–Ismallia.	" 27–3.30 p.m. Arrived Port Said.
	" 28–11.00 a.m. Arrived Ismallia, 9.00 p.m. Suez.
Dec. 3–Aden.	Dec. 3–11.00 Arrived Aden.
" 10–Colombo (Ceylon).	" 8–11.00 a.m. Arrived Colombo (Ceylon).
" 16–Penang.	" 16–7.00 a.m. Arrived Penang.
" 18–Singapore.	" 18–5.00 a.m. Arrived Singapore.

" 25–Hong Kong.	" 25–7.00 a.m. Arrived Hong Kong.
" 28–Leave Hong Kong for Yokohama, Japan.	" 28–2.30 p.m. Left Hong Kong for Yokohama.
Jan. 7–Leave Yokohama, via Pacific Mail Steamship.	Jan. 7–10.55 a.m. Left Yokohama via Occidental and Oriental Steamship.
" 22–Due San Francisco.	" 21–8.00 a.m. Arrived San Francisco
	" 23–7.05 a.m. Arrived Chicago.
" 27–Due New York.	" 25–3.51 p.m. Arrived New York.
Nov. 14 to Jan. 27-seventy-five days.	Nov. 14 to Jan. 25–Seventy-two days.

	Miles	Hours Traveling	Hours Delayed
Hoboken to Southampton	3,041	184 50	50
To London	90	2 15	14 25 *
" Brindisi	1,450	53 30	1 30
" Port Said	930	62 30	3 30

" Aden	1,394	110	6
" Colombo	2,093	138	98 05
" Penang	1,278	89 55	7
" Singapore	381	39	11
" Hong Kong	1,437	111	127 20
" Yokohama	1,597	131 40	104 55
" San Francisco	4,525	333 05	
" Chicago	2,573	71 05	2 55
" Jersey City	951	29 51	
	21,740	1356 41	377 30

Total time occupied in tour, 1,734 hours and 11 minutes, being 72 days, 6 hours and 11 minutes.

Average rate of speed per hour, exclusive of stops, 22.47 miles.

Average rate of speed, including stops, 28.71 miles per hour.

The names of the steamers and the different routes by which I traveled were the "Augusta Victoria" of the Hamburg American Steamship Line, the London and South Western Railway, the South Eastern Railway, the India Mail, the "Victoria" and the "Oriental" of the Peninsular and Oriental Steamship Line, the "Oceanic," of the Occidental and Oriental Steamship Line, the Southern Pacific Railway, the Atlantic and Pacific Railway, the Atchison, Topeka and Sante Fé Railway and the Pennsylvania Railway.

I spent 56 days 12 hours and 41 minutes in actual travel and lost by delay 15 days 17 hours and 30 minutes.

The second table shows the miles traveled, hours spent in traveling and hours delayed. The "hours delayed" marked by a star shows the time spent in diverging from my original line of travel to visit M. and Mme. Jules Verne at Amiens. I traveled 179-1/2 miles out of my way to visit the great novelist which is not considered in my number of miles traveled, nor do I count the miles traveled at the ports where I was detained, which taken together would not fall short of 1,500 miles.

Up to date, my trip is the fastest on record between San Francisco and Chicago. One run was 250 miles in 250 minutes, and that, counting the minutes lost stopping at a half dozen different towns. Another run was 59 miles in 50 minutes. Between Topeka and Kansas City we ran 13 miles in 11 minutes. Later we ran a mile in 53 seconds, and again 26 miles in 23 minutes. We made 2,566 miles in 69 hours, which is the fastest time, I am informed, that has been made for this distance. Although the Sante Fe route is over 500 miles longer than the Union Pacific, we beat the time of the fastest mail to Chicago by ten hours. If we had had the same distance to travel we would have beaten it twenty-four hours. The Santa Fé had only one day to prepare for my trip, and yet everything was perfect. They tell me when the Palmer-Jarrett "Across the Continent" trip was made they had been preparing for it for six months in advance, and when the start was made a flagman was posted at every switch and crossing between New York and San Francisco, and yet without any preparations my train traveled 500 miles farther and beat their time by 24 hours.

It is not possible to quote my fares and expenses as a criterion for prospective tourists, as I was traveling for a newspaper, and what it cost is their secret. Not counting the extra train, if first-class tickets had been bought from New York to New York it would only have cost $805. By using economy, outside expenses should not exceed $300.

On my tour I traversed the following waters: North River, New York Bay, Atlantic Ocean, English Channel, Adriatic Sea, Ionian Sea, Mediterranean Sea, Suez Canal, Gulf of Suez, Red Sea, Straits of Bab el Mandeb, Gulf of Aden, Arabian Sea, Indian Ocean, Straits of Malacca, China Sea, Pacific Ocean, San Francisco Bay.

I visited or passed through the following countries: England, France, Italy, Egypt, Japan, the United States, and the following British possessions: Aden, Arabia; Colombo, Isle of Ceylon; Penang, Prince of Wales Island; Singapore, Malay Peninsula; and the Island of Hong Kong.

L'envoi.

To so many people this wide world over am I indebted for kindnesses that I cannot, in a little book like this, thank them all individually. They form a chain around the earth. To each and all of you, men, women and children, in my land and in the lands I visited, I am most truly grateful. Every kind act and thought, if but an unuttered wish, a cheer, a tiny flower, is imbedded in my memory as one of the pleasant things of my novel tour.

From you and from all those who read the chronicle of my trip I beg indulgence. These pages have been written in the spare moments snatched from the exactions of a busy life.

Ten Days in a Mad-House

Introduction.

SINCE my experiences in Blackwell's Island Insane Asylum were published in the *World* I have received hundreds of letters in regard to it. The edition containing my story long since ran out, and I have been prevailed upon to allow it to be published in book form, to satisfy the hundreds who are yet asking for copies.

I am happy to be able to state as a result of my visit to the asylum and the exposures consequent thereon, that the City of New York has appropriated $1,000,000 more per annum than ever before for the care of the insane. So I have at least the satisfaction of knowing that the poor unfortunates will be the better cared for because of my work.

Nellie Bly

Chapter I: A Delicate Mission.

ON the 22d of September I was asked by the *World* if I could have myself committed to one of the asylums for the insane in New York, with a view to writing a plain and unvarnished narrative of the treatment of the patients therein and the methods of management, etc. Did I think I had the courage to go through such an ordeal as the mission would demand? Could I assume the characteristics of insanity to such a degree that I could pass the doctors, live for a week among the insane without the authorities there finding out that I was only a "chiel amang 'em takin' notes?" I said I believed I could. I had some faith in my own ability as an actress and thought I could assume insanity long enough to accomplish any mission intrusted to me. Could I pass a week in the insane ward at Blackwell's Island? I said I could and I would. And I did.

My instructions were simply to go on with my work as soon as I felt that I was ready. I was to chronicle faithfully the experiences I underwent, and when once within the walls of the asylum to find out and describe its inside workings, which are always, so effectually hidden by white-capped nurses, as well as by bolts and bars, from the knowledge of the public. "We do not ask you to go there for the purpose of making sensational revelations. Write up things as you find them, good or bad; give praise or blame as you think best, and the truth all the time. But I am afraid of that chronic smile of yours," said the editor. "I will smile no more," I said, and I went away to execute my delicate and, as I found out, difficult mission.

If I did get into the asylum, which I hardly hoped to do, I had no idea that my experiences would contain aught else than a simple tale of life in an asylum. That such an institution could be mismanaged, and that cruelties could exist 'neath its roof, I did not deem possible. I always had a desire to know asylum life more thoroughly-a desire to be convinced that the most helpless of God's creatures, the insane, were cared for kindly and properly. The many stories I had read of abuses in such institutions I had regarded as wildly exaggerated or else romances, yet there was a latent desire to know positively.

I shuddered to think how completely the insane were in the power of their keepers, and how one could weep and plead for release, and all of no avail, if the keepers were so minded. Eagerly I accepted the mission to learn the inside workings of the Blackwell Island Insane Asylum.

"How will you get me out," I asked my editor, "after I once get in?"

"I do not know," he replied, "but we will get you out if we have to tell who you are, and for what purpose you feigned insanity-only get in."

I had little belief in my ability to deceive the insanity experts, and I think my editor had less.

All the preliminary preparations for my ordeal were left to be planned by myself. Only one thing was decided upon, namely, that I should pass under the pseudonym of Nellie Brown, the initials of which would agree with my own name and my linen, so that there would be no difficulty in keeping track of my movements and assisting me out of any difficulties or dangers I might get into. There were ways of getting into the insane ward, but I did not know them. I might adopt one of two courses. Either I could feign insanity at the house of friends, and get myself committed on the decision of two competent physicians, or I could go to my goal by way of the police courts.

On reflection I thought it wiser not to inflict myself upon my friends or to get any good-natured doctors to assist me in my purpose. Besides, to get to Blackwell's Island my friends would have had to feign poverty, and, unfortunately for the end I had in view, my

acquaintance NELLIE PRACTICES INSANITY AT HOME. with the struggling poor, except my own self, was only very superficial. So I determined upon the plan which led me to the successful accomplishment of my mission. I succeeded in getting committed to the insane ward at Blackwell's Island, where I spent ten days and nights and had an experience which I shall never forget. I took upon myself to enact the part of a poor, unfortunate crazy girl, and felt it my duty not to shirk any of the disagreeable results that should follow. I became one of the city's insane wards for that length of time, experienced much, and saw and heard more of the treatment accorded to this helpless class of our population, and when I had seen and heard enough, my release was promptly secured. I left the insane ward with pleasure and regret-pleasure that I was once more able to enjoy the free breath of heaven; regret that I could not have brought with me some of the unfortunate women who lived and suffered with me, and who, I am convinced, are just as sane as I was and am now myself.

But here let me say one thing: From the moment I entered the insane ward on the Island, I made no attempt to keep up the assumed *role* of insanity. I talked and acted just as I do in ordinary life. Yet strange to say, the more sanely I talked and acted the crazier I was thought to be by all except one physician, whose kindness and gentle ways I shall not soon forget.

Chapter II: Preparing for the Ordeal.

BUT to return to my work and my mission. After receiving my instructions I returned to my boarding-house, and when evening came I began to practice the *role* in which I was to make my *debut* on the morrow. What a difficult task, I thought, to appear before a crowd of people and convince them that I was insane. I had never been near insane persons before in my life, and had not the faintest idea of what their actions were like. And then to be examined by a number of learned physicians who make insanity a specialty, and who daily come in contact with insane people! How could I hope to pass these doctors and convince them that I was crazy? I feared that they could not be deceived. I began to think my task a hopeless one; but it had to be done. So I flew to the mirror and examined my face. I remembered all I had read of the doings of crazy people, how first of all they have staring eyes, and so I opened mine as wide as possible and stared unblinkingly at my own reflection. I assure you the sight was not reassuring, even to myself, especially in the dead of night. I tried to turn the gas up higher in hopes that it would raise my courage. I succeeded only partially, but I consoled myself with the thought that in a few nights more I would not be there, but locked up in a cell with a lot of lunatics.

The weather was not cold; but, nevertheless, when I thought of what was to come, wintery chills ran races up and down my back in very mockery of the perspiration which was slowly but surely taking the curl out of my bangs. Between times, practicing before the mirror and picturing my future as a lunatic, I read snatches of improbable and impossible ghost stories, so that when the dawn came to chase away the night, I felt that I was in a fit mood for my mission, yet hungry enough to feel keenly that I wanted my breakfast. Slowly and sadly I took my morning bath and quietly bade farewell to a few of the most precious articles known to modern civilization. Tenderly I put my tooth-brush aside, and, when taking a final rub of the soap, I murmured, "It may be for days, and it may be-for longer." Then I donned the old clothing I had selected for the occasion. I was in the mood to look at everything through very serious glasses. It's just as well to take a last "fond look," I mused, for who could tell but that the strain of playing crazy, and being shut up with a crowd of mad people, might turn my own brain, and I would never get back. But not once did I think of shirking my mission. Calmly, outwardly at least, I went out to my crazy business.

I first thought it best to go to a boarding-house, and, after securing lodging, confidentially tell the landlady, or lord, whichever it might chance to be, that I was seeking work, and, in a few days after, apparently go insane. When I reconsidered the idea, I feared it would take too long to mature. Suddenly I thought how much easier it would be to go to a boarding-home for working women. I knew, if once I made a houseful of women believe me crazy, that they would never rest until I was out of their reach and in secure quarters.

From a directory I selected the Temporary Home for Females, No. 84 Second Avenue. As I walked down the avenue, I determined that, once inside the Home, I should do the best I could to get started on my journey to Blackwell's Island and the Insane Asylum.

Chapter III: In the Temporary Home.

I WAS left to begin my career as Nellie Brown, the insane girl. As I walked down the avenue I tried to assume the look which maidens wear in pictures entitled "Dreaming." "Far-away" expressions have a crazy air. I passed through the little paved yard to the entrance of the Home. I pulled the bell, which sounded loud enough for a church chime, and nervously awaited the opening of the door to the Home, which I intended should ere long cast me forth and out upon the charity of the police. The door was thrown back with a vengeance, and a short, yellow-haired girl of some thirteen summers stood before me.

"Is the matron in?" I asked, faintly.

"Yes, she's in; she's busy. Go to the back parlor," answered the girl, in a loud voice, without one change in her peculiarly matured face.

I followed these not overkind or polite instructions and found myself in a dark, uncomfortable back-parlor. There I awaited the arrival of my hostess. I had been

AT THE TEMPORARY HOME FOR WOMEN. seated some twenty minutes at the least, when a slender woman, clad in a plain, dark dress entered and, stopping before me, ejaculated inquiringly, "Well?"

"Are you the matron?" I asked.

"No," she replied, "the matron is sick; I am her assistant. What do you want?"

"I want to stay here for a few days, if you can accommodate me."

"Well, I have no single rooms, we are so crowded; but if you will occupy a room with another girl, I shall do that much for you."

"I shall be glad of that," I answered. "How much do you charge?" I had brought only about seventy cents along with me, knowing full well that the sooner my funds were exhausted the sooner I should be put out, and to be put out was what I was working for.

"We charge thirty cents a night," was her reply to my question, and with that I paid her for one night's lodging, and she left me on the plea of having something else to look after. Left to amuse myself as best I could, I took a survey of my surroundings.

They were not cheerful, to say the least. A wardrobe, desk, book-case, organ, and several chairs completed the furnishment of the room, into which the daylight barely came.

By the time I had become familiar with my quarters a bell, which rivaled the door-bell in its loudness, began clanging in the basement, and simultaneously women went trooping down-stairs from all parts of the house. I imagined, from the obvious signs, that dinner was served, but as no one had said anything to me I made no effort to follow in the hungry train. Yet I did wish that some one would invite me down. It always produces such a lonely, homesick feeling to know others are eating, and we haven't a chance, even if we are not hungry. I was glad when the assistant matron came up and asked me if I did not want something to eat. I replied that I did, and then I asked her what her name was. Mrs. Stanard, she said, and I immediately wrote it down in a notebook I had taken with me for the purpose of making memoranda, and in which I had written several pages of utter nonsense for inquisitive scientists.

Thus equipped I awaited developments. But my dinner-well, I followed Mrs. Stanard down the uncarpeted stairs into the basement; where a large number of women were eating. She found room for me at a table with three other women. The short-haired slavey who had opened the door now put in an appearance as waiter. Placing her arms akimbo and staring me out of countenance she said:

"Boiled mutton, boiled beef, beans, potatoes, coffee or tea?"

"Beef, potatoes, coffee and bread," I responded.

"Bread goes in," she explained, as she made her way to the kitchen, which was in the rear. It was not very long before she returned with what I had ordered on a large, badly battered tray, which she banged down before me. I began my simple meal. It was not very enticing, so while making a feint of eating I watched the others.

I have often moralized on the repulsive form charity always assumes! Here was a home for deserving women and yet what a mockery the name was. The floor was bare, and the little wooden tables were sublimely ignorant of such modern beautifiers as varnish, polish and table-covers. It is useless to talk about the cheapness of linen and its effect on civilization. Yet these honest workers, the most deserving of women, are asked to call this spot of bareness-home.

When the meal was finished each woman went to the desk in the corner, where Mrs. Stanard sat, and paid her bill. I was given a much-used, and abused, red check, by the original piece of humanity in shape of my waitress. My bill was about thirty cents.

After dinner I went up-stairs and resumed my former place in the back parlor. I was quite cold and uncomfortable, and had fully made up my mind that I could not endure that sort of business long, so the sooner I assumed my insane points the sooner I would be released from enforced idleness. Ah! that was indeed the longest day I had ever lived. I listlessly watched the women in the front parlor, where all sat except myself.

One did nothing but read and scratch her head and occasionally call out mildly, "Georgie," without lifting her eyes from her book. "Georgie" was her over-frisky boy, who had more noise in him than any child I ever saw before. He did everything that was rude and unmannerly, I thought, and the mother never said a word unless she heard some one else yell at him. Another woman always kept going to sleep and waking herself up with her own snoring. I really felt wickedly thankful it was only herself she awakened. The majority of the women sat there doing nothing, but there were a few who made lace and knitted unceasingly. The enormous door-bell seemed to be going all the time, and so did the short-haired girl. The latter was, besides, one of those girls who sing all the time snatches of all the songs and hymns that have been composed for the last fifty years. There is such a thing as martyrdom in these days. The ringing of the bell brought more people who wanted shelter for the night. Excepting one woman, who was from the country on a day's shopping expedition, they were working women, some of them with children.

As it drew toward evening Mrs. Stanard came to me and said:

"What is wrong with you? Have you some sorrow or trouble?"

"No," I said, almost stunned at the suggestion. "Why?"

"Oh, because," she said, womanlike, "I can see it in your face. It tells the story of a great trouble."

"Yes, everything is so sad," I said, in a haphazard way, which I had intended to reflect my craziness.

"But you must not allow that to worry you. We all have our troubles, but we get over them in good time. What kind of work are you trying to get?"

"I do not know; it's all so sad," I replied.

"Would you like to be a nurse for children and wear a nice white cap and apron?" she asked.

I put my handkerchief up to my face to hide a smile, and replied in a muffled tone, "I never worked; I don't know how."

"But you must learn," she urged; "all these women here work."

"Do they?" I said, in a low, thrilling whisper. "Why, they look horrible to me; just like crazy women. I am so afraid of them."

"They don't look very nice," she answered, assentingly, "but they are good, honest working women. We do not keep crazy people here."

I again used my handkerchief to hide a smile, as I thought that before morning she would at least think she had one crazy person among her flock.

"They all look crazy," I asserted again, "and I am afraid of them. There are so many crazy people about, and one can never tell what they will do. Then there are so many murders committed, and the police never catch the murderers," and I finished with a sob that would have broken up an audience of *blase* critics. She gave a sudden and convulsive start, and I knew my first stroke had gone home. It was amusing to see what a remarkably short time it took her to get up from her chair and to whisper hurriedly: "I'll come back to talk with you after a while." I knew she would not come back and she did not.

When the supper-bell rang I went along with the others to the basement and partook of the evening meal, which was similar to dinner, except that there was a spaner bill of fare and more people, the women who are employed outside during the day having returned. After the evening meal we all adjourned to the parlors, where all sat, or stood, as there were not chairs enough to go round.

It was a wretchedly lonely evening, and the light which fell from the solitary gas jet in the parlor, and oil-lamp the hall, helped to envelop us in a dusky hue and dye our spirits navy blue. I felt it would not require many inundations of this atmosphere to make me a fit subject for the place I was striving to reach.

I watched two women, who seemed of all the crowd to be the most sociable, and I selected them as the ones to work out my salvation, or, more properly speaking, my condemnation and conviction. Excusing myself and saying that I felt lonely, I asked if I might join their company. They graciously consented, so with my hat and gloves on, which no one had asked me to lay aside, I sat down and listened to the rather wearisome conversation, in which I took no part, merely keeping up my sad look, saying "Yes," or "No," or "I can't say," to their observations. Several times I told them I thought everybody in the house looked crazy, but they were slow to catch on to my very original remark. One said her name was Mrs. King and that she was a Southern woman. Then she said that I had a Southern accent. She asked me bluntly if I did not really come from the South. I said "Yes." The other woman got to talking about the Boston boats and asked me if I knew at what time they left.

For a moment I forgot my *role* of assumed insanity, and told her the correct hour of departure. She then asked me what work I was going to do, or if I had ever done any. I replied that I thought it very sad that there were so many working people in the world. She said in reply that she had been unfortunate and had come to New York, where she had worked at correcting proofs on a medical dictionary for some time, but that her health had given way under the task, and that she was now going to Boston again. When the maid came to tell us to go to bed I remarked that I was afraid, and again ventured the assertion that all the women in the house seemed to be crazy. The nurse insisted on my going to bed. I asked if I could not sit on the stairs, but she said, decisively: "No; for every one in the house would think you were crazy." Finally I allowed them to take me to a room.

Here I must introduce a new personage by name into my narrative. It is the woman who had been a proofreader, and was about to return to Boston. She was a Mrs. Caine, who was as courageous as she was good-hearted. She came into my room, and sat and talked with me a long time, taking down my hair with gentle ways. She tried to persuade me to undress and go to bed, but I stubbornly refused to do so. During this time a number of the inmates of the house had gathered around us. They expressed themselves in various ways. "Poor loon!" they said. "Why, she's crazy enough!" "I am afraid to stay with such a crazy being in house." "She will murder us all before morning." One woman was for sending for a policeman to take me at once. They were all in a terrible and real state of fright.

No one wanted to be responsible for me, and the woman who was to occupy the room with me declared that she would not stay with that "crazy woman" for all the money of the Vanderbilts. It was then that Mrs. Caine said she would stay with me. I told her I would like to have her do so. So she was left with me. She didn't undress, but lay down on the bed, watchful of my movements. She tried to induce me to lie down, but I was afraid to do this. I knew that if I once gave way I should fall asleep and dream as pleasantly and peacefully as a child. I should, to use a slang expression, be liable to "give myself dead away." So I insisted on sitting on the side of the bed and staring blankly at vacancy. My poor companion was put into a wretched state of unhappiness. Every few moments she would rise up to look at me. She told me that my eyes shone terribly brightly and then began to question me, asking me where I had had been in New York, what I had been doing, and many things besides. To a I had but one response–I told her that I had forgotten everything, that ever since my headache had come on I could not remember.

Poor soul! How cruelly I tortured her, and what a kind heart she had! But how I tortured all of them! One of them dreamed of me–as a nightmare. After I had been in the room an hour or so, I was myself startled by hearing a woman screaming in the next room. I began to imagine that I was really in an insane asylum.

Mrs. Caine woke up, looked around, frightened, and listened. She then went out and into the next room, and I heard her asking another woman some questions. When she came back she told me that the woman had had a hideous nightmare. She had been dreaming of me. She had seen me, she said, rushing at her with a knife in my hand, with the intention of killing her. In trying to escape me she had fortunately been able to scream, and so to awaken herself and scare off her nightmare. Then Mrs. Caine got into bed again, considerably agitated, but very sleepy.

I was weary, too, but I had braced myself up to the work, and was determined to keep awake all night so as to carry on my work of impersonation to a successful end in the morning. I heard midnight. I had yet six hours to wait for daylight. The time passed with excruciating slowness. Minutes appeared hours. The noises in the house and on the avenue ceased.

Fearing that sleep would coax me into its grasp, I commenced to review my life. How strange it all seems! One incident, if never so trifling, is but a link more to chain us to our unchangeable fate. I began at the beginning, and lived again the story of my life. Old friends were recalled with a pleasurable thrill; old enmities, old heartaches, old joys were once again present. The turned-down pages of my life were turned up, and the past was present.

When it was completed, I turned my thoughts bravely to the future, wondering, first, what the next day would bring forth, then making plans for the carrying out of my project. I wondered if I should be able to pass over the river to the goal of my strange ambition, to become eventually an inmate of the halls inhabited by my mentally wrecked sisters. And then, once in, what would be my experience? And after? How to get out? Bah! I said, they will get me out.

That was the greatest night of my existence. For a few hours I stood face to face with "self!"

I looked out toward the window and hailed with joy the slight shimmer of dawn. The light grew strong and gray, but the silence was strikingly still. My companion slept. I had still an hour or two to pass over. Fortunately I found some employment for my mental activity. Robert Bruce in his captivity had won confidence in the future, and passed his time as pleasantly as possible under the circumstances, by watching the celebrated spider building his web. I had less noble vermin to interest me. Yet I believe I made some valuable discoveries in natural history. I was about to drop off to sleep in spite of myself when I was suddenly startled to wakefulness. I thought I heard something crawl and fall down upon the counterpane with an almost inaudible thud.

I had the opportunity of studying these interesting animals very thoroughly. They had evidently come for breakfast, and were not a little disappointed to find that their principal *plat* was not there. They scampered up and down the pillow, came together, seemed to hold interesting converse, and acted in every way as if they were puzzled by the absence of an appetizing breakfast. After one consultation of some length they finally disappeared, seeking victims elsewhere, and leaving me to pass the long minutes by giving my attention to cockroaches, whose size and agility were something of a surprise to me.

My room companion had been sound asleep for a long time, but she now woke up, and expressed surprise at seeing me still awake and apparently as lively as a cricket. She was as sympathetic as ever. She came to me and took my hands and tried her best to console me, and asked me if I did not want to go home. She kept me up-stairs until nearly everybody was out of the house, and then took me down to the basement for coffee and a bun. After that, partaken in silence, I went back to my room, where I sat down, moping. Mrs. Caine grew more and more anxious. "What is to be done?" she kept exclaiming. "Where are your friends?" "No," I answered, "I have no friends, but I have some trunks. Where are they? I want them." The good woman tried to pacify me, saying that they would be found in good time. She believed that I was insane.

Yet I forgive her. It is only after one is in trouble that one realizes how little sympathy and kindness there are in the world. The women in the Home who were not afraid of me had wanted to have some amusement at my expense, and so they had bothered me with questions and remarks that had I been insane would have been cruel and inhumane. Only this one woman among the crowd, pretty and delicate Mrs. Caine, displayed true womanly feeling. She compelled the others to cease teasing me and took the bed of the woman who refused to sleep near me. She protested against the suggestion to leave me alone and to have me locked up for the night so that I could harm no one. She insisted on remaining with me in order to administer aid should I need it. She smoothed my hair and bathed my brow and talked as soothingly to me as a mother would do to an ailing child. By every means she tried to have me go to bed and rest, and when it drew toward morning she got up and wrapped a blanket around me for fear I might get cold; then she kissed me on the brow and whispered, compassionately:

"Poor child, poor child!"

How much I admired that little woman's courage and kindness. How I longed to reassure her and whisper that I was not insane, and how I hoped that, if any poor girl should ever be so unfortunate as to be what I was pretending to be, she might meet with one who possessed the same spirit of human kindness possessed by Mrs. Ruth Caine.

Chapter IV: Judge Duffy and the Police.

BUT to return to my story. I kept up my *role* until the assistant matron, Mrs. Stanard, came in. She tried to persuade me to be calm. I began to see clearly that she wanted to get me out of the house at all hazards, quietly if possible. This I did not want. I refused to move, but kept up ever the refrain of my lost trunks. Finally some one suggested that an officer be sent for. After awhile Mrs. Stanard put on her bonnet and went out. Then I knew that I was making an advance toward the home of the insane. Soon she returned, bringing with her two policemen-big, strong men-who entered the room rather unceremoniously, evidently expecting to meet with a person violently crazy. The name of one of them was Tom Bockert.

When they entered I pretended not to see them. "I want you to take her quietly," said Mrs. Stanard. "If she don't come along quietly," responded one of the men, "I will drag her through the streets." I still took no notice of them, but certainly wished to avoid raising a scandal outside. Fortunately Mrs. Caine came to my rescue. She told the officers about my outcries for my lost trunks, and together they made up a plan to get me to go along with them quietly by telling me they would go with me to look for my lost effects. They asked me if I would go. I said I was afraid to go alone. Mrs. Stanard then said she would accompany me, and she arranged that the two policemen should follow us at a respectful distance. She tied on my veil for me, and we left the house by the basement and started across town, the two officers following at some distance behind. We walked along very quietly and finally came to the station house, which the good woman assured me was the express office, and that there we should certainly find my missing effects. I went inside with fear and trembling, for good reason.

A few days previous to this I had met Captain McCullagh at a meeting held in Cooper Union. At that time I had asked him for some information which he had given me. If he were in, would he not recognize me? And then all would be lost so far as getting to the island was concerned. I pulled my sailor hat as low down over my face as I possibly could, and prepared for the ordeal. Sure enough there was sturdy Captain McCullagh standing near the desk.

He watched me closely as the officer at the desk conversed in a low tone with Mrs. Stanard and the policeman who brought me.

"Are you Nellie Brown?" asked the officer. I said I supposed I was. "Where do you come from?" he asked. I told him I did not know, and then Mrs. Stanard gave him a lot of information about me-told him how strangely I had acted at her home; how I had not slept a wink all night, and that in her opinion I was a poor unfortunate who had been driven crazy by inhuman treatment. There was some discussion between Mrs. Standard and the two officers, and Tom Bockert was told to take us down to the court in a car.

"Come along," Bockert said, "I will find your trunk for you." We all went together, Mrs.

IN THE HANDS OF THE POLICE.

Stanard, Tom Bockert, and myself. I said it was very kind of them to go with me, and I should not soon forget them. As we walked along I kept up my refrain about my trucks, injecting occasionally some remark about the dirty condition of the streets and the curious character of the people we met on the way. "I don't think I have ever seen such people before," I said. "Who are they?" I asked, and my companions looked upon me with expressions of pity, evidently believing I was a foreigner, an emigrant or something of the sort. They told me that the people around me were working people. I remarked once more that I thought there were too many working people in the world for the amount of work to be done, at which remark Policeman P. T. Bockert eyed me closely, evidently thinking that my mind was gone for good. We passed several other policemen, who generally asked my sturdy guardians what was the matter with me. By this time quite a number of ragged children were following us too, and they passed remarks about me that were to me original as well as amusing.

"What's she up for?" "Say, kop, where did ye get her?" "Where did yer pull 'er?" "She's a daisy!"

Poor Mrs. Stanard was more frightened than I was. The whole situation grew interesting, but I still had fears for my fate before the judge.

At last we came to a low building, and Tom Bockert kindly volunteered the information: "Here's the express office. We shall soon find those trunks of yours."

The entrance to the building was surrounded by a curious crowd and I did not think my case was bad enough to permit me passing them without some remark, so I asked if all those people had lost their trunks.

"Yes," he said, "nearly all these people are looking for trunks."

I said, "They all seem to be foreigners, too." "Yes," said Tom, "they are all foreigners just landed. They have all lost their trunks, and it takes most of our time to help find them for them."

We entered the courtroom. It was the Essex Market Police Courtroom. At last the question of my sanity or insanity was to be decided. Judge Duffy sat behind the high desk, wearing a look which seemed to indicate that he was dealing out the milk of human kindness by wholesale. I rather feared I would not get the fate I sought, because of the kindness I saw on every line of his face, and it was with rather a sinking heart that I followed Mrs. Stanard as she answered the summons to go up to the desk, where Tom Bockert had just given an account of the affair.

"Come here," said an officer. "What is your name?"

"Nellie Brown," I replied, with a little accent. "I have lost my trunks, and would like if you could find them."

"When did you come to New York?" he asked.

"I did not come to New York," I replied (while I added, mentally, "because I have been here for some time.")

"But you are in New York now," said the man.

"No," I said, looking as incredulous as I thought a crazy person could, "I did not come to New York."

"That girl is from the west," he said, in a tone that made me tremble. "She has a western accent."

Some one else who had been listening to the brief dialogue here asserted that he had lived south and that my accent was southern, while another officer was positive it was eastern. I felt much relieved when the first spokesman turned to the judge and said:

"Judge, here is a peculiar case of a young woman who doesn't know who she is or where she came from. You had better attend to it at once."

I commenced to shake with more than the cold, and I looked around at the strange crowd about me, composed of poorly dressed men and women with stories printed on their faces of hard lives, abuse and poverty. Some were consulting eagerly with friends, while others sat still with a look of utter hopelessness. Everywhere was a sprinkling of well-dressed, well-fed officers watching the scene passively and almost indifferently. It was only an old story with

NELLIE BEFORE JUDGE DUFFY.

them. One more unfortunate added to a long list which had long since ceased to be of any interest or concern to them.

"Come here, girl, and lift your veil," called out Judge Duffy, in tones which surprised me by a harshness which I did not think from the kindly face he possessed.

"Who are you speaking to?" I inquired, in my stateliest manner.

"Come here, my dear, and lift your veil. You know the Queen of England, if she were here, would have to lift her veil," he said, very kindly.

"That is much better," I replied. "I am not the Queen of England, but I'll lift my veil."

As I did so the little judge looked at me, and then, in a very kind and gentle tone, he said:

"My dear child, what is wrong?"

"Nothing is wrong except that I have lost my trunks, and this man," indicating Policeman Bockert, "promised to bring me where they could be found."

"What do you know about this child?" asked the judge, sternly, of Mrs. Stanard, who stood, pale and trembling, by my side.

"I know nothing of her except that she came to the home yesterday and asked to remain overnight."

"The home! What do you mean by the home?" asked Judge Duffy, quickly.

"It is a temporary home kept for working women at No. 84 Second Avenue."

"What is your position there?"

"I am assistant matron."

"Well, tell us all you know of the case."

"When I was going into the home yesterday I noticed her coming down the avenue. She was all alone. I had just got into the house when the bell rang and she came in. When I talked with her she wanted to know if she could stay all night, and I said she could. After awhile she said all the people in the house looked crazy, and she was afraid of them. Then she would not go to bed, but sat up all the night."

"Had she any money?"

"Yes," I replied, answering for her, "I paid her for everything, and the eating was the worst I ever tried."

There was a general smile at this, and some murmurs of "She's not so crazy on the food question."

"Poor child," said Judge Duffy, "she is well dressed, and a lady. Her English is perfect, and I would stake everything on her being a good girl. I am positive she is somebody's darling."

At this announcement everybody laughed, and I put my handkerchief over my face and endeavored to choke the laughter that threatened to spoil my plans, in despite of my resolutions.

"I mean she is some woman's darling," hastily amended the judge. "I am sure some one is searching for her. Poor girl, I will be good to her, for she looks like my sister, who is dead."

There was a hush for a moment after this announcement, and the officers glanced at me more kindly, while I silently blessed the kind-hearted judge, and hoped that any poor creatures who might be afflicted as I pretended to be should have as kindly a man to deal with as Judge Duffy.

"I wish the reporters were here," he said at last. "They would be able to find out something about her."

I got very much frightened at this, for if there is any one who can ferret out a mystery it is a reporter. I felt that I would rather face a mass of expert doctors, policemen, and detectives than two bright specimens of my craft, so I said:

"I don't see why all this is needed to help me find my trunks. These men are impudent, and I do not want to be stared at. I will go away. I don't want to stay here."

So saying, I pulled down my veil and secretly hoped the reporters would be detained elsewhere until I was sent to the asylum.

"I don't know what to do with the poor child," said the worried judge. "She must be taken care of."

"Send her to the Island," suggested one of the officers.

"Oh, don't!" said Mrs. Stanard, in evident alarm. "Don't! She is a lady and it would kill her to be put on the Island."

For once I felt like shaking the good woman. To think the Island was just the place I wanted to reach and here she was trying to keep me from going there! It was very kind of her, but rather provoking under the circumstances.

"There has been some foul work here," said the judge. "I believe this child has been drugged and brought to this city. Make out the papers and we will send her to Bellevue for examination. Probably in a few days the effect of the drug will pass off and she will be able to tell us a story that will be startling. If the reporters would only come!"

I dreaded them, so I said something about not wishing to stay there any longer to be gazed at. Judge Duffy then told Policeman Bockert to take me to the back office. After we were seated there Judge Duffy came in and asked me if my home was in Cuba.

"Yes," I replied, with a smile. "How did you know?"

"Oh, I knew it, my dear. Now, tell me were was it? In what part of Cuba?"

"On the hacienda," I replied.

"Ah," said the judge, "on a farm. Do you remember Havana?"

"Si, senor," I answered; "it is near home. How did you know?"

"Oh, I knew all about it. Now, won't you tell me the name of your home?" he asked, persuasively.

"That's what I forget," I answered, sadly. "I have a headache all the time, and it makes me forget things. I don't want them to trouble me. Everybody is asking me questions, and it makes my head worse," and in truth it did.

"Well, no one shall trouble you any more. Sit down here and rest awhile," and the genial judge left me alone with Mrs. Stanard.

Just then an officer came in with a reporter. I was so frightened, and thought I would be recognized as a journalist, so I turned my head away and said, "I don't want to see any reporters; I will not see any; the judge said I was not to be troubled."

"Well, there is no insanity in that," said the man who had brought the reporter, and together they left the room. Once again I had a fit of fear. Had I gone too far in not wanting to see a reporter, and was my sanity detected? If I had given the impression that I was sane, I was determined to undo it, so I jumped up and ran back and forward through the office, Mrs. Stanard clinging terrified to my arm.

"I won't stay here; I want my trunks! Why do they bother me with so many people?" and thus I kept on until the ambulance surgeon came in, accompanied by the judge.

Chapter V: Pronounced Insane.

"HERE is a poor girl who has been drugged," explained the judge. "She looks like my sister, and any one can see she is a good girl. I am interested in the child, and I would do as much for her as if she were my own. I want you to be kind to her," he said to the ambulance surgeon. Then, turning to Mrs. Stanard, he asked her if she could not keep me for a few days until my case was inquired into. Fortunately, she said she could not, because all the women at the Home were afraid of me, and would leave if I were kept there. I was very much afraid she would keep me if the pay was assured her, and so I said something about the bad cooking and that I did not intend to go back to the Home. Then came the examination; the doctor looked clever and I had not one hope of deceiving him, but I determined to keep up the farce.

"Put out your tongue," he ordered, briskly.

I gave an inward chuckle at the thought.

"Put out your tongue when I tell you," he said.

"I don't want to," I answered, truthfully enough.

"You must. You are sick, and I am a doctor."

"I am not sick and never was. I only want my trunks."

But I put out my tongue, which he looked at in a sagacious manner. Then he felt my pulse and listened to the beating of my heart. I had not the least idea how the heart of an insane person

beat, so I held my breath all the while he   AN INSANITY EXPERT AT WORK.   listened, until, when he quit, I had to give a gasp to regain it. Then he tried the effect of the light on the pupils of my eyes. Holding his hand within a half inch of my face, he told me to look at it, then, jerking it hastily away, he would examine my eyes. I was puzzled to know what insanity was like in the eye, so I thought the best thing under the circumstances was to stare. This I did. I held my eyes riveted unblinkingly upon his hand, and when he removed it I exerted all my strength to still keep my eyes from blinking.

"What drugs have you been taking?" he then asked me.

"Drugs!" I repeated, wonderingly. "I do not know what drugs are."

"The pupils of her eyes have been enlarged ever since she came to the Home. They have not changed once," explained Mrs. Stanard. I wondered how she knew whether they had or not, but I kept quiet.

"I believe she has been using belladonna," said the doctor, and for the first time I was thankful that I was a little near-sighted, which of course answers for the enlargement of the pupils. I thought I might as well be truthful when I could without injuring my case, so I told him

I was near-sighted, that I was not in the least ill, had never been sick, and that no one had a right to detain me when I wanted to find my trunks. I wanted to go home. He wrote a lot of things in a long, slender book, and then said he was going to take me home. The judge told him to take me and to be kind to me, and to tell the people at the hospital to be kind to me, and to do all they could for me. If we only had more such men as Judge Duffy, the poor unfortunates would not find life all darkness.

I began to have more confidence in my own ability now, since one judge, one doctor, and a mass of people had pronounced me insane, and I put on my veil quite gladly when I was told that I was to be taken in a carriage, and that afterward I could go home. "I am so glad to go with you," I said, and I meant it. I was very glad indeed. Once more, guarded by Policeman Brockert, I walked through the little, crowded courtroom. I felt quite proud of myself as I went out a side door into an alleyway, where the ambulance was waiting. Near the closed and barred gates was a span office occupied by several men and large books. We all went in there, and when they began to ask me questions the doctor interposed and said he had all the papers, and that it was useless to ask me anything further, because I was unable to answer questions. This was a great relief to me, for my nerves were already feeling the strain. A rough-looking man wanted to put me into the ambulance, but I refused his aid so decidedly that the doctor and policeman told him to desist, and they performed that gallant office themselves. I did not enter the ambulance without protest. I made the remark that I had never seen a carriage of that make before, and that I did not want to ride in it, but after awhile I let them persuade me, as I had right along intended to do.

I shall never forget that ride. After I was put in flat on the yellow blanket, the doctor got in and sat near the door. The large gates were swung open, and the curious crowd which had collected swayed back to make way for the ambulance as it backed out. How they tried to get a glimpse at the supposed crazy girl! The doctor saw that I did not like the people gazing at me, and considerately put down the curtains, after asking my wishes in regard to it. Still that did not keep the people away. The children raced after us, yelling all sorts of slang expressions, and trying to get a peep under the curtains. It was quite an interesting drive, but I must say that it was an excruciatingly rough one. I held on, only there was not much to hold on to, and the driver drove as if he feared some one would catch up with us.

Chapter VI: In Bellevue Hospital.

AT last Bellevue was reached, the third station on my way to the island. I had passed through successfully the ordeals at the home and at Essex Market Police Court, and now felt confident that I should not fail. The ambulance stopped with a sudden jerk and the doctor jumped out. "How many have you?" I heard some one inquire. "Only one, for the pavilion," was the reply. A rough-looking man came forward, and catching hold of me attempted to drag me out as if I had the strength of an elephant and would resist. The doctor, seeing my look of disgust, ordered him to leave me alone, saying that he would take charge of me himself. He then lifted me carefully out and I walked with the grace of a queen past the crowd that had gathered curious to see the new unfortunate. Together with the doctor I entered a span dark office, where there were several men. The one behind the desk opened a book and began on the long string of questions which had been asked me so often.

I refused to answer, and the doctor told him it was not necessary to trouble me further, as he had all the papers made out, and I was too insane to be able to tell anything that would be of consequence. I felt relieved that it was so easy here, as, though still undaunted, I had begun to feel faint for want of food. The order was then given to take me to the insane pavilion, and a muscular man came forward and caught me so tightly by the arm that a pain ran clear through me. It made me angry, and for a moment I forgot my *role* as I turned to him and said:

"How dare you touch me?" At this he loosened his hold somewhat, and I shook him off with more strength than I thought I possessed.

"I will go with no one but this man," I said, pointing to the ambulance-surgeon. "The judge said that he was to take care of me, and I will go with no one else."

At this the surgeon said that he would take me, and so we went arm in arm, following the man who had at first been so rough with me. We passed through the well-cared-for grounds and finally reached the insane ward. A white-capped nurse was there to receive me.

"This young girl is to wait here for the boat," said the surgeon, and then he started to leave me. I begged him not to go, or to take me with him, but he said he wanted to get his dinner first, and that I should wait there for him. When I insisted on accompanying him he claimed that he had to assist at an amputation, and it would not look well for me to be present. It was evident that he believed he was dealing with an insane person. Just then the most horrible insane cries came from a yard in the rear. With all my bravery I felt a chill at the prospect of being shut up with a fellow-creature who was really insane. The doctor evidently noticed my nervousness, for he said to the attendant;

"What a noise the carpenters make."

Turning to me he offered me explanation to the effect that new buildings were being erected, and that the noise came from some of the workmen engaged upon it. I told him I did not want to stay there without him, and to pacify me he promised soon to return. He left me and I found myself at last an occupant of an insane asylum.

I stood at the door and contemplated the scene before me. The long, uncarpeted hall was scrubbed to that peculiar whiteness seen only in public institutions. In the rear of the hall were large iron doors fastened by a padlock. Several still-looking benches and a number of willow chairs were the only articles of furniture. On either side of the hall were doors leading into what I supposed and what proved to be bedrooms. Near the entrance door, on the right-hand side, was a span sitting-room for the nurses, and opposite it was a room where dinner was dished out. A nurse in a black dress, white cap and apron and armed with a bunch of keys had charge of the hall. I soon learned her name, Miss Ball.

An old Irishwoman was maid-of-all-work. I heard her called Mary, and I am glad to know that there is such a good-hearted woman in that place. I experienced only kindness and the utmost consideration from her. There were only three patients, as they are called. I made the fourth. I thought I might as well begin work at once, for I still expected that the very first doctor might declare me sane and send me out again into the wide, wide world. So I went down to the rear of the room and introduced myself to one of the women, and asked her all about herself. Her name, she said, was Miss Anne Neville, and she had been sick from overwork. She had been working as a chambermaid, and when her health gave way she was sent to some Sisters' Home to be treated. Her nephew, who was a waiter, was out of work, and, being unable to pay her expenses at the Home, had had her transferred to Bellevue.

"Is there anything wrong with you mentally as well?" I asked her.

"No," she said. "The doctors have been asking me many curious questions and confusing me as much as possible, but I have nothing wrong with my brain."

"Do you know that only insane people are sent to this pavilion?" I asked.

"Yes, I know; but I am unable to do anything. The doctors refuse to listen to me, and it is useless to say anything to the nurses."

Satisfied from various reasons that Miss Neville was as sane as I was myself, I transferred my attentions to one of the other patients. I found her in need of medical aid and quite silly mentally, although I have seen many women in the lower walks of life, whose sanity was never questioned, who were not any brighter.

The third patient, Mrs. Fox, would not say much. She was very quiet, and after telling me that her case was hopeless refused to talk. I began now to feel surer of my position, and I determined that no doctor should convince me that I was sane so long as I had the hope of accomplishing my mission. A span, fair-complexioned nurse arrived, and, after putting on her cap, told Miss Ball to go to dinner. The new nurse, Miss Scott by name, came to me and said, rudely:

"Take off your hat."

"I shall not take off my hat," I answered. "I am waiting for the boat, and I shall not remove it."

"Well, you are not going on any boat. You might as well know it now as later. You are in an asylum for the insane."

Although fully aware of that fact, her unvarnished words gave me a shock. "I did not want to come here; I am not sick or insane, and I will not stay," I said.

"It will be a long time before you get out if you don't do as you are told," answered Miss Scott. "You might as well take off your hat, or I shall use force, and if I am not able to do it, I have but to touch a bell and I shall get assistance. Will you take it off?"

"No, I will not. I am cold, and I want my hat on, and you can't make me take it off."

"I shall give you a few more minutes, and if you don't take it off then I shall use force, and I warn you it will not be very gentle."

"If you take my hat off I shall take your cap off; so now."

Miss Scott was called to the door then, and as I feared that an exhibition of temper might show too much sanity I took off my hat and gloves and was sitting quietly looking into space when she returned. I was hungry, and was quite pleased to see Mary make preparations for dinner. The preparations were simple. She merely pulled a straight bench up along the side of a bare table and ordered the patients to gather 'round the feast; then she brought out a span tin plate on which was a piece of boiled meat and a potato. It could not have been colder had it been cooked the week before, and it had no chance to make acquaintance with salt or pepper. I would not go up to the table, so Mary came to where I sat in a corner, and while handing out the tin plate, asked:

"Have ye any pennies about ye, dearie?"

"What?" I said, in my surprise.

"Have ye any pennies, dearie, that ye could give me. They'll take them all from ye any way, dearie, so I might as well have them."

I understood it fully now, but I had no intention of feeing Mary so early in the game, fearing it would have an influence on her treatment of me, so I said I had lost my purse, which was quite true. But though I did not give Mary any money, she was none the less kind to me. When I objected to the tin plate in which she had brought my food she fetched a china one for me, and when I found it impossible to eat the food she presented she gave me a glass of milk and a soda cracker.

All the windows in the hall were open and the cold air began to tell on my Southern blood. It grew so cold indeed as to be almost unbearable, and I complained of it to Miss Scott and Miss Ball. But they answered curtly that as I was in a charity place I could not expect much else. All the other women were suffering from the cold, and the nurses themselves had to wear heavy garments to keep themselves warm. I asked if I could go to bed. They said "No!" At last Miss Scott got an old gray shawl, and shaking some of the moths out of it, told me to put it on.

"It's rather a bad-looking shawl," I said.

"Well, some people would get along better if they were not so proud," said Miss Scott. "People on charity should not expect anything and should not complain."

So I put the moth-eaten shawl, with all its musty smell, around me, and sat down on a wicker chair, wondering what would come next, whether I should freeze to death or survive. My nose was very cold, so I covered up my head and was in a half doze, when the shawl was suddenly jerked from my face and a strange man and Miss Scott stood before me. The man proved to be a doctor, and his first greetings were:

"I've seen that face before."

"Then you know me?" I asked, with a great show of eagerness that I did not feel.

"I think I do. Where did you come from?"

"From home."

"Where is home?"

"Don't you know? Cuba."

POSITIVELY DEMENTED.

He then sat down beside me, felt my pulse, and examined my tongue, and at last said:

"Tell Miss Scott all about yourself."

"No, I will not. I will not talk with women."

"What do you do in New York?"

"Nothing."

"Can you work?"

"No, senor."

"Tell me, are you a woman of the town?"

"I do not understand you," I replied, heartily disgusted with him.

"I mean have you allowed the men to provide for you and keep you?"

I felt like slapping him in the face, but I had to maintain my composure, so I simply said:

"I do not know what you are talking about. I always lived at home."

After many more questions, fully as useless and senseless, he left me and began to talk with the nurse. "Positively demented," he said. "I consider it a hopeless case. She needs to be put where some one will take care of her."

And so I passed my second medical expert.

After this, I began to have a spaner regard for the ability of doctors than I ever had before, and a greater one for myself. I felt sure now that no doctor could tell whether people were insane or not, so long as the case was not violent.

Later in the afternoon a boy and a woman came. The woman sat down on a bench, while the boy went in and talked with Miss Scott. In a short time he came out, and, just nodding good-bye to the woman, who was his mother, went away. She did not look insane, but as she was German I could not learn her story. Her name, however, was Mrs. Louise Schanz. She seemed quite lost, but when the nurses put her at some sewing she did her work well and quickly. At three in the afternoon all the patients were given a gruel broth, and at five a cup of tea and a piece of bread. I was favored; for when they saw that it was impossible for me to eat the bread or drink the stuff honored by the name of tea, they gave me a cup of milk and a cracker, the same as I had had at noon.

Just as the gas was being lighted another patient was added. She was a young girl, twenty-five years old. She told me that she had just gotten up from a sick bed. Her appearance confirmed her story. She looked like one who had had a severe attack of fever. "I am now suffering from nervous debility," she said, "and my friends have sent me here to be treated for it." I did not tell her where she was, and she seemed quite satisfied. At 6.15 Miss Ball said that she wanted to go away, and so we would all have to go to bed. Then each of us-we now numbered six-were assigned a room and told to undress. I did so, and was given a short, cotton-flannel gown to wear during the night. Then she took every particle of the clothing I had worn during the day, and, making it up in a bundle, labeled it "Brown," and took it away. The iron-barred window was locked, and Miss Ball, after giving me an extra blanket, which, she said, was a favor rarely granted, went out and left me alone. The bed was not a comfortable one. It was so hard, indeed, that I could not make a dent in it; and the pillow was stuffed with straw. Under the sheet was an oilcloth spread. As the night grew colder I tried to warm that oilcloth. I kept on trying, but when morning dawned and it was still as cold as when I went to bed, and had reduced me too, to the temperature of an iceberg, I gave it up as an impossible task.

I had hoped to get some rest on this my first night in an insane asylum. But I was doomed to disappointment. When the night nurses came in they were curious to see me and to find out what I was like. No sooner had they left than I heard some one at my door inquiring for Nellie Brown, and I began to tremble, fearing always that my sanity would be discovered. By listening to the conversation I found it was a reporter in search of me, and I heard him ask for my clothing so that he might examine it. I listened quite anxiously to the talk about me, and was relieved to learn that I was considered hopelessly insane. That was encouraging. After the reporter left I heard new arrivals, and I learned that a doctor was there and intended to see me. For what purpose I knew not, and I imagined all sorts of horrible things, such as examinations and the rest of it, and when they got to my room I was shaking with more than fear.

"Nellie Brown, here is the doctor; he wishes to speak with you," said the nurse. If that's all he wanted I thought I could endure it. I removed the blanket which I had put over my head in my sudden fright and looked up. The sight was reassuring.

He was a handsome young man. He had the air and address of a gentleman. Some people have since censured this action; but I feel sure, even if it was a little indiscreet, that they young doctor only meant kindness to me. He came forward, seated himself on the side of my bed, and put his arm soothingly around my shoulders. It was a terrible task to play insane before this young man, and only a girl can sympathize with me in my position.

"How do you feel to-night, Nellie?" he asked, easily.

"Oh, I feel all right."

"But you are sick, you know," he said.

"Oh, am I?" I replied, and I turned by head on the pillow and smiled.

"When did you leave Cuba, Nellie?"

"Oh, you know my home?" I asked.

"Yes, very well. Don't you remember me? I remember you."

"Do you?" and I mentally said I should not forget him. He was accompanied by a friend who never ventured a remark, but stood staring at me as I lay in bed. After a great many questions, to which I answered truthfully, he left me. Then came other troubles. All night long the nurses read one to the other aloud, and I know that the other patients, as well as myself, were unable to sleep. Every half-hour or hour they would walk heavily down the halls, their boot-heels resounding like the march of a private of dragoons, and take a look at every patient. Of course this helped to keep us awake. Then as it came toward morning, they began to beat eggs for breakfast, and the sound made me realize how horribly hungry I was. Occasional yells and cries came from the male department, and that did not aid in making the night pass more cheerfully. Then the ambulance-gong, as it brought in more unfortunates, sounded as a knell to life and liberty. Thus I passed my first night as an insane girl at Bellevue.

Chapter VII: The Goal in Sight.

AT 6 o'clock on Sunday morning, Sept. 25, the nurses pulled the covering from my bed. "Come, it's time for you to get out of bed," they said, and opened the window and let in the cold breeze. My clothing was then returned to me. After dressing I was shown to a washstand, where all the other patients were trying to rid their faces of all traces of sleep. At 7 o'clock we were given some horrible mess, which Mary told us was chicken broth. The cold, from which we had suffered enough the day previous, was bitter, and when I complained to the nurse she said it was one of the rules of the institution not to turn the heat on until October, and so we would have to endure it, as the steam-pipes had not even been put in order. The night nurses then, arming themselves with scissors, began to play manicure on the patients. They cut my nails to the quick, as they did those of several of the other patients. Shortly after this a handsome young doctor made his appearance and I was conducted into the sitting-room.

"Who are you?" he asked.

"Nellie Moreno," I replied.

"Then why did you give the name of Brown?" he asked. "What is wrong with you?"

"Nothing. I did not want to come here, but they brought me. I want to go away. Won't you let me out?"

"If I take you out will you stay with me? Won't you run away from me when you get on the street?"

"I can't promise that I will not," I answered, with a smile and a sigh, for he was handsome.

He asked me many other questions. Did I ever see faces on the wall? Did I ever hear voices around? I answered him to the best of my ability.

"Do you ever hear voices at night?" he asked.

"Yes, there is so much talking I cannot sleep."

"I thought so," he said to himself. Then turning to me, he asked: "What do these voices say?"

"Well, I do not listen to them always. But sometimes, very often, they talk about Nellie Brown, and then on other subjects that do not interest me half so much," I answered, truthfully.

"That will do," he said to Miss Scott, who was just on the outside.

"Can I go away?" I asked.

"Yes," he said, with a satisfied laugh, "we'll soon send you away."

"It is so very cold here, I want to go out," I said.

"That's true," he said to Miss Scott. "The cold is almost unbearable in here, and you will have some cases of pneumonia if you are not careful."

With this I was led away and another patient was taken in. I sat right outside the door and waited to hear how he would test the sanity of the other patients. With little variation the examination was exactly the same as mine. All the patients were asked if they saw faces on the wall, heard voices, and what they said. I might also add each patient denied any such peculiar freaks of sight and hearing. At 10 o'clock we were given a cup of unsalted beef tea; at noon a bit of cold meat and a potatoe, at 3 o'clock a cup of oatmeal gruel and at 5.30 a cup of tea and a slice of unbuttered bread. We were all cold and hungry. After the physician left we were given shawls and told to walk up and down the halls in order to get warm. During the day the pavilion was visited by a number of people who were curious to see the crazy girl from Cuba. I kept my head covered, on the plea of being cold, for fear some of the reporters would recognize me. Some of the visitors were apparently in search of a missing girl, for I was made take down the shawl repeatedly, and after they looked at me they would say, "I don't know her," or [sic], "she is not the one," for which I was secretly thankful. Warden O'Rourke visited me, and tried his arts on an examination. Then he brought some well-dressed women and some gentlemen at different times to have a glance at the mysterious Nellie Brown.

The reporters were the most troublesome. Such a number of them! And they were all so bright and clever that I was terribly frightened lest they should see that I was sane. They were very kind and nice to me, and very gentle in all their questionings. My late visitor the night previous came to the window while some reporters were interviewing me in the sitting-room, and told the nurse to allow them to see me, as they would be of assistance in finding some clew as to my identity.

In the afternoon Dr. Field came and examined me. He asked me only a few questions, and one that had no bearing on such a case. The chief question was of my home and friends, and if I had any lovers or had ever been married. Then he made me stretch out my arms and move my fingers, which I did without the least hesitation, yet I heard him say my case was hopeless. The other patients were asked the same questions.

As the doctor was about to leave the pavilion Miss Tillie Mayard discovered that she was in an insane ward. She went to Dr. Field and asked him why she had been sent there.

"Have you just found out you are in an insane asylum?" asked the doctor.

"Yes; my friends said they were sending me to a convalescent ward to be treated for nervous debility, from which I am suffering since my illness. I want to get out of this place immediately."

"Well, you won't get out in a hurry," he said, with a quick laugh.

"If you know anything at all," she responded, "you should be able to tell that I am perfectly sane. Why don't you test me?"

"We know all we want to on that score," said the doctor, and he left the poor girl condemned to an insane asylum, probably for life, without giving her one feeble chance to prove her sanity.

Sunday night was but a repetition of Saturday. All night long we were kept awake by the talk of the nurses and their heavy walking through the uncarpeted halls. On Monday morning we were told that we should be taken away at 1.30. The nurses questioned me unceasingly about my home, and all seemed to have an idea that I had a lover who had cast me forth on the world and wrecked my brain. The morning brought many reporters. How untiring they are in their efforts to get something new. Miss Scott refused to allow me to be seen, however, and for this I was thankful. Had they been given free access to me, I should probably not have been a mystery long, for many of them knew me by sight. Warden O'Rourke came for a final visit and had a short conversation with me. He wrote his name in my notebook, saying to the nurse that I would forget all about it in an hour. I smiled and thought I wasn't sure of that. Other people called to see me, but none knew me or could give any information about me.

Noon came. I grew nervous as the time approached to leave for the Island. I dreaded every new arrival, fearful that my secret would be discovered at the last moment. Then I was given a shawl and my hat and gloves. I could hardly put them on, my nerves were so unstrung. At last the attendant arrived, and I bade good-bye to Mary as I slipped "a few pennies" into her hand. "God bless you," she said; "I shall pray for you. Cheer up, dearie. You are young, and will get over this." I told her I hoped so, and then I said good-bye to Miss Scott in Spanish. The rough-looking attendant twisted his arms around mine, and half-led, half-dragged me to an ambulance. A crowd of the students had assembled, and they watched us curiously. I put the shawl over my face, and sank thankfully into the wagon. Miss Neville, Miss Mayard, Mrs. Fox, and Mrs. Schanz were all put in after me, one at a time. A man got in with us, the doors were locked, and we were driven out of the gates in great style on toward the Insane Asylum and victory! The patients made no move to escape. The odor of the male attendant's breath was enough to make one's head swim.

When we reached the wharf such a mob of people crowded around the wagon that the police were called to put them away, so that we could reach the boat. I was the last of the procession. I was escorted down the plank, the fresh breeze blowing the attendants' whisky breath into my face until I staggered. I was taken into a dirty cabin, where I found my companions seated on a narrow bench. The span windows were closed, and, with the smell of the filthy room, the air was stifling. At one end of the cabin was a span bunk in such a condition that I had to hold my nose when I went near it. A sick girl was put on it. An old woman, with an enormous bonnet and a dirty basket filled with chunks of bread and bits of scrap meat, completed our company. The door was guarded by two female attendants. One

ON BOARD THE ISLAND BOAT.
was clad in a dress made of bed-ticking and the other was dressed with some attempt at style. They were coarse, massive women, and expectorated tobacco juice about on the floor in a manner more skillful than charming. One of these fearful creatures seemed to have much faith in the power of the glance on insane people, for, when any one of us would move or go to look out of the high window she would say "Sit down," and would lower her brows and glare in a way that was simply terrifying. While guarding the door they talked with some men on the outside. They discussed the number of patients and then their own affairs in a manner neither edifying nor refined.

The boat stopped and the old woman and the sick girl were taken off. The rest of us were told to sit still. At the next stop my companions were taken off, one at a time. I was last, and it seemed to require a man and a woman to lead me up the plank to reach the shore. An ambulance was standing there, and in it were the four other patients.

"What is this place?" I asked of the man, who had his fingers sunk into the flesh of my arm.

"Blackwell's Island, an insane place, where you'll never get out of."

With this I was shoved into the ambulance, the springboard was put up, an officer and a mail-carrier jumped on behind, and I was swiftly driven to the Insane Asylum on Blackwell's Island.

Chapter VIII: Inside the Madhouse.

As the wagon was rapidly driven through the beautiful lawns up to the asylum my feelings of satisfaction at having attained the object of my work were greatly dampened by the look of distress on the faces of my companions. Poor women, they had no hopes of a speedy delivery. They were being driven to a prison, through no fault of their own, in all probability for life. In comparison, how much easier it would be to walk to the gallows than to this tomb of living horrors! On the wagon sped, and I, as well as my comrades, gave a despairing farewell glance at freedom as we came in sight of the long stone buildings. We passed one low building, and the stench was so horrible that I was compelled to hold my breath, and I mentally decided that it was the kitchen. I afterward found I was correct in my surmise, and smiled at the signboard at the end of the walk: "Visitors are not allowed on this road." I don't think the sign would be necessary if they once tried the road, especially on a warm day.

The wagon stopped, and the nurse and officer in charge told us to get out. The nurse added: "Thank God! they came quietly." We obeyed orders to go ahead up a flight of narrow, stone steps, which had evidently been built for the accommodation of people who climb stairs three at a time. I wondered if my companions knew where we were, so I said to Miss Tillie Mayard:

"Where are we?"

"At the Blackwell's Island Lunatic Asylum," she answered, sadly.

"Are you crazy?" I asked.

"No," she replied; "but as we have been sent here we will have to be quiet until we find some means of escape. They will be few, though, if all the doctors, as Dr. Field, refuse to listen to me or give me a chance to prove my sanity." We were ushered into a narrow vestibule, and the door was locked behind us.

In spite of the knowledge of my sanity and the assurance that I would be released in a few days, my heart gave a sharp twinge. Pronounced insane by four expert doctors and shut up behind the unmerciful bolts and bars of a madhouse! Not to be confined alone, but to be a companion, day and night, of senseless, chattering lunatics; to sleep with them, to eat with them, to be considered one of them, was an uncomfortable position. Timidly we followed the nurse up the long uncarpeted hall to a room filled by so-called crazy women. We were told to sit down, and some of the patients kindly made room for us. They looked at us curiously, and one came up to me and asked:

"Who sent you here?"

"The doctors," I answered.

"What for?" she persisted.

"Well, they say I am insane," I admitted.

"Insane!" she repeated, incredulously. "It cannot be seen in your face."

This woman was too clever, I concluded, and was glad to answer the roughly given orders to follow the nurse to see the doctor. This nurse, Miss Grupe, by the way, had a nice German face, and if I had not detected certain hard lines about the mouth I might have expected, as did my companions, to receive but kindness from her. She left us in a span waiting-room at the end of the hall, and left us alone while she went into a span office opening into the sitting or receiving-room.

"I like to go down in the wagon," she said to the invisible party on the inside. "It helps to break up the day." He answered her that the open air improved her looks, and she again appeared before us all smiles and simpers.

"Come here, Tillie Mayard," she said. Miss Mayard obeyed, and, though I could not see

into the office, I could hear THE INSANE ASYLUM. her gently but firmly pleading her case. All her remarks were as rational as any I ever heard, and I thought no good physician could help but be impressed with her story. She told of her recent illness, that she was suffering from nervous debility. She begged that they try all their tests for insanity, if they had any, and give her justice. Poor girl, how my heart ached for her! I determined then and there that I would try by every means to make my mission of benefit to my suffering sisters; that I would show how they are committed without ample trial. Without one word of sympathy or encouragement she was brought back to where we sat.

Mrs. Louise Schanz was taken into the presence of Dr. Kinier, the medical man.

"Your name?" he asked, loudly. She answered in German, saying she did not speak English nor could she understand it. However, when he said Mrs. Louise Schanz, she said "Yah, yah." Then he tried other questions, and when he found she could not understand one world of English, he said to Miss Grupe:

"You are German; speak to her for me."

Miss Grupe proved to be one of those people who are ashamed of their nationality, and she refused, saying she could understand but few worlds of her mother tongue.

"You know you speak German. Ask this woman what her husband does," and they both laughed as if they were enjoying a joke.

"I can't speak but a few words," she protested, but at last she managed to ascertain the occupation of Mr. Schanz.

"Now, what was the use of lying to me?" asked the doctor, with a laugh which dispelled the rudeness.

"I can't speak any more," she said, and she did not.

Thus was Mrs. Louise Schanz consigned to the asylum without a chance of making herself understood. Can such carelessness be excused, I wonder, when it is so easy to get an interpreter? If the confinement was but for a few days one might question the necessity. But here was a woman taken without her own consent from the free world to an asylum

THE FRONT HALLWAY.

and there given no chance to prove her sanity. Confined most probably for life behind asylum bars, without even being told in her language the why and wherefore. Compare this with a criminal, who is given every chance to prove his innocence. Who would not rather be a murderer and take the chance for life than be declared insane, without hope of escape? Mrs. Schanz begged in German to know where she was, and pleaded for liberty. Her voice broken by sobs, she was led unheard out to us.

Mrs. Fox was then put through this weak, trifling examination and brought from the office, convicted. Miss Annie Neville took her turn, and I was again left to the last. I had by this time determined to act as I do when free, except that I would refuse to tell who I was or where my home was.

Chapter IX: An Expert(?) At Work.

"NELLIE BROWN, the doctor wants you," said Miss Grupe. I went in and was told to sit down opposite Dr. Kinier at the desk.

"What is your name?" he asked, without looking up.

"Nellie Brown," I replied easily.

"Where is your home?" writing what I had said down in a large book.

"In Cuba."

"Oh!" he ejaculated, with sudden understanding-then, addressing the nurse:

"Did you see anything in the papers about her?"

"Yes," she replied, "I saw a long account of this girl in the *Sun* on Sunday." Then the doctor said:

"Keep her here until I go to the office and see the notice again."

He left us, and I was relieved of my hat and shawl. On his return, he said he had been unable to find the paper, but he related the story of my*debut*, as he had read it, to the nurse.

"What's the color of her eyes?"

Miss Grupe looked, and answered "gray," although everybody had always said my eyes were brown or hazel.

"What's your age?" he asked; and as I answered, "Nineteen last May," he turned to the nurse, and said, "When do you get your next pass?" This I ascertained was a leave of absence, or "a day off."

"Next Saturday," she said, with a laugh.

"You will go to town?" and they both laughed as she answered in the affirmative, and he said:

"Measure her." I was stood under a measure, and it was brought down tightly on my head.

"What is it?" asked the doctor.

"Now you know I can't tell," she said.

"Yes, you can; go ahead. What height?"

"I don't know; there are some figures there, but I can't tell."

"Yes, you can. Now look and tell me."

"I can't; do it yourself," and they laughed again as the doctor left his place at the desk and came forward to see for himself.

"Five feet five inches; don't you see?" he said, taking her hand and touching the figures.

By her voice I knew she did not understand yet, but that was no concern of mine, as the doctor seemed to find a pleasure in aiding her. Then I was put on the scales, and she worked around until she got them to balance.

"How much?" asked the doctor, having resumed his position at the desk.

"I don't know. You will have to see for yourself," she replied, calling him by his Christian name, which I have forgotten. He turned and also addressing her by her baptismal name, he said:

"You are getting too fresh!" and they both laughed. I then told the weight–112 pounds-to the nurse, and she in turn told the doctor.

"What time are you going to supper?" he asked, and she told him. He gave the nurse more attention than he did me, and asked her six questions to every one of me. Then he wrote my fate in the book before him. I said, "I am not sick and I do not want to stay here. No one has a right to shut me up in this manner." He took no notice of my remarks, and having completed his writings, as well as his talk with the nurse for the moment, he said that would do, and with my companions, I went back to the sitting-room.

"You play the piano?" they asked.

"Oh, yes; ever since I was a child," I replied.

Then they insisted that I should play, and they seated me on a wooden chair before an old-fashioned square. I struck a few notes, and the untuned response sent a grinding chill through me.

"How horrible," I exclaimed, turning to a nurse, Miss McCarten, who stood at my side. "I never touched a piano as much out of tune."

"It's a pity of you," she said, spitefully; "we'll have to get one made to order for you."

I began to play the variations of "Home Sweet Home." The talking ceased and every patient sat silent, while my cold fingers moved slowly and stiffly over the keyboard. I finished in an aimless fashion and refused all requests to play more. Not seeing an available place to sit, I still occupied the chair in the front of the piano while I "sized up" my surroundings.

It was a long, bare room, with bare yellow benches encircling it. These benches, which were perfectly straight, and just as uncomfortable, would hold five people, although in almost every instance six were crowded on them. Barred windows, built about five feet from the floor, faced the two double doors which led into the hall. The bare white walls were somewhat relieved by three lithographs, one of Fritz Emmet and the others of negro minstrels. In the center of the room was a large table covered with a white bed-spread, and around it sat the nurses. Everything was spotlessly clean and I thought what good workers the nurses must be to keep such order. In a few days after how I laughed at my own stupidity to think the nurses would work. When they found I would not play any more, Miss McCarten came up to me saying, roughly:

"Get away from here," and closed the piano with a bang.

"Brown, come here," was the next order I got from a rough, red-faced woman at the table. "What have you on?"

"My clothing," I replied.

She lifted my dress and skirts and wrote down one pair shoes, one pair stockings, one cloth dress, one straw sailor hat, and so on.

Chapter X: My First Supper.

THIS examination over, we heard some one yell, "Go out into the hall." One of the patients kindly explained that this was an invitation to supper. We late comers tried to keep together, so we entered the hall and stood at the door where all the women had crowded. How we shivered as we stood there! The windows were open and the draught went whizzing through the hall. The patients looked blue with cold, and the minutes stretched into a quarter of an hour. At last one of the nurses went forward and unlocked a door, through which we all crowded to a landing of the stairway. Here again came a long halt directly before an open window.

"How very imprudent for the attendants to keep these thinly clad women standing here in the cold," said Miss Neville.

I looked at the poor crazy captives shivering, and added, emphatically, "It's horribly brutal." While they stood there I thought I would not relish supper that night. They looked so lost and hopeless. Some were chattering nonsense to invisible persons, others were laughing or crying aimlessly, and one old, gray-haired woman was nudging me, and, with winks and sage noddings of the head and pitiful uplifting of the eyes and hands, was assuring me that I must not mind the poor creatures, as they were all mad. "Stop at the heater," was then ordered, "and get in line, two by two." "Mary, get a companion." "How many times must I tell you to keep in line?" "Stand still," and, as the orders were issued, a shove and a push were administered, and often a slap on the ears. After this third and final halt, we were marched into a long, narrow dining-room, where a rush was made for the table.

The table reached the length of the room and was uncovered and uninviting. Long benches without backs were put for the patients to sit on, and over these they had to crawl in order to face the table. Placed closed together all along the table were large dressing-bowls filled with a pinkish-looking stuff which the patients called tea. By each bowl was laid a piece of bread, cut thick and buttered. A span saucer containing five prunes accompanied the bread. One fat woman made a rush, and jerking up several saucers from those around her emptied their contents into her own saucer. Then while holding to her own bowl she lifted up another and drained its contents at one gulp. This she did to a second bowl in shorter time than it takes to tell it. Indeed, I was so amused at her successful grabbings that when I looked at my own share the woman opposite, without so much as by your leave, grabbed my bread and left me without any.

Another patient, seeing this, kindly offered me hers, but I declined with thanks and turned to the nurse and asked for more. As she flung a thick piece down on the table she made some remark about the fact that if I forgot where my home was I had not forgotten how to eat. I tried the bread, but the butter was so horrible that one could not eat it. A blue-eyed German girl on the opposite side of the table told me I could have bread unbuttered if I wished, and that very few were able to eat the butter. I turned my attention to the prunes and found that very few of them would be sufficient. A patient near asked me to give them to her. I did so. My bowl of tea was all that was left. I tasted, and one taste was enough. It had no sugar, and it tasted as if it had been made in copper. It was as weak as water. This was also transferred to a hungrier patient, in spite of the protest of Miss Neville.

"You must force the food down," she said, "else you will be sick, and who know but what, with these surroundings, you may go crazy. To have a good brain the stomach must be cared for."

"It is impossible for me to eat that stuff," I replied, and, despite all her urging, I ate nothing that night.

It did not require much time for the patients to consume all that was eatable on the table, and then we got our orders to form in line in the hall. When this was done the doors before us were unlocked and we were ordered to proceed back to the sitting-room. Many of the patients crowded near us, and I was again urged to play, both by them and by the nurses. To please the patients I promised to play and Miss Tillie Mayard was to sing. The first thing she asked me to play was "Rock-a-bye Baby," and I did so. She sang it beautifully.

Chapter XI: In the Bath.

A FEW more songs and we were told to go with Miss Grupe. We were taken into a cold, wet bathroom, and I was ordered to undress. Did I protest? Well, I never grew so earnest in my life as when I tried to beg off. They said if I did not they would use force and that it would not be very gentle. At this I noticed one of the craziest women in the ward standing by the filled bathtub with a large, discolored rag in her hands. She was chattering away to herself and chuckling in a manner which seemed to me fiendish. I knew now what was to be done with me. I shivered. They began to undress me, and one by one they pulled off my clothes. At last everything was gone excepting one garment. "I will not remove it," I said vehemently, but they took it off. I gave one glance at the group of patients gathered at the door watching the scene, and I jumped into the bathtub with more energy than grace.

The water was ice-cold, and I again began to protest. How useless it all was! I begged, at least, that the patients be made to go away, but was ordered to shut up. The crazy woman began to scrub me. I can find no other word that will express it but scrubbing. From a span tin pan she

THE RECEPTION-ROOM.

took some soft soap and rubbed it all over me, even all over my face and my pretty hair. I was at last past seeing or speaking, although I had begged that my hair be left untouched. Rub, rub, rub, went the old woman, chattering to herself. My teeth chattered and my limbs were goose-fleshed and blue with cold. Suddenly I got, one after the other, three buckets of water over my head-ice-cold water, too-into my eyes, my ears, my nose and my mouth. I think I experienced some of the sensations of a drowning person as they dragged me, gasping, shivering and quaking, from the tub. For once I did look insane. I caught a glance of the indescribable look on the faces of my companions, who had witnessed my fate and knew theirs was surely following. Unable to control myself at the absurd picture I presented, I burst into roars of laughter. They put me, dripping wet, into a short canton flannel slip, labeled across the extreme end in large black letters, "Lunatic Asylum, B. I., H. 6." The letters meant Blackwell's Island, Hall 6.

By this time Miss Mayard had been undressed, and, much as I hated my recent bath, I would have taken another if by it I could have saved her the experience. Imagine plunging that sick girl into a cold bath when it made me, who have never been ill, shake as if with ague. I heard her explain to Miss Grupe that her head was still sore from her illness. Her hair was short and had mostly come out, and she asked that the crazy woman be made to rub more gently, but Miss Grupe said:

"There isn't much fear of hurting you. Shut up, or you'll get it worse." Miss Mayard did shut up, and that was my last look at her for the night.

I was hurried into a room where there were six beds, and had been put into bed when some one came along and jerked me out again, saying:

"Nellie Brown has to be put in a room alone to-night, for I suppose she's noisy."

I was taken to room 28 and left to try and make an impression on the bed. It was an impossible task. The bed had been made high in the center and sloping on either side. At the first touch my head flooded the pillow with water, and my wet slip transferred some of its dampness to the sheet. When Miss Grupe came in I asked if I could not have a night-gown.

"We have not such things in this institution," she said.

"I do not like to sleep without," I replied.

"Well, I don't care about that," she said. "You are in a public institution now, and you can't expect to get anything. This is charity, and you should be thankful for what you get."

"But the city pays to keep these places up," I urged, "and pays people to be kind to the unfortunates brought here."

"Well, you don't need to expect any kindness here, for you won't get it," she said, and she went out and closed the door.

A sheet and an oilcloth were under me, and a sheet and black wool blanket above. I never felt anything so annoying as that wool blanket as I tried to keep it around my shoulders to stop

HER BEDROOM.

the chills from getting underneath. When I pulled it up I left my feet bare, and when I pulled it down my shoulders were exposed. There was absolutely nothing in the room but the bed and myself. As the door had been locked I imagined I should be left alone for the night, but I heard the sound of the heavy tread of two women down the hall. They stopped at every door, unlocked it, and in a few moments I could hear them relock it. This they did without the least attempt at quietness down the whole length of the opposite side of the hall and up to my room. Here they paused. The key was inserted in the lock and turned. I watched those about to enter. In they came, dressed in brown and white striped dresses, fastened by brass buttons, large, white aprons, a heavy green cord about the waist, from which dangled a bunch of large keys, and span, white caps on their heads. Being dressed as were the attendants of the day, I knew they were nurses. The first one carried a lantern, and she flashed its light into my face while she said to her assistant:

"This is Nellie Brown." Looking at her, I asked:

"Who are you?"

"The night nurse, my dear," she replied, and, wishing that I would sleep well, she went out and locked the door after her. Several times during the night they came into my room, and even had I been able to sleep, the unlocking of the heavy door, their loud talking, and heavy tread, would have awakened me.

I could not sleep, so I lay in bed picturing to myself the horrors in case a fire should break out in the asylum. Every door is locked separately and the windows are heavily barred, so that escape is impossible. In the one building alone there are, I think Dr. Ingram told me, some three hundred women. They are locked, one to ten to a room. It is impossible to get out unless these doors are unlocked. A fire is not improbable, but one of the most likely occurrences. Should the building burn, the jailers or nurses would never think of releasing their crazy patients. This I can prove to you later when I come to tell of their cruel treatment of the poor things intrusted to their care. As I say, in case of fire, not a dozen women could escape. All would be left to roast to death. Even if the nurses were kind, which they are not, it would require more presence of mind than women of their class possess to risk the flames and their own lives while they unlocked the hundred doors for the insane prisoners. Unless there is a change there will some day be a tale of horror never equaled.

In this connection is an amusing incident which happened just previous to my release. I was talking with Dr. Ingram about many things, and at last told him what I thought would be the result of a fire.

"The nurses are expected to open the doors," he said.

"But you know positively that they would not wait to do that," I said, "and these women would burn to death."

He sat silent, unable to contradict my assertion.

"Why don't you have it changed?" I asked.

"What can I do?" he replied. "I offer suggestions until my brain is tired, but what good does it do? What would you do?" he asked, turning to me, the proclaimed insane girl.

"Well, I should insist on them having locks put in, as I have seen in some places, that by turning a crank at the end of the hall you can lock or unlock every door on the one side. Then there would be some chance of escape. Now, every door being locked separately, there is absolutely none."

Dr. Ingram turned to me with an anxious look on his kind face as he asked, slowly:

"Nellie Brown, what institution have you been an inmate of before you came here?"

"None. I never was confined in any institution, except boarding-school, in my life."

"Where then did you see the locks you have described?"

I had seen them in the new Western Penitentiary at Pittsburg, Pa., but I did not dare say so. I merely answered:

"Oh, I have seen them in a place I was in–I mean as a visitor."

"There is only one place I know of where they have those locks," he said, sadly, "and that is at Sing Sing."

The inference is conclusive. I laughed very heartily over the implied accusation, and tried to assure him that I had never, up to date, been an inmate of Sing Sing or even ever visited it.

Just as the morning began to dawn I went to sleep. It did not seem many moments until I was rudely awakened and told to get up, the window being opened and the clothing pulled off me. My hair was still wet and I had pains all through me, as if I had the rheumatism. Some clothing was flung on the floor and I was told to put it on. I asked for my own, but was told to take what I got and keep quiet by the apparently head nurse, Miss Grady. I looked at it. One underskirt made of coarse dark cotton goods and a cheap white calico dress with a black spot in it. I tied the strings of the skirt around me and put on the little dress. It was made, as are all those worn by the patients, into a straight tight waist sewed on to a straight skirt. As I buttoned the waist I noticed the underskirt was about six inches longer than the upper, and for a moment I sat down on the bed and laughed at my own appearance. No woman ever longed for a mirror more than I did at that moment.

I saw the other patients hurrying past in the hall, so I decided not to lose anything that might be going on. We numbered forty-five patients in Hall 6, and were sent to the bathroom, where there were two coarse towels. I watched crazy patients who had the most dangerous eruptions all over their faces dry on the towels and then saw women with clean skins turn to use them. I went to the bathtub and washed my face at the running faucet and my underskirt did duty for a towel.

Before I had completed my ablutions a bench was brought into the bathroom. Miss Grupe and Miss McCarten came in with combs in their hands. We were told to sit down on the bench, and the hair of forty-five women was combed with one patient, two nurses, and six combs. As I saw some of the sore heads combed I thought this was another dose I had not bargained for. Miss Tillie Mayard had her own comb, but it was taken from her by Miss Grady. Oh, that combing! I never realized before what the expression "I'll give you a combing" meant, but I knew then. My hair, all matted and wet from the night previous, was pulled and jerked, and, after expostulating to no avail, I set my teeth and endured the pain. They refused to give me my hairpins, and my hair was arranged in one plait and tied with a red cotton rag. My curly bangs refused to stay back, so that at least was left of my former glory.

After this we went to the sitting-room and I looked for my companions. At first I looked vainly, unable to distinguish them from the other patients, but after awhile I recognized Miss Mayard by her short hair.

"How did you sleep after your cold bath?"

"I almost froze, and then the noise kept me awake. It's dreadful! My nerves were so unstrung before I came here, and I fear I shall not be able to stand the strain."

I did the best I could to cheer her. I asked that we be given additional clothing, at least as much as custom says women shall wear, but they told me to shut up; that we had as much as they intended to give us.

We were compelled to get up at 5.30 o'clock, and at 7.15 we were told to collect in the hall, where the experience of waiting, as on the evening previous, was repeated. When we got into the dining-room at last we found a bowl of cold tea, a slice of buttered bread and a saucer of oatmeal, with molasses on it, for each patient. I was hungry, but the food would not down. I asked for unbuttered bread and was given it. I cannot tell you of anything which is the same dirty, black color. It was hard, and in places nothing more than dried dough. I found a spider in my slice, so I did not eat it. I tried the oatmeal and molasses, but it was wretched, and so I endeavored, but without much show of success, to choke down the tea.

After we were back to the sitting-room a number of women were ordered to make the beds, and some of the patients were put to scrubbing and others given different duties which covered all the work in the hall. It is not the attendants who keep the institution so nice for the poor patients, as I had always thought, but the patients, who do it all themselves-even to cleaning the nurses' bedrooms and caring for their clothing.

About 9.30 the new patients, of which I was one, were told to go out to see the doctor. I was taken in and my lungs and my heart were examined by the flirty young doctor who was the first to see us the day we entered. The one who made out the report, if I mistake not, was the assistant superintendent, Ingram. A few questions and I was allowed to return to the sitting-room.

I came in and saw Miss Grady with my note-book and long lead pencil, bought just for the occasion.

"I want my book and pencil," I said, quite truthfully. "It helps me remember things."

I was very anxious to get it to make notes in and was disappointed when she said:

"You can't have it, so shut up."

Some days after I asked Dr. Ingram if I could have it, and he promised to consider the

AN INSANE HALL.

matter. When I again referred to it, he said that Miss Grady said I only brought a book there; and that I had no pencil. I was provoked, and insisted that I had, whereupon I was advised to fight against the imaginations of my brain.

After the housework was completed by the patients, and as day was fine, but cold, we were told to go out in the hall and get on shawls and hats for a walk. Poor patients! How eager they were for a breath of air; how eager for a slight release from their prison. They went swiftly into the hall and there was a skirmish for hats. Such hats!

Chapter XII: Promenading with Lunatics.

ISHALL never forget my first walk. When all the patients had donned the white straw hats, such as bathers wear at Coney Island, I could not but laugh at their comical appearances. I could not distinguish one woman from another. I lost Miss Neville, and had to take my hat off and search for her. When we met we put our hats on and laughed at one another. Two by two we formed in line, and guarded by the attendants we went out a back way on to the walks.

We had not gone many paces when I saw, proceeding from every walk, long lines of women guarded by nurses. How many there were! Every way I looked I could see them in the queer dresses, comical straw hats and shawls, marching slowly around. I eagerly watched the passing lines and a thrill of horror crept over me at the sight. Vacant eyes and meaningless faces, and their tongues uttered meaningless nonsense. One crowd passed and I noted by nose as well as eyes, that they were fearfully dirty.

"Who are they?" I asked of a patient near me.

"They are considered the most violent on the island," she replied. "They are from the Lodge, the first building with the high steps." Some were yelling, some were cursing, others were singing or praying or preaching, as the fancy struck them, and they made up the most miserable collection of humanity I had ever seen. As the din of their passing faded in the distance there came another sight I can never forget:

A long cable rope fastened to wide leather belts, and these belts locked around the waists of fifty-two women. At the end of the rope was a heavy iron cart, and in it two women-one nursing a sore foot, another screaming at some nurse, saying: "You beat me and I shall not forget it. You want to kill me," and then she would sob and cry. The women "on the rope," as the patients call it, were each busy on their individual freaks. Some were yelling all the while. One who had blue eyes saw me look at her, and she turned as far as she could, talking and smiling, with that terrible, horrifying look of absolute insanity stamped on her. The doctors might safely judge on her case. The horror of that sight to one who had never been near an insane person before, was something unspeakable.

"God help them!" breathed Miss Neville. "It is so dreadful I cannot look."

On they passed, but for their places to be filled by more. Can you imagine the sight? According to one of the physicians there are 1600 insane women on Blackwell's Island.

Mad! what can be half so horrible? My heart thrilled with pity when I looked on old, gray-haired women talking aimlessly to space. One woman had on a straightjacket, and two women had to drag her along. Crippled, blind, old, young, homely, and pretty; one senseless mass of humanity. No fate could be worse.

I looked at the pretty lawns, which I had once thought was such a comfort to the poor creatures confined on the Island, and laughed at my own notions. What enjoyment is it to them? They are not allowed on the grass-it is only to look at. I saw some patients eagerly and caressingly lift a nut or a colored leaf that had fallen on the path. But they were not permitted to keep them. The nurses would always compel them to throw their little bit of God's comfort away.

As I passed a low pavilion, where a crowd of helpless lunatics were confined, I read a motto on the wall, "While I live I hope." The absurdity of it struck me forcibly. I would have liked to put above the gates that open to the asylum, "He who enters here leaveth hope behind."

During the walk I was annoyed a great deal by nurses who had heard my romantic story calling to those in charge of us to ask which one I was. I was pointed out repeatedly.

It was not long until the dinner hour arrived and I was so hungry that I felt I could eat anything. The same old story of standing for a half and three-quarters of an hour in the hall was repeated before we got down to our dinners. The bowls in which we had had our tea were now filled with soup, and on a plate was one cold boiled potato and a chunk of beef, which on investigation, proved to be slightly spoiled. There were no knives or forks, and the patients looked fairly savage as they took the tough beef in their fingers and pulled in opposition to their teeth. Those toothless or with poor teeth could not eat it. One tablespoon was given for the soup, and a piece of bread was the final entree. Butter is never allowed at dinner nor coffee or tea. Miss Mayard could not eat, and I saw many of the sick ones turn away in disgust. I was getting very weak from the want of food and tried to eat a slice of bread. After the first few bites hunger asserted itself, and I was able to eat all but the crusts of the one slice.

Superintendent Dent went through the sitting-room, giving an occasional "How do you do?" "How are you to-day?" here and there among the patients. His voice was as cold as the hall, and the patients made no movement to tell him of their sufferings. I asked some of them to tell how they were suffering from the cold and insufficiency of clothing, but they replied that the nurse would beat them if they told.

I was never so tired as I grew sitting on those benches. Several of the patients would sit on one foot or sideways to make a change, but they were always reproved and told to sit up straight. If they talked they were scolded and told to shut up; if they wanted to walk around in order to take the stiffness out of them, they were told to sit down and be still. What, excepting torture, would produce insanity quicker than this treatment? Here is a class of women sent to be cured. I would like the expert physicians who are condemning me for my action, which has proven their ability, to take a perfectly sane and healthy woman, shut her up and make her sit from 6 A. M. until 8 P. M. on straight-back benches, do not allow her to talk or move during these hours, give her no reading and let her know nothing of the world or its doings, give her bad food and harsh treatment, and see how long it will take to make her insane. Two months would make her a mental and physical wreck.

I have described my first day in the asylum, and as my other nine were exactly the same in the general run of things it would be tiresome to tell about each. In giving this story I expect to be contradicted by many who are exposed. I merely tell in common words, without exaggeration, of my life in a mad-house for ten days. The eating was one of the most horrible things. Excepting the first two days after I entered the asylum, there was no salt for the food. The hungry and even famishing women made an attempt to eat the horrible messes. Mustard and vinegar were put on meat and in soup to give it a taste, but it only helped to make it worse. Even that was all consumed after two days, and the patients had to try to choke down fresh fish, just boiled in water, without salt, pepper or butter; mutton, beef and potatoes without the faintest seasoning. The most insane refused to swallow the food and were threatened with punishment. In our short walks we passed the kitchen were food was prepared for the nurses and doctors. There we got glimpses of melons and grapes and all kinds of fruits, beautiful white bread and nice meats, and the hungry feeling would be increased tenfold. I spoke to some of the physicians, but it had no effect, and when I was taken away the food was yet unsalted.

My heart ached to see the sick patients grow sicker over the table. I saw Miss Tillie Mayard so suddenly overcome at a bite that she had to rush from the dining-room and then got a scolding for doing so. When the patients complained of the food they were told to shut up; that they would not have as good if they were at home, and that it was too good for charity patients.

A German girl, Louise–I have forgotten her last name-did not eat for several days and at last one morning she was missing. From the conversation of the nurses I found she was suffering from a high fever. Poor thing! she told me she unceasingly prayed for death. I watched the nurses make a patient carry such food as the well ones were refusing up to Louise's room. Think of that stuff for a fever patient! Of course, she refused it. Then I saw a nurse, Miss McCarten, go to test her temperature, and she returned with a report of it being some 150 degrees. I smiled at the report, and Miss Grupe, seeing it, asked me how high my temperature had ever run. I refused to answer. Miss Grady then decided to try her ability. She returned with the report of 99 degrees.

Miss Tillie Mayard suffered more than any of us from the cold, and yet she tried to follow my advice to be cheerful and try to keep up for a short time. Superintendent Dent brought in a man to see me. He felt my pulse and my head and examined my tongue. I told them how cold it was, and assured them that I did not need medical aid, but that Miss Mayard did, and they should transfer their attentions to her. They did not answer me, and I was pleased to see Miss Mayard leave her place and come forward to them. She spoke to the doctors and told them she was ill, but they paid no attention to her. The nurses came and dragged her back to the bench, and after the doctors left they said, "After awhile, when you see that the doctors will not notice you, you will quit running up to them." Before the doctors left me I heard one say—I cannot give it in his exact words—that my pulse and eyes were not that of an insane girl, but Superintendent Dent assured him that in cases such as mine such tests failed. After watching me for awhile he said my face was the brightest he had ever seen for a lunatic. The nurses had on heavy undergarments and coats, but they refused to give us shawls.

Nearly all night long I listened to a woman cry about the cold and beg for God to let her die. Another one yelled "Murder!" at frequent intervals and "Police!" at others until my flesh felt creepy.

The second morning, after we had begun our endless "set" for the day, two of the nurses, assisted by some patients, brought the woman in who had begged the night previous for God to take her home. I was not surprised at her prayer. She appeared easily seventy years old, and she was blind. Although the halls were freezing-cold, that old woman had no more clothing on than the rest of us, which I have described. When she was brought into the sitting-room and placed on the hard bench, she cried:

"Oh, what are you doing with me? I am cold, so cold. Why can't I stay in bed or have a shawl?" and then she would get up and endeavor to feel her way to leave the room. Sometimes the attendants would jerk her back to the bench, and again they would let her walk and heartlessly laugh when she bumped against the table or the edge of the benches. At one time she said the heavy shoes which charity provides hurt her feet, and she took them off. The nurses made two patients put them on her again, and when she did it several times, and fought against having them on, I counted seven people at her at once trying to put the shoes on her. The old woman then tried to lie down on the bench, but they pulled her up again. It sounded so pitiful to hear her cry:

"Oh, give me a pillow and pull the covers over me, I am so cold."

At this I saw Miss Grupe sit down on her and run her cold hands over the old woman's face and down inside the neck of her dress. At the old woman's cries she laughed savagely, as did the other nurses, and repeated her cruel action. That day the old woman was carried away to another ward.

Chapter XIII: Choking and Beating Patients.

MISS TILLIE MAYARD suffered greatly from cold. One morning she sat on the bench next to me and was livid with the cold. Her limbs shook and her teeth chattered. I spoke to the three attendants who sat with coats on at the table in the center of the floor.

"It is cruel to lock people up and then freeze them," I said. They replied she had on as much as any of the rest, and she would get no more. Just then Miss Mayard took a fit and every patient looked frightened. Miss Neville caught her in her arms and held her, although the nurses roughly said:

"Let her fall on the floor and it will teach her a lesson." Miss Neville told them what she thought of their actions, and then I got orders to make my appearance in the office.

Just as I reached there Superintendent Dent came to the door and I told him how we were suffering from the cold, and of Miss Mayard's condition. Doubtless, I spoke incoherently, for I told of the state of the food, the treatment of the nurses and their refusal to give more clothing, the condition of Miss Mayard, and the nurses telling us, because the asylum was a public institution we could not expect even kindness. Assuring him that I needed no medical aid, I told him to go to Miss Mayard. He did so. From Miss Neville and other patients I learned what transpired. Miss Mayard was still in the fit, and he caught her roughly between the eyebrows or thereabouts, and pinched until her face was crimson from the rush of blood to the head, and her senses returned. All day afterward she suffered from terrible headache, and from that on she grew worse.

Insane? Yes, insane; and as I watched the insanity slowly creep over the mind that had appeared to be all right I secretly cursed the doctors, the nurses and all public institutions. Some one may say that she was insane at some time previous to her consignment to the asylum. Then if she were, was this the proper place to send a woman just convalescing, to be given cold baths, deprived of sufficient clothing and fed with horrible food?

On this morning I had a long conversation with Dr. Ingram, the assistant superintendent of the asylum. I found that he was kind to the helpless in his charge. I began my old complaint of the cold, and he called Miss Grady to the office and ordered more clothing given the patients. Miss Grady said if I made a practice of telling it would be a serious thing for me, she warned me in time.

Many visitors looking for missing girls came to see me. Miss Grady yelled in the door from the hall one day:

"Nellie Brown, you're wanted."

I went to the sitting-room at the end of the hall, and there sat a gentleman who had known me intimately for years. I saw by the sudden blanching of his face and his inability to speak that the sight of me was wholly unexpected and had shocked him terribly. In an instant I determined, if he betrayed me as Nellie Bly, to say I had never seen him before. However, I had one card to play and I risked it. With Miss Grady within touching distance I whispered hurriedly to him, in language more expressive than elegant:

"Don't give me away."

I knew by the expression of his eye that he understood, so I said to Miss Grady:

"I do not know this man."

"Do you know her?" asked Miss Grady.

"No; this is not the young lady I came in search of," he replied, in a strained voice.

"If you do not know her you cannot stay here," she said, and she took him to the door. All at once a fear struck me that he would think I had been sent there through some mistake and would tell my friends and make an effort to have me released. So I waited until Miss Grady had the door unlocked. I knew that she would have to lock it before she could leave, and the time required to do so would give me opportunity to speak, so I called:

"One moment, senor." He returned to me and I asked aloud:

"Do you speak Spanish, senor?" and then whispered, "It's all right. I'm after an item. Keep still." "No," he said, with a peculiar emphasis, which I knew meant that he would keep my secret.

People in the world can never imagine the length of days to those in asylums. They seemed never ending, and we welcomed any event that might give us something to think about as well as talk of. There is nothing to read, and the only bit of talk that never wears out is conjuring up delicate food that they will get as soon as they get out. Anxiously the hour was watched for when the boat arrived to see if there were any new unfortunates to be added to our ranks. When they came and were ushered into the sitting-room the patients would express sympathy to one another for them and were anxious to show them little marks of attention. Hall 6 was the receiving hall, so that was how we saw all newcomers.

Soon after my advent a girl called Urena Little-Page was brought in. She was, as she had been born, silly, and her tender spot was, as with many sensible women, her age. She claimed eighteen, and would grow very angry if told to the contrary. The nurses were not long in finding this out, and then they teased her.

"Urena," said Miss Grady, "the doctors say that you are thirty-three instead of eighteen," and the other nurses laughed. They kept up this until the simple creature began to yell and cry, saying she wanted to go home and that everybody treated her badly. After they had gotten all the amusement out of her they wanted and she was crying, they began to scold and tell her to keep quiet. She grew more hysterical every moment until they pounced upon her and slapped her face and knocked her head in a lively fashion. This made the poor creature cry the more, and so they choked her. Yes, actually choked her. Then they dragged her out to the closet, and I heard her terrified cries hush into smothered ones. After several hours' absence she returned to the sitting-room, and I plainly saw the marks of their fingers on her throat for the entire day.

This punishment seemed to awaken their desire to administer more. They returned to the sitting-room and caught hold of an old gray-haired woman whom I have heard addressed both as Mrs. Grady and Mrs. O'Keefe. She was insane, and she talked almost continually to herself and to those near her. She never spoke very loud, and at the time I speak of was sitting harmlessly chattering to herself. They grabbed her, and my heart ached as she cried:

"For God sake, ladies, don't let them beat me."

"Shut up, you hussy!" said Miss Grady as she caught the woman by her gray hair and dragged her shrieking and pleading from the room. She was also taken to the closet, and her cries grew lower and lower, and then ceased.

The nurses returned to the room and Miss Grady remarked that she had "settled the old fool for awhile." I told some of the physicians of the occurrence, but they did not pay any attention to it.

One of the characters in Hall 6 was Matilda, a little old German woman, who, I believe, went insane over the loss of money. She was span, and had a pretty pink complexion. She was not much trouble, except at times. She would take spells, when she would talk into the steam-heaters or get up on a chair and talk out of the windows. In these conversations she railed at the lawyers who had taken her property. The nurses seemed to find a great deal of amusement in teasing the harmless old soul. One day I sat beside Miss Grady and Miss Grupe, and heard them tell her perfectly vile things to call Miss McCarten. After telling her to say these things they would send her to the other nurse, but Matilda proved that she, even in her state, had more sense than they.

"I cannot tell you. It is private," was all she would say. I saw Miss Grady, on a pretense of whispering to her, spit in her ear. Matilda quietly wiped her ear and said nothing.

Chapter XIV: Some Unfortunate Stories.

BY this time I had made the acquaintance of the greater number of the forty-five women in hall 6. Let me introduce a few. Louise, the pretty German girl who I have spoken of formerly as being sick with fever, had the delusion that the spirits of her dead parents were with her. "I have gotten many beatings from Miss Grady and her assistants," she said, "and I am unable to eat the horrible food they give us. I ought not to be compelled to freeze for want of proper clothing. Oh! I pray nightly that I may be taken to my papa and mamma. One night, when I was confined at Bellevue, Dr. Field came; I was in bed, and weary of the examination. At last I said: 'I am tired of this. I will talk no more.' 'Won't you?' he said, angrily. 'I'll see if I can't make you.' With this he laid his crutch on the side of the bed, and, getting up on it, he pinched me very severely in the ribs. I jumped up straight in bed, and said: 'What do you mean by this?' 'I want to teach you to obey when I speak to you,' he replied. If I could only die and go to papa!" When I left she was confined to bed with a fever, and maybe by this time she has her wish.

There is a Frenchwoman confined in hall 6, or was during my stay, whom I firmly believe to be perfectly sane. I watched her and talked with her every day, excepting the last three, and I was unable to find any delusion or mania in her. Her name is Josephine Despreau, if that is spelled correctly, and her husband and all her friends are in France. Josephine feels her position keenly. Her lips tremble, and she breaks down crying when she talks of her helpless condition. "How did you get here?" I asked.

"One morning as I was trying to get breakfast I grew deathly sick, and two officers were called in by the woman of the house, and I was taken to the station-house. I was unable to understand their proceedings, and they paid little attention to my story. Doings in this country were new to me, and before I realized it I was lodged as an insane woman in this asylum. When I first came I cried that I was here without hope of release, and for crying Miss Grady and her assistants choked me until they hurt my throat, for it has been sore ever since."

A pretty young Hebrew woman spoke so little English I could not get her story except as told by the nurses. They said her name is Sarah Fishbaum, and that her husband put her in the asylum because she had a fondness for other men than himself. Granting that Sarah was insane, and about men, let me tell you how the nurses tried to cure(?) her. They would call her up and say:

"Sarah, wouldn't you like to have a nice young man?"

"Oh, yes; a young man is all right," Sarah would reply in her few English words.

"Well, Sarah, wouldn't you like us to speak a good word to some of the doctors for you? Wouldn't you like to have one of the doctors?"

And then they would ask her which doctor she preferred, and advise her to make advances to him when he visited the hall, and so on.

I had been watching and talking with a fair-complexioned woman for several days, and I was at a loss to see why she had been sent there, she was so sane.

"Why did you come here?" I asked her one day, after we had indulged in a long conversation.

"I was sick," she replied.

"Are you sick mentally?" I urged.

"Oh, no; what gave you such an idea? I had been overworking myself, and I broke down. Having some family trouble, and being penniless and nowhere to go, I applied to the commissioners to be sent to the poorhouse until I would be able to go to work."

"But they do not send poor people here unless they are insane," I said. "Don't you know there are only insane women, or those supposed to be so, sent here?"

"I knew after I got here that the majority of these women were insane, but then I believed them when they told me this was the place they sent all the poor who applied for aid as I had done."

"How have you been treated?" I asked. "Well, so far I have escaped a beating, although I have been sickened at the sight of many and the recital of more. When I was brought here they went to give me a bath, and the very disease for which I needed doctoring and from which I was suffering made it necessary that I should not bathe. But they put me in, and my sufferings were increased greatly for weeks thereafter."

A Mrs. McCartney, whose husband is a tailor, seems perfectly rational and has not one fancy. Mary Hughes and Mrs. Louise Schanz showed no obvious traces of insanity.

One day two new-comers were added to our list. The one was an idiot, Carrie Glass, and the other was a nice-looking German girl-quite young, she seemed, and when she came in all the patients spoke of her nice appearance and apparent sanity. Her name was Margaret. She told me she had been a cook, and was extremely neat. One day, after she had scrubbed the kitchen floor, the chambermaids came down and deliberately soiled it. Her temper was aroused and she began to quarrel with them; an officer was called and she was taken to an asylum.

"How can they say I am insane, merely because I allowed my temper to run away with me?" she complained. "Other people are not shut up for crazy when they get angry. I suppose the only thing to do is to keep quiet and so avoid the beatings which I see others get. No one can say one word about me. I do everything I am told, and all the work they give me. I am obedient in every respect, and I do everything to prove to them that I am sane."

One day an insane woman was brought in. She was noisy, and Miss Grady gave her a beating and blacked her eye. When the doctors noticed it and asked if it was done before she came there the nurses said it was.

While I was in hall 6 I never heard the nurses address the patients except to scold or yell at them, unless it was to tease the. They spent much of their time gossiping about the physicians and about the other nurses in a manner that was not elevating. Miss Grady nearly always interspersed her conversation with profane language, and generally began her sentences by calling on the name of the Lord. The names she called the patients were of the lowest and most profane type. One evening she quarreled with another nurse while we were at supper about the bread, and when the nurse had gone out she called her bad names and made ugly remarks about her.

In the evenings a woman, whom I supposed to be head cook for the doctors, used to come up and bring raisins, grapes, apples, and crackers to the nurses. Imagine the feelings of the hungry patients as they sat and watched the nurses eat what was to them a dream of luxury.

One afternoon, Dr. Dent was talking to a patient, Mrs. Turney, about some trouble she had had with a nurse or matron. A short time after we were taken down to supper and this woman who had beaten Mrs. Turney, and of whom Dr. Dent spoke, was sitting at the door of our dining-room. Suddenly Mrs. Turney picked up her bowl of tea, and, rushing out of the door flung it at the woman who had beat her. There was some loud screaming and Mrs. Turney was returned to her place. The next day she was transferred to the "rope gang," which is supposed to be composed of the most dangerous and most suicidal women on the island.

At first I could not sleep and did not want to so long as I could hear anything new. The night nurses may have complained of the fact. At any rate one night they came in and tried to make me take a dose of some mixture out of a glass "to make me sleep," they said. I told them I would do nothing of the sort and they left me, I hoped, for the night. My hopes were vain, for in a few minutes they returned with a doctor, the same that received us on our arrival. He insisted that I take it, but I was determined not to lose my wits even for a few hours. When he saw that I was not to be coaxed he grew rather rough, and said he had wasted too much time with me already. That if I did not take it he would put it into my arm with a needle. It occurred to me that if he put it into my arm I could not get rid of it, but if I swallowed it there was one hope, so I said I would take it. I smelt it and it smelt like laudanum, and it was a horrible dose. No sooner had they left the room and locked me in than I tried so see how far down my throat my finger would go, and the chloral was allowed to try its effect elsewhere.

I want to say that the night nurse, Burns, in hall 6, seemed very kind and patient to the poor, afflicted people. The other nurses made several attempts to talk to me about lovers, and asked me if I would not like to have one. They did not find me very communicative on the-to them-popular subject.

Once a week the patients are given a bath, and that is the only time they see soap. A patient handed me a piece of soap one day about the size of a thimble, I considered it a great compliment in her wanting to be kind, but I thought she would appreciate the cheap soap more than I, so I thanked her but refused to take it. On bathing day the tub is filled with water, and the patients are washed, one after the other, without a change of water. This is done until the water is really thick, and then it is allowed to run out and the tub is refilled without being washed. The same towels are used on all the women, those with eruptions as well as those without. The healthy patients fight for a change of water, but they are compelled to submit to the dictates of the lazy, tyrannical nurses. The dresses are seldom changed oftener than once a month. If the patient has a visitor, I have seen the nurses hurry her out and change her dress before the visitor comes in. This keeps up the appearance of careful and good management.

The patients who are not able to take care of themselves get into beastly conditions, and the nurses never look after them, but order some of the patients to do so.

For five days we were compelled to sit in the room all day. I never put in such a long time. Every patient was stiff and sore and tired. We would get in little groups on benches and torture our stomachs by conjuring up thoughts of what we would eat first when we got out. If I had not known how hungry they were and the pitiful side of it, the conversation would have been very amusing. As it was it only made me sad. When the subject of eating, which seemed to be the favorite one, was worn out, they used to give their opinions of the institution and its management. The condemnation of the nurses and the eatables was unanimous.

As the days passed Miss Tillie Mayard's condition grew worse. She was continually cold and unable to eat of the food provided. Day after day she sang in order to try to maintain her memory, but at last the nurse made her stop it. I talked with her daily, and I grieved to find her grow worse so rapidly. At last she got a delusion. She thought that I was trying to pass myself off for her, and that all the people who called to see Nellie Brown were friends in search of her, but that I, by some means, was trying to deceive them into the belief that I was the girl. I tried to reason with her, but found it impossible, so I kept away from her as much as possible, lest my presence should make her worse and feed the fancy.

One of the patients, Mrs. Cotter, a pretty, delicate woman, one day thought she saw her husband coming up the walk. She left the line in which she was marching and ran to meet him. For this act she was sent to the Retreat. She afterward said:

"The remembrance of that is enough to make me mad. For crying the nurses beat me with a broom-handle and jumped on me, injuring me internally, so that I shall never get over it. Then they tied my hands and feet, and, throwing a sheet over my head, twisted it tightly around my throat, so I could not scream, and thus put me in a bathtub filled with cold water. They held me under until I gave up every hope and became senseless. At other times they took hold of my ears and beat my head on the floor and against the wall. Then they pulled out my hair by the roots, so that it will never grow in again."

Mrs. Cotter here showed me proofs of her story, the dent in the back of her head and the bare spots where the hair had been taken out by the handful. I give her story as plainly as possible: "My treatment was not as bad as I have seen others get in there, but it has ruined my health, and even if I do get out of here I will be a wreck. When my husband heard of the treatment given me he threatened to expose the place if I was not removed, so I was brought here. I am well mentally now. All that old fear has left me, and the doctor has promised to allow my husband to take me home."

I made the acquaintance of Bridget McGuinness, who seems to be sane at the present time. She said she was sent to Retreat 4, and put on the "rope gang." "The beating I got there were something dreadful. I was pulled around by the hair, held under the water until I strangled, and I was choked and kicked. The nurses would always keep a quiet patient stationed at the window to tell them when any of the doctors were approaching. It was hopeless to complain to the doctors, for they always said it was the imagination of our diseased brains, and besides we would get another beating for telling. They would hold patients under the water and threaten to leave them to die there if they did not promise not to tell the doctors. We would all promise, because we knew the doctors would not help us, and we would do anything to escape the punishment. After breaking a window I was transferred to the Lodge, the worst place on the island. It is dreadfully dirty in there, and the stench is awful. In the summer the flies swarm the place. The food is worse than we get in other wards and we are given only tin plates. Instead of the bars being on the outside, as in this ward, they are on the inside. There are many quiet patients there who have been there for years, but the nurses keep them to do the work. Among other beating I got there, the nurses jumped on me once and broke two of my ribs.

"While I was there a pretty young girl was brought in. She had been sick, and she fought against being put in that dirty place. One night the nurses took her and, after beating her, they held her naked in a cold bath, then they threw her on her bed. When morning came the girl was dead. The doctors said she died of convulsions, and that was all that was done about it.

"They inject so much morphine and chloral that the patients are made crazy. I have seen the patients wild for water from the effect of the drugs, and the nurses would refuse it to them. I have heard women beg for a whole night for one drop and it was not given them. I myself cried for water until my mouth was so parched and dry that I could not speak."

I saw the same thing myself in hall 7. The patients would beg for a drink before retiring, but the nurses–Miss Hart and the others–refused to unlock the bathroom that they might quench their thirst.

Chapter XV: Incidents of Asylum Life.

THERE is little in the wards to help one pass the time. All the asylum clothing is made by the patients, but sewing does not employ one's mind. After several months' confinement the thoughts of the busy world grow faint, and all the poor prisoners can do is to sit and ponder over their hopeless fate. In the upper halls a good view is obtained of the passing boats and New York. Often I tried to picture to myself as I looked out between the bars to the lights faintly glimmering in the city, what my feelings would be if I had no one to obtain my release.

I have watched patients stand and gaze longingly toward the city they in all likelihood will never enter again. It means liberty and life; it seems so near, and yet heaven is not further from hell.

Do the women pine for home? Excepting the most violent cases, they are conscious that they are confined in an asylum. An only desire that never dies is the one for release, for home.

One poor girl used to tell me every morning, "I dreamed of my mother last night. I think she may come to-day and take me home." That one thought, that longing, is always present, yet she has been confined some four years.

What a mysterious thing madness is. I have watched patients whose lips are forever sealed in a perpetual silence. They live, breathe, eat; the human form is there, but that something, which the body can live without, but which cannot exist without the body, was missing. I have wondered if behind those sealed lips there were dreams we ken not of, or if all was blank?

Still, as sad are those cases when the patients are always conversing with invisible parties. I have seen them wholly unconscious of their surroundings and engrossed with an invisible being. Yet, strange to say, that any command issued to them is always obeyed, in about the same manner as a dog obeys his master. One of the most pitiful delusions of any of the patients was that of a blue-eyed Irish girl, who believed she was forever damned because of one act in her life. Her horrible cry, morning and night, "I am damned for all eternity!" would strike horror to my soul. Her agony seemed like a glimpse of the inferno.

After being transferred to hall 7 I was locked in a room every night with six crazy women. Two of them seemed never to sleep, but spent the night in raving. One would get out of her bed and creep around the room searching for some one she wanted to kill. I could not help but think how easy it would be for her to attack any of the other patients confined with her. It did not make the night more comfortable.

One middle-aged woman, who used to sit always in the corner of the room, was very strangely affected. She had a piece of newspaper, and from it she continually read the most wonderful things I ever heard. I often sat close by her and listened. History and romance fell equally well from her lips.

I saw but one letter given a patient while I was there. It awakened a big interest. Every patient seemed thirsty for a word from the world, and they crowded around the one who had been so fortunate and asked hundreds of questions.

Visitors make but little interest and a great deal of mirth. Miss Mattie Morgan, in hall 7, played for the entertainment of some visitors one day. They were close about her until one whispered that she was a patient. "Crazy!" they whispered, audibly, as they fell back and left her alone. She was amused as well as indignant over the episode. Miss Mattie, assisted by several girls she has trained, makes the evenings pass very pleasantly in hall 7. They sing and dance. Often the doctors come up and dance with the patients.

One day when we went down to dinner we heard a weak little cry in the basement. Every one seemed to notice it, and it was not long until we knew there was a baby down there. Yes, a baby. Think of it-a little, innocent babe born in such a chamber of horrors! I can imagine nothing more terrible.

A visitor who came one day brought in her arms her babe. A mother who had been separated from her five little children asked permission to hold it. When the visitor wanted to leave, the woman's grief was uncontrollable, as she begged to keep the babe which she imagined was her own. It excited more patients than I had ever seen excited before at one time.

The only amusement, if so it may be called, given the patients outside, is a ride once a week, if the weather permits, on the "merry-go-round." It is a change, and so they accept it with some show of pleasure.

A scrub-brush factory, a mat factory, and the laundry, are where the mild patients work. They get no recompense for it, but they get hungry over it.

Chapter XVI: The Last Good-Bye.

THE day Pauline Moser was brought to the asylum we heard the most horrible screams, and an Irish girl, only partly dressed, came staggering like a drunken person up the hall, yelling, "Hurrah! Three cheers! I have killed the divil! Lucifer, Lucifer, Lucifer," and so on, over and over again. Then she would pull a handful of hair out, while she exultingly cried, "How I deceived the divils. They always said God made hell, but he didn't." Pauline helped the girl to make the place hideous by singing the most horrible songs. After the Irish girl had been there an hour or so, Dr. Dent came in, and as he walked down the hall, Miss Grupe whispered to the demented girl, "Here is the devil coming, go for him." Surprised that she would give a mad woman such instructions, I fully expected to see the frenzied creature rush at the doctor. Luckily she did not, but commenced to repeat her refrain of "Oh, Lucifer." After the doctor left, Miss Grupe again tried to excite the woman by saying the pictured minstrel on the wall was the devil, and the poor creature began to scream, "You divil, I'll give it to you," so that two nurses had to sit on her to keep her down. The attendants seemed to find amusement and pleasure in exciting the violent patients to do their worst.

I always made a point of telling the doctors I was sane and asking to be released, but the more I endeavored to assure them of my sanity the more they doubted it.

"What are you doctors here for?" I asked one, whose name I cannot recall.

"To take care of the patients and test their sanity," he replied.

"Very well," I said. "There are sixteen doctors on this island, and excepting two, I have never seen them pay any attention to the patients. How can a doctor judge a woman's sanity by merely bidding her good morning and refusing to hear her pleas for release? Even the sick ones know it is useless to say anything, for the answer will be that it is their imagination." "Try every test on me," I have urged others, "and tell me am I sane or insane? Try my pulse, my heart, my eyes; ask me to stretch out my arm, to work my fingers, as Dr. Field did at Bellevue, and then tell me if I am sane." They would not heed me, for they thought I raved.

Again I said to one, "You have no right to keep sane people here. I am sane, have always been so and I must insist on a thorough examination or be released. Several of the women here are also sane. Why can't they be free?"

"They are insane," was the reply, "and suffering from delusions."

After a long talk with Dr. Ingram, he said, "I will transfer you to a quieter ward." An hour later Miss Grady called me into the hall, and, after calling me all the vile and profane names a woman could ever remember, she told me that it was a lucky thing for my "hide" that I was transferred, or else she would pay me for remembering so well to tell Dr. Ingram everything. "You d — n hussy, you forget all about yourself, but you never forget anything to tell the

INSANE HALL NO. 7.

doctor." After calling Miss Neville, whom Dr. Ingram also kindly transferred, Miss Grady took us to the hall above, No. 7.

In hall 7 there are Mrs. Kroener, Miss Fitzpatrick, Miss Finney, and Miss Hart. I did not see as cruel treatment as down-stairs, but I heard them make ugly remarks and threats, twist the fingers and slap the faces of the unruly patients. The night nurse, Conway I believe her name is, is very cross. In hall 7, if any of the patients possessed any modesty, they soon lost it. Every one was compelled to undress in the hall before their own door, and to fold their clothes and leave them there until morning. I asked to undress in my room, but Miss Conway told me if she ever caught me at such a trick she would give me cause not to want to repeat it.

The first doctor I saw here–Dr. Caldwell-chucked me under the chin, and as I was tired refusing to tell where my home was, I would only speak to him in Spanish.

Hall 7 looks rather nice to a casual visitor. It is hung with cheap pictures and has a piano, which is presided over by Miss Mattie Morgan, who formerly was in a music store in this city. She has been training several of the patients to sing, with some show of success. The artiste of the hall is Under, pronounced Wanda, a Polish girl. She is a gifted pianist when she chooses to display her ability. The most difficult music she reads at a glance, and her touch and expression are perfect.

On Sunday the quieter patients, whose names have been handed in by the attendants during the week, are allowed to go to church. A span Catholic chapel is on the island, and other services are also held.

A "commissioner" came one day, and made the rounds with Dr. Dent. In the basement they found half the nurses gone to dinner, leaving the other half in charge of us, as was always done. Immediately orders were given to bring the nurses back to their duties until after the patients had finished eating. Some of the patients wanted to speak about their having no salt, but were prevented.

The insane asylum on Blackwell's Island is a human rat-trap. It is easy to get in, but once there it is impossible to get out. I had intended to have myself committed to the violent wards, the Lodge and Retreat, but when I got the testimony of two sane women and could give it, I decided not to risk my health-and hair-so I did not get violent.

I had, toward the last, been shut off from all visitors, and so when the lawyer, Peter A. Hendricks, came and told me that friends of mine were willing to take charge of me if I would rather be with them than in the asylum, I was only too glad to give my consent. I asked him to send me something to eat immediately on his arrival in the city, and then I waited anxiously for my release.

It came sooner than I had hoped. I was out "in line" taking a walk, and had just gotten interested in a poor woman who had fainted away while the nurses were trying to compel her to walk. "Good-bye; I am going home," I called to Pauline Moser, as she went past with a woman on either side of her. Sadly I said farewell to all I knew as I passed them on my way to freedom and life, while they were left behind to a fate worse than death. "*Adios*," I murmured to the Mexican woman. I kissed my fingers to her, and so I left my companions of hall 7.

I had looked forward so eagerly to leaving the horrible place, yet when my release came and I knew that God's sunlight was to be free for me again, there was a certain pain in leaving. For ten days I had been one of them. Foolishly enough, it seemed intensely selfish to leave them to their sufferings. I felt a Quixotic desire to help them by sympathy and presence. But only for a moment. The bars were down and freedom was sweeter to me than ever.

Soon I was crossing the river and nearing New York. Once again I was a free girl after ten days in the mad-house on Blackwell's Island.

Chapter XVII: The Grand Jury Investigation.

SOON after I had bidden farewell to the Blackwell's Island Insane Asylum, I was summoned to appear before the Grand Jury. I answered the summons with pleasure, because I longed to help those of God's most unfortunate children whom I had left prisoners behind me. If I could not bring them that boon of all boons, liberty, I hoped at least to influence others to make life more bearable for them. I found the jurors to be gentlemen, and that I need not tremble before their twenty-three august presences.

I swore to the truth of my story, and then I related all-from my start at the Temporary Home until my release. Assistant District-Attorney Vernon M. Davis conducted the examination. The jurors then requested that I should accompany them on a visit to the Island. I was glad to consent.

No one was expected to know of the contemplated trip to the Island, yet we had not been there very long before one of the commissioners of charity and Dr. MacDonald, of Ward's Island, were with us. One of the jurors told me that in conversation with a man about the asylum, he heard that they were notified of our coming an hour before we reached the Island. This must have been done while the Grand Jury were examining the insane pavilion at Bellevue.

The trip to the island was vastly different to my first. This time we went on a clean new boat, while the one I had traveled in, they said, was laid up for repairs.

Some of the nurses were examined by the jury, and made contradictory statements to one another, as well as to my story. They confessed that the jury's contemplated visit had been talked over between them and the doctor. Dr. Dent confessed that he had no means by which to tell positively if the bath was cold and of the number of women put into the same water. He knew the food was not what it should be, but said it was due to the lack of funds.

If nurses were cruel to their patients, had he any positive means of ascertaining it? No, he had not. He said all the doctors were not competent, which was also due to the lack of means to secure good medical men. In the conversation with me, he said:

"I am glad you did this now, and had I known your purpose, I would have aided you. We have no means of learning the way things are going except to do as you did. Since your story was published I found a nurse at the Retreat who had watches set for our approach, just as you had stated. She was dismissed."

Miss Anne Neville was brought down, and I went into the hall to meet her, knowing that the sight of so many strange gentlemen would excite her, even if she be sane. It was as I feared. The attendants had told her she was going to be examined by a crowd of men, and she was shaking with fear. Although I had left her only two weeks before, yet she looked as if she had suffered a severe illness, in that time, so changed was her appearance. I asked her if she had taken any medicine, and she answered in the affirmative. I then told her that all I wanted her to do was tell the jury all we had done since I was brought with her to the asylum, so they would be convinced that I was sane. She only knew me as Miss Nellie Brown, and was wholly ignorant of my story.

She was not sworn, but her story must have convinced all hearers of the truth of my statements.

"When Miss Brown and I were brought here the nurses were cruel and the food was too bad to eat. We did not have enough clothing, and Miss Brown asked for more all the time. I thought she was very kind, for when a doctor promised her some clothing she said she would give it to me. Strange to say, ever since Miss Brown has been taken away everything is different. The nurses are very kind and we are given plenty to wear. The doctors come to see us often and the food is greatly improved."

Did we need more evidence?

The jurors then visited the kitchen. It was very clean, and two barrels of salt stood conspicuously open near the door! The bread on exhibition was beautifully white and wholly unlike what was given us to eat.

We found the halls in the finest order. The beds were improved, and in hall 7 the buckets in which we were compelled to wash had been replaced by bright new basins.

The institution was on exhibition, and no fault could be found.

But the women I had spoken of, where were they? Not one was to be found where I had left them. If my assertions were not true in regard to these patients, why should the latter be changed, so to make me unable to find them? Miss Neville complained before the jury of being changed several times. When we visited the hall later she was returned to her old place.

Mary Hughes, of whom I had spoken as appearing sane, was not to be found. Some relatives had taken her away. Where, they knew not. The fair woman I spoke of, who had been sent here because she was poor, they said had been transferred to another island. They denied all knowledge of the Mexican woman, and said there never had been such a patient. Mrs. Cotter had been discharged, and Bridget McGuinness and Rebecca Farron had been transferred to other quarters. The German girl, Margaret, was not to be found, and Louise had been sent elsewhere from hall 6. The Frenchwoman, Josephine, a great, healthy woman, they said was dying of paralysis, and we could not see her. If I was wrong in my judgment of these patients' sanity, why was all this done? I saw Tillie Mayard, and she had changed so much for the worse that I shuddered when I looked at her.

I hardly expected the grand jury to sustain me, after they saw everything different from what it had been while I was there. Yet they did, and their report to the court advises all the changes made that I had proposed.

I have one consolation for my work-on the strength of my story the committee of appropriation provides $1,000,000 more than was ever before given, for the benefit of the insane.

Made in the USA
Middletown, DE
29 August 2017